ASHANT

ASHANTI GOLD

JAMES CROSBIE

To Eddie

With best wishes.

James

BLACK & WHITE PUBLISHING

First published 2009
by Black & White Publishing Ltd
29 Ocean Drive, Edinburgh EH6 6JL

1 3 5 7 9 10 8 6 4 2   09 10 11 12

ISBN: 978–1–84502–251–8

A CIP catalogue record for this book is available from the
British Library.

Typeset by RefineCatch Limited, Bungay, Suffolk
Printed and bound by Cox & Wyman, Reading

For what might have been

PROLOGUE

The mining complex was quiet, the looted earth offering nothing to sustain life. On the steep slope behind the silent workings the last window of the living quarters had long since darkened, with only the pallid, yellow glow of sparse gantry lights betraying the lie of abandonment.

Four crouching black men inched their sweating bodies deep into the shadow of a shale-heap, their eyes following two armed soldiers as they completed a circuit of the building they were guarding. Artu Koffi, their leader, cocked his head, absorbing the sounds of the night. Then he signed with his hand, sending his men deeper into the shale as the alien whine of an approaching vehicle disturbed the still night air. The noise of the engine grew louder and they sunk even lower, pressing themselves into the loose shale as twin beams of light threw long dark shadows accusingly towards them. Body hugging the ground, Artu carefully raised his head just enough to see the squat shape of an army Land Rover materialise from behind the glare of headlights. He looked at his watch and allowed himself a satisfied smile as the vehicle turned a full circle and crunched to a halt outside the building where the two soldiers had snapped to parade-ground attention.

Two sergeants, one of them a white man from a special training group, and two privates dismounted from the Land Rover. There was a flurry of stamping boots and shouldered weapons as the sentries were relieved. The black sergeant set the new detail at ease, then easy, before stepping forward with the white sergeant to check the solid-looking door of the squat, windowless building. One of the soldiers going off duty said something to the newcomers and held out a hand. The whites of Artu's eyes grew big as the new arrival passed over his water bottle; this was something no one had considered. Sweat dampened the ground beneath him as the soldier raised the bottle to his mouth and took a deep, refreshing draught before passing it to his colleague. Blinking against the sweat that suddenly stung his eyes, Artu watched the second soldier take a long, slow pull from the bottle. Then he saw both sergeants walk to the corner of the building and stare along its side. *Surely they weren't going to carry out a full site inspection?* Anxiously eyeing the two guards for any signs of sluggishness, Artu willed the

8

sergeants to return to their vehicle, knowing the potion his agent had put in the water bottle was powerful and quick-acting. If the guards fell asleep now, the entire plan would be ruined, and his people desperately needed the gold, *their* gold.

He was relieved to see both sergeants returning to the Land Rover and chivvying the tired men aboard. A minute later the sound of its engine was swallowed by the darkness of the night.

The fresh sentries completed their first circuit and sat down on the verandah, backs against the door, chatting quietly as they passed the water bottle to and fro. Within a few minutes their voices faded and both men seemed to sag lower against the door. Artu grudgingly gave them another two minutes before he and his men moved in.

Both sentries were out cold and Artu's men quickly dragged them clear of the doorway. One weapon was kicked aside, the other picked up and cradled in the arms of the man posted as lookout. Two of the men pulled tools from rucksacks and set to work on the heavy, hardwood door, the wrenching, tearing sounds drawing nervous glances from the lookout who watched the buildings on the hill. There was a sharp, louder crack of splintering wood as both crowbars pulled together and the door burst open, allowing the cloying scent of polished floors and woodwork to sweep over them. Artu stepped inside the open doorway, nodding in satisfaction as he stared at the huge iron safe behind the barrier of steel bars that bisected the office. Quickly, he unslung his backpack and ordered his men forward; they had urgent work to perform.

*

The barracks of the 4th Ghanaian Rifles lay about six miles to the north of the mine and normally the return to camp was a cheerful, talkative run. Tonight, however, after an initial exchange of banter, both guards sank into an uncharacteristic silence. Sergeant Nunsu, always alert to the moods of his men, looked over his shoulder at them. They seemed tired, almost on the edge of sleep. Still, he reasoned, the mine duty, even at night, was a hot, strength-sapping chore. He glanced at the white sergeant who sat beside him, quietly pleased that his men had been alert at the end of their long stag.

By the time the Land Rover had turned into the camp gates, privates Joseph Nati and Adame Katey were in a deep sleep. When his second command to dismount was ignored, Sergeant Nunsu became annoyed and pulled Nati roughly by the shoulder, snorting back in surprise when the soldier toppled from his seat and flopped to the floor of the vehicle, dead to the world. He checked for the smell of alcohol but there was nothing. *Ganja!* The thought leapt into his mind and his face became a mask of anger.

Two minutes later both unconscious men had been manhandled into the sick-bay and a grumbling nurse rudely wakened from his stolen catnap. The nurse flicked a pen-light in both soldiers' eyes, took their pulses and checked their blood pressure. Like the sergeant, he dismissed alcohol, but unlike him, he also dismissed ganja. His voice sounded puzzled when he reported to the sergeant that both men appeared to be heavily sedated.

'Sedated?' Sergeant Nunsu stared blankly at the nurse. 'How can they be sedated? They have just come off duty at the mine.'

The tired nurse shrugged his shoulders. 'I do not know how this is so. I only know I speak true.'

A puzzled Sergeant Nunsu ran his hand across his bullet-smooth head. 'But they are unconscious . . . Sedated, you say?'

'I speak true,' the nurse agreed. 'Maybe they eat something. Or drink,' he added.

Sergeant Nunsu shook his head. 'They would have eaten hours ago. And their water was finished. I saw the relief guards let them drink from their bottle when they took over.'

The nurse held his palms out in front of him. 'So . . . They take drink and now they are . . . sedated.' He looked up from the unconscious men and stared into the suddenly narrowing eyes of the sergeant.

Despite the heat of the night, an icy chill stabbed through Nunsu's body. Urgently, he grabbed for a telephone.

*

Artu and his men had been working furiously, filling the almost airless room with the musky stink of stale sweat as they laboured at their task. Two of them worked with a car-jack, widening a gap they had made in the steel bars that divided the room in half. Inside the barred area, Artu knelt in front of the large safe, wiping his streaming forehead as he delicately pushed a detonator into the wedge of gelignite he had force fed into the space behind the keyhole. Making certain the detonator was firmly in place, he backed off, paying out the blue touch-cord until he reached the opening in the bars. Quickly, he checked that the narrow gap he had squeezed through had been widened enough to permit a speedy exit. Artu knew that time would be short once the explosion blasted the night apart. But the men had done a good job and he slipped quickly through the gap to join them on the other side.

The three intruders huddled round the touch-cord and looked along its length, eyes focused on the shiny copper head of the detonator. Artu impatiently waved the other two outside and reached into his pocket for a lighter. Three times his sweat-slicked thumb slid uselessly across the ribbed wheel until finally it gripped and a stream of glowing sparks ignited spurting butane gas. He stared once more at the door of the safe, offered a prayer to his tribal gods and applied the flame, rolling the touch-cord between his fingers as it hissed into fiery life. Carefully, he placed the cord on the floor and watched the sparks dance and splutter towards the detonator in the keyhole of the safe. It was good and he nodded to himself before hurrying outside to join the others.

The men crouched against the wall of the building in a tense waiting silence, exchanging worried looks, as seconds seemed to drag too long. Suddenly the blast reverberated round the mine-head, echoing off the silent living quarters like a ricocheting shellshot. Momentarily paralysed, they pressed themselves against the wall. Then, as the last echoes died away, they rose and charged into the dust-filled building, the excitement drawing the lookout from his post as he joined them in the rush, jostling and pushing to be the first through the gap in the metal bars.

The heavy steel door of the safe hung askew and with ecstatic whoops they bounded forward. There were a few seconds of jubilant confusion until Artu's voice barked out, bringing them to order. Remembering instructions, they quickly helped each other to fill the rucksacks they carried on their backs. The work took only minutes and soon, weighed down with their booty, they headed for the door, anxious now to get away.

The first man out looked up towards the living quarters, seeing lights flick on in the windows high on the hill. He grinned confidently, knowing that there was plenty of time to reach the shelter of the bush before the first investigators arrived. He was pushed aside as the others crowded out behind him and together they turned towards the shelter of the shale-heaps. There was a shouted command, and instantly a blinding arc of floodlights illuminated the front of the building.

The four men froze. The sheer volume of light fixed them against the whitewashed wall like dead insects pinned on a display board. Then the armed lookout blazed off a pointless, frustrated shot. The return volley was immediate and murderous. One man's head disappeared in an eruption of blood, bone and brain matter that splattered high and wide against the wall behind him. A second man was hurled against the building by the explosive force of high-velocity bullets, his chest suddenly spouting blood, his back leaving a vertical, dragging red mess down the wall as he sagged lifeless to the ground. Another man stared unbelievingly at the stump of his right forearm, which was gouting dark arterial blood in a thick, viscous stream. His moans of pain rose to a keening, high-pitched scream as anaesthetising shock faded and agony bit hard.

Amazingly, Artu Koffi found himself unscathed. He stood, legs apart, arms raised, the whites of his eyes wide with shock as he stared into the blinding brightness. Then he heard the deliberate, measured crunch crunch crunch of approaching footsteps and an army officer came slowly into focus, the round brim of his cap a dark halo against the glaring light. Artu saw the face as the man marched close, noted the narrow lips thinned tight in a sneer of triumph and recognised Judas Akaba, the army captain in charge of mine security. For a long moment the uniformed figure stood smartly to attention, staring calmly at the four men who had dared every-thing and come so very, very close to success. Then soldiers were running past him to strip the haversacks from the two dead men, ignoring the screams of the wounded man as they tore the straps of his rucksack over his mutilated stump, finally rifle-butting Artu to his knees in order to rip the bag from his back.

The officer's voice hissed an order and his soldiers stepped clear, dropping the rucksacks at his feet and turning to point their weapons at Artu and the man still writhing on the ground. The low, cruel voice sounded again, echoed by the sharp, metallic rattle of weapons being cocked. The sound was loud and ominous against the moans of the wounded man.

'No! No!' The white sergeant burst into the pool of light. 'No! No!' he shouted again, breaking into a run. 'They've surren . . .'

A fusillade of machine-gun fire drowned his voice and he stumbled to an impotent halt as bullets smashed into fragile flesh, sending limbs flailing wildly as the living joined the dead.

Captain Akaba stepped forward, bending to lift the flap of one of the rucksacks. Slowly, deliberately, he allowed its contents to spill out into the glaring light, forcing an involuntary gasp from the wide-eyed soldiers. Artu Koffi stared with fast-failing eyes at his people's birthright gleaming on the ground before him. Then, painfully, slowly, he raised his head to look into the merciless eyes of Judas Akaba.

'One day . . .' he dredged up the last strength of the dying man he was. 'One day our gold will return to the Ashanti people. One day.' He fell back gasping for breath, the gleam of gold reflected in his dying eyes. He was unaware of Akaba drawing his sidearm, already dead when the heavy 9mm bullet smashed into his skull.

'You murdering bastard!' The white sergeant swung his fist at the grinning Akaba.

I

Colin Grant felt the morning air knife through his clothing and shivered as a flurry of cold January wind buffeted him. The wicket gate slammed shut and he heard the metallic clatter of its lock being thrown, the underlining clash as the bolt slammed home. Familiar, nerve-jarring sounds, yet somehow they sounded different this time, and he felt no urge to turn. Chin raised, eyes half-closed, he leant back and slowly inhaled, feeling the cold, fresh, free air invade his long starved lungs. *Yes!* It felt *good!* And his senses, after years of stifled strangulation, were suddenly alive again. He became conscious of his chest swelling against the clean, soft material of a white linen shirt and he breathed again, more deeply this time, as he quite literally enjoyed the taste of freedom. *Four years*, he thought. Four years of breathing in the stink of prison. He tasted the air again, turning his head slowly from left to right, savouring the unfamiliar smell of wet leaves on a cold winter's morning. The freshness almost stung his eyes to tears.

'Oi!' He heard a yell from the Judas grille in the door. 'What's up Grant? Nowhere to go?'

'Bollocks!' Colin tossed the word over his shoulder, following it with an insolent finger jab, eloquent in its casual contempt.

'Less of that Grant.' The voice was suddenly brisk with authority. 'You're still on prison property. On yer bike or I'll have you back inside again. Move!'

Colin spun round, body tensed, chin taut, eyes suddenly flashing anger as he glared at the face behind the grille. 'You'll have fuck all again, mister!' he snapped back, pushing his face up to the grille. 'Want to try?' he challenged, stepping back, making room for the screw to step out as he flexed his lean, well muscled shoulders.

A furrow of doubt creased the screw's forehead above suddenly wary eyes.

'Come on then!' Colin invited him with his hand. 'Come on. Come and get me. Let's see how you manage on my side of the wall.'

'On your way, Grant.' The screw's voice was subdued, his face drawn back from the grille as if he feared some kind of attack. Colin shook his head in disgust and turned away to step out to freedom, feet strangely light in unfamiliar civvy shoes. His step became livelier the further he left the prison gate behind until, reaching the end of the drive, he stopped to look back at the blackened architectural scab that was Wandsworth prison.

'Beat you!' He spat the words out loud at the bleak, brooding walls and glared angrily at the gates, remembering some of the harder times he had endured behind them. Then the tightened muscles of his face relaxed in a slow smile of achievement.

Beat you! For the first time in years, he felt some of his old natural exuberance bubbling up and it was all he could do to prevent himself from yelling out in sheer exhilaration.

Colin had yelled out many times during his thirty-six years of life – when he first saw the light of day in a dingy Glasgow tenement where, despite knowing nothing but the barest essentials, he grew up an attractive, if rebellious, lad. Again, when he discovered the joy of winning, whether it was a playground fight or a game. And again, when he left the restrictions of school behind him to take up the adventure of shipyard working, keen to learn a trade and contribute towards the upkeep of the neat two-bedroom tenement flat he shared with his widowed mother.

For more than three years he had been conscientious at his work and content at home. Then the world's shipping surplus began to bite. A series of mergers and big-business takeovers saw his job disappear as recession, rationalisation and redundancy became familiar words in the working man's vocabulary. At just eighteen he had found himself in the dole queue, facing a life of unemployment. Soon after that his mother had died – *viral infection*, they said. Silent in his grief, he began to question the fairness of it all. Was he to live and die on government handouts? Signing on every week for his dole money . . . sliding deeper and deeper into despair? To do nothing and own nothing in this life but cheap clothes and some sticks of chain-store furniture? Deep inside he yelled rebellion.

With his mother gone, there was nothing to keep him in Scotland and a week after the funeral, with only an aunt in Greenock, an uncle abroad, and unemployment in Glasgow, he had accepted £100 from a vulture furniture dealer for the contents of the flat. That same day he packed his bags and like thousands of hopefuls before him took the high road to London.

Life in the capital was an adventure at first, but rents were high and shipyard welders in low demand in central London. Within a month he had been thrown out of his digs, his promises to pay when he found work worthless currency in the grasping city.

Had his mother still been alive Colin would never have surrendered to a life of crime, but she was gone now and although he revered her memory and appreciated the standards she had taught him, he knew that he couldn't hurt her. Besides, all his efforts to find proper work had failed, and the thought of living in poverty or existing on handouts and petty crime for the rest of his days held no attraction for him. Reluctantly at first, but out of sheer necessity, he began by stealing food from street stalls and supermarkets, then, as his needs and nerve increased, cars and their contents became an easy target. He could pick up twenty quid here and there for a radio – thirty if it was a good one. The occasional bonus of a set of golf clubs or a tempting parcel meant that he was able to eat and pay rent on a modest bedsit and almost against his will he began to like the life. Inevitably his talents brought him to the attention of some of the local 'chaps' who offered him more serious and lucrative opportunities.

Never a person to do things by halves, Colin decided to commit himself to this new life, willingly accepting the comradeship, risks and rewards it gave him. Suddenly he was wearing good clothes, enjoying fast cars, gorgeous girls and flashy nightclubs. He was on his way; living like a king, with a freewheeling lifestyle that could only be supported through crime. Colin reigned successfully for over four years, until one day an alert assistant in a high-class jewellery shop checked his plastic and the fraud squad caught up with him. He was only trying to buy a watch on this occasion, but there was one big fault with plastic fraud; once captured, every previous purchase on the card becomes immediately exposed. Colin had no option but to plead guilty to three sample charges of fraud, with fifteen other offences taken into consideration. It was considered 'organised crime' and a strict Old Bailey judge sent him down for a six-stretch. With time off for good behaviour he had served four long years. But now it was over. He took a last look at the prison and turned away to walk towards the Tube.

Across the road a car drew into the kerb, tooting urgently for attention. Colin stared for a moment, taking in the mop of unruly black hair over a healthy, well-bronzed face – it had to be a lamp job this time of the year – and recognised Joey 'Doc' Docherty grinning over at him. Wary of the unfamiliar traffic, he negotiated the crossing and ducked into the front seat of the car.

Doc's expression showed how delighted he was to see him, his hair bouncing around as he jostled Colin's shoulder, face wreathed in smiles, repeating the words, 'Well done, old son! Well done!' as if Colin had just accomplished some extraordinary achievement.

Colin smiled widely, pleased at the friendly spontaneity of his welcome, and eyed up his pal's appearance. Four years seemed to have made little difference to Doc. He still favoured dark-coloured silk shirts, unbuttoned halfway down his chest to display heavy gold chains amongst abundant, curling tufts of black hair. The same devil-may-care face stared at him through clear blue eyes, and a single gold earring – an affectation Colin usually disliked – winked wickedly against Doc's dark skin.

'Good to see you, mate.' Doc thumped him on the shoulder again. 'Bet'cha thought I hadn't turned up, eh?' He grasped Colin's hand in a strong, clean grip. 'Didn't want to pick you up too near the gate,' he explained. 'The less those bastards see the better.'

'I wondered where you'd got to,' Colin admitted, his harsh Glasgow accent somewhat softened by the years of close confinement in a London prison. 'But you're right to be careful.'

'Yea . . . Bastards think they're fucking cops an' all now. Anyway, here you are and here we go. Where will it be? Fernhead Road?'

'Only to pick up my gear. I can't stay there; it's down as my *last known* address.'

'No problem. Bert's trouble'n strife is staying with her sister up Watford way for a few weeks. She's about ready to drop a sprog – the sister, I mean. Bert

24

said to tell you that you're welcome at his flat until you find a place of your own.'

'That's good,' Colin nodded, relieved that his immediate accommodation problem had been solved. Already the hard lines on his face were softening as the pressures of prison receded. He smiled and settled back in his seat, content to watch the world go by.

'How'd it go then?' Doc glanced across at him as he revved impatiently at traffic lights. 'In there, I mean.'

'Stinking dump!' The question immediately affected Colin's easy manner. 'Locked up twenty-three hours a day. No association. And, fuck me, a work party's even considered a privilege! It's so fucking boring you even go to church for a break.'

'Yeah . . . I heard old Wanno' was a bit rough,' Doc nodded sympathetically.

'It was a bastard!'

'Well, you've done it now. It's over. You'll soon settle back into the swing of things again.'

'Aye,' Colin rubbed his hands together. 'I expect so.'

'You've not turned it in? You are coming back on the firm?'

'Aye, I'm coming back on the firm,' Colin nodded. 'But I don't fancy getting into the old plastic game again. We'll have to find work that's really tasty; jobs that will throw us big lumps of money. And they're there to be had too.' He looked over at Doc. 'Look at that job they pulled at the airport; the bullion vans they've hijacked. I'm telling you, the work's there if you look for it.'

'Well, if you can sort one out we'll be only too pleased to take it on.' Doc dropped a gear and charged past a startled driver. 'You always were pretty good at spotting a piece of work.'

'Aye,' Colin nodded his head. 'It's just a matter of raising our sights. The fraud game is over as far as I'm concerned. It's time to move on. But I think I'm due a bit of a holiday before I get into any sort of business.' He pulled a well-creased letter from his pocket. 'I've got an invitation here from an uncle of mine. Lives in a place called Takoradi, somewhere in Ghana, West Africa. I fancy a look at the place and it sounds a lot better than the Costa Del Sol to me.'

'It certainly sounds different,' Doc acknowledged. 'And you're well entitled to a rest. But after . . . ?'

'After . . . ? Well, once I've had a bit of a rest it'll be straight back to business.'

'Good.' Doc sounded pleased. 'Here.' He held out a wad of notes. 'There's a grand there. Keep you going for a couple of weeks.'

Colin shook his head. 'Thanks, Doc, but I don't need it. I've still got a few quid stashed away. I'll be all right for a few months, or until we have an earner.'

'Take it, mate,' Doc insisted. 'You're back on the firm, aren't you? Call it mad money. Fritter it away on a bit of fun and keep your stash for living on.' He pushed the wad of notes into Colin's lap. 'C'mon – you're entitled!'

'Well . . . thanks.' Colin pocketed the notes, pleased more by the gesture than the actual cash.

By mid-morning they had successfully retrieved Colin's belongings from his old landlord and were pulling up outside a row of elderly terraced flats in Eustace Road, Fulham. 'You'll be all right here for a week or two,' Doc told him as they mounted the well-worn steps to Bert's front door.

Colin saw little change in the stocky-looking man who opened the door to them. True, Bert looked a little heavier than he remembered, especially around his belly and shoulders. His face had beefed out a little too, intensifying a belligerent, bulldoggish appearance. With thinning fair hair and gold-rimmed spectacles glinting on a well-scrubbed face, Albert Maddren could easily have been mistaken for an earnest, old-style family grocer as he stretched out a hand in greeting.

'You all right?' Bert asked in a concerned voice, looking Colin up and down for signs of wear and tear.

Colin held both hands out from his side. 'I'm as right as four years in Wanno' can make me,' he joked as Bert welcomed him in, making no fuss, simply accepting the fact that Colin was back in circulation and needed a place to stay until he was on his feet again.

Arranging to meet Doc in the evening, Colin spent the rest of the morning at the public baths in North End Road, filling and refilling a huge, old-fashioned tub as he scrubbed the stench of prison from his body. A relaxed afternoon amble round the shops enabled him to replenish his wardrobe with some up-to-date shirts and other accessories and by early evening he was ready to venture out to sample some of the things he had missed during his four years of incarceration. The tacit understanding that he would have the flat to himself that night gave him a tingling sensation of expectancy as he left with Bert to meet up with Doc again and Eddie Ferns, the fourth member of the firm.

The scene inside the Red Lion was unchanged. The same hard-drinking, vociferous crowd of street traders from the North End Road market were still arguing in their loud, matey fashion, berating one another in friendly rivalry, or boasting of the strokes they had pulled on the unsuspecting public during the day's business.

Through the smoke-hazed bar-room, Colin caught sight of Doc waving over the heads of the noisy drinkers. Most of the local market men greeted Bert as he led Colin through the crowd, one or two of them directing enquiring looks at Colin as memories stirred. One of the men stared a little longer then smiled in sudden recognition, holding up a thumb in congratulation. It felt good to be in the hubbub of a lively pub again.

There were two empty places at the corner table Doc had commandeered and sitting on a third chair was the neatly dressed figure of Eddie Ferns.

'T'riffic! Great to see you again.' There was a tangible aura of awareness and capability about Eddie as he rose to his feet and reached for Colin's hand, his eyes keenly assessing. 'Well, it doesn't seem to have done you any harm,' he said, completing his inspection and loosening his grip. 'How'd it go then? Inside, I mean?' he asked, regaining his seat as Bert pushed his way through to the bar.

'Wasn't too bad after the first four years,' Colin quipped in the hoary old ex-con style. 'I could hardly tear myself away.'

Eddie laughed appreciatively. 'Nice one, nice one.

Maybe you should've signed on for a bit longer then, if you were getting to like it that much?'

They passed friendly banter back and forth until Bert returned from the bar to place overflowing pints on the table. 'There you go!' He slid a foaming beer over to Colin. 'Try a sup of that – it'll beat your Wandsworth tea a mile!'

The three men watched expectantly as Colin took a small, tasting mouthful, holding their breath as he rolled it over his tongue and sucked in his cheeks to saturate his taste buds. Finally, he took a long, savouring draught, swallowing slowly before lowering the half-empty glass to the table. 'De . . . licious!' He smacked his lips in loud appreciation. 'I'd forgotten just how good a pint could taste.'

'Glad to have you back, mate,' Eddie broke the silence and lifted his glass, waiting a little for the others to follow him, and together they toasted Colin's return.

'We've got a table booked at the Celebrity Club, up west,' Bert informed him as they each sank their second pints. 'Got it all laid on for you – birds and booze all night.'

'Did you say birds?' Colin looked at him, a happy smile pasted on his face.

'That's what I said,' Bert confirmed. 'Wine, women and song – that's the buzz tonight.'

'Let's get up west then.' Colin knocked back the remains of his pint and licked his lips in anticipation. 'I've waited a long time for a night like this.'

★

It was three-thirty in the morning when Bert helped a drunk but happy Colin back into the flat, the young woman accompanying them fussing and fluttering uselessly as they laid him on the bed, loosened his tie and removed his shoes.

'Well . . . Sharon,' Bert turned to the girl, eyeing her shapely figure and attractive features, letting his hand wander through abundant auburn hair.

Her eyebrows arched. 'He won't be much good to me like that, will he?' she pouted.

Bert restrained himself with an effort. It was, after all, Colin's night. 'He'll be fine in the morning, love,' he finally said. 'Just you make sure you do your job when he does come round – it'll be a nice surprise for him.'

She patted his face cheekily. 'Just you leave him to me.'

★

Colin woke slowly, gradually becoming aware of soft, gentle hands caressing his body. He stirred and immediately felt the hands slip down his stomach to

31

his groin and softly grip him. Gently her hands worked slowly up and down, doing their job.

What a dream! He squirmed on his back, enjoying the pleasurable sensations coursing through him. And the bed felt unbelievably soft. Then he remembered. This was no dream. He was out. *OUT!* The nightclub. The dancing. The girls. A girl! Memory flooded back and he opened his eyes to look at her.

He had only a vague recollection of meeting the girl and couldn't even remember her name, but the situation was crystal clear and he rolled over to embrace her eagerly.

His happiness was almost euphoric as he kissed and caressed her sensual, willing body, letting his hands cup the indescribably soft, silky breast, slowly massaging a swollen nipple between his fingers. It had been so long since . . .

'What's your name?' he whispered, afraid that if he spoke out loud he would wake up and find himself back on his metal bunk in Wandsworth.

'I'm Sharon.' She kissed him with full red lips and punctuated each word with a peck. 'I'm here to help you make up for lost time. Four years, I believe you told me last night, or don't you remember?'

'I remember,' Colin assured her as he drew her body close. 'Far too long to be missing out on this.'

And gently savouring every moment, he entered her, sighing deeply, oblivious to everything except the eroticism of the moment.

It was good to be back.

2

Sharon left the flat by midday, leaving a sated Colin recovering in the well-tumbled bed. He was still there savouring the memory when the front door rattled and Bert let himself into the flat, quickly followed by a grinning Doc and Eddie.

'Remembered where to put it, did you?' Doc leered at him as they entered the bedroom.

'I'm knackered!' he admitted. 'Really fucked!'

'You're fucked?' Bert gave a snuffling laugh. 'I wonder how Sharon feels!'

Colin closed his eyes for a few seconds in blissful memory, then he looked up at his grinning mates. 'Thanks,' he said. 'Thanks for a great night. Almost worth doing a four-stretch for.' A sudden burst of energy got him out of bed and with an insouciance born of shared-cell living he padded naked to the bathroom.

Half an hour later, refreshed and contented, he was lounging in the living room with his friends.

'So what are you going to do?' Bert's voice was

serious as he broached the subject of Colin's future. 'You coming back on the firm?'

'I've already told Doc,' Colin replied after a pause. 'I'm on the firm all right, but I think we should look for a better class of work; something with a bit more money. But before I do anything I want a rest. Go and stay with an uncle of mine for a couple of months; get rid of the taste of Wandsworth and see a bit of sun for a change.'

'It's up to you,' Bert leant forward, speaking earnestly, 'but Eddie's been put onto a nice little earner over Kilburn way. Inside job. The cashier is in debt to the bookies for a few grand and he's desperate for the money. He'll pass the bag, no problem. But there's still his escort and the driver to take care of, so we need a bit of weight just in case. We could do it three-handed, but another man would be useful. Give you a nice few quid for a starter.'

'I'm not exactly skint,' Colin admitted. 'Still got a few grand stashed in the building society.'

'Well, it's not exactly big time, but it's a sweet enough little blag. Comes to about fifty grand. Cashier wants ten off the top, but it's still forty grand to us. Handy bonus to take on that holiday,' he teased.

'What's it like?' Colin asked, tempted by the offer despite his reservations.

'Nothing to it,' Doc told him. 'Small factory payroll. Our man and his clerk carry the money from the bank to a car waiting round the back in the parking lot – that's where we take it. Shouldn't be any bother for us.'

'Not really a four-handed job, is it?' Colin pointed out. 'Three's enough for that kind of work.'

'Yeah,' Bert agreed. 'But it doesn't do any harm to be careful. Remember, we've only got one man on our side. And the driver is supposed to be a bit of a minder too.'

'What we thought, seeing as you're just out,' Eddie leant forward to add encouragement, 'was to use you as insurance, in case someone decides to have a go at us. If there's no trouble you just sit until the fuss dies down then make your way home.'

Doc waved a gold-laden wrist. 'It'll be a canter, Colin,' he said. 'We've watched it for three weeks now. Believe me, it's a job just begging to be done.'

Despite his intention of taking a well-earned rest, Colin felt a familiar shiver course the length of his spine. The job was a *lay on* and he knew he was being offered the soft end – practically a spectator. It would be an easy re-entry to villainy and the money *would* make a difference.

'Sounds all right,' he agreed cautiously. 'But are you sure you want me in on it? I mean . . .

I don't want to start off practically poncing on you.'

'Poncing!' Bert exclaimed. 'You're on the firm, aren't you? Besides, the way the robbery squad's going on just now, a little bit of insurance might come in useful.'

'OK!' Colin made up his mind. 'I'm in.'

3

It was nearing eight o'clock on Thursday morning when Colin drove into the Council car park behind the main shopping centre in Kilburn High Street. He came to a halt just inside the entrance and looked on as Doc drove ahead in a stolen Cortina to park in the far corner. In another minute Doc had locked up and was walking towards him, hurrying in the cold morning air.

'Brrr,' Doc exaggerated a shiver, moving his shoulders and rubbing his hands as he settled in beside Colin. 'Bit parky out there, mate.'

'Motor all right?' Colin asked as he turned the ignition key, stirring the car into life.

'Yeah. We've got a clear view from there. Should be able to spot them right away. See exactly where they park.'

'Don't they always park in the same place?'

'Nah,' Doc shook his head, dismissing the idea. 'The car park's usually pretty full by the time they arrive. There's a fair number of local workers use this

38

place and once they've parked that's them for the day. The wages car arrives just after ten o'clock and the driver always tries to get as close to the front as he can.'

Colin reached forward and switched off the engine – Doc was a willing worker all right, but he had his flaws. He looked at three gold chains dangling ostentatiously against Doc's black T-shirt, the thick links of a monogrammed gold bracelet, bright against the expensive leather of his jacket, and wished he would pay as much attention to his planning as he did to his appearance. 'So they could be parked a good bit from the footpath then? Anywhere in the car park, come to that?'

Doc cocked his head and glanced across at him. 'Yeah, I've seen them right up here once. But they usually manage to get a place about the second or third row down.' He looked at Colin with a puzzled expression. 'Something about it you don't like?'

'I'm not sure,' Colin replied. 'The idea's good enough. But I'm not too happy about them parking just anywhere. Could be a problem there.'

Doc's eyes narrowed. 'What sort of a problem?' he demanded. 'I've checked this job out. It's a good'un – a nice straightforward blag.'

'The blag seems straightforward enough, I'll grant you that,' Colin conceded. 'But there's only one road in and out of here and . . .' he pointed at the access road, '. . . if they happen to be parked near the exit and their driver is a bit lively . . . there's every chance he could block your getaway.'

'Yeah, yeah,' Doc nodded impatiently. 'We thought about that. But you know how these things go – crash bang wallop and away. We don't reckon their driver would think that fast.'

'You're probably right,' Colin agreed. 'But I still don't like it. Why don't you get them to park down the front? Pick your own spot for them?'

'Oh yeah!' snorted Doc. 'Would you please park here, sir?' He spoke in an exaggeratedly polite voice. 'It would make it much easier for us to blag you, thank you very much. Come off it Colin!' he snorted scornfully.

'But you would rather have them in the front row, wouldn't you?' Colin persisted.

'Of course we would,' Doc replied. 'But we can't just pick and choose a parking place for them . . .' His voice tailed off and he looked cautiously at Colin, the flesh around his eyes crinkled in query. 'Can we?'

Colin sighed inwardly and pointed at the Cortina. 'Park that motor in the slot you want them to use. When they drive in, you pull out and they'll nick into the empty space. That way you'll have them exactly

40

where you want them. Then you drive off and reposition yourself ready for the job.' He winked at Doc. 'Right?'

Doc looked at the Cortina, then at the empty parking slots in the front row. Slowly, his eyes moved between the two locations, thinking over Colin's words. His hand thumped the dashboard. 'I like it! We'll be in control of them and they won't even know it. Great!' He opened the door to get out of the car. 'You're a wide bastard, Colin,' he grinned. 'Double wide!'

In a few minutes he had moved the Cortina into a front row slot close to where the footpath entered the car park and rejoined Colin.

'Better?' Colin looked at him.

'Yeah,' Doc agreed. 'Ideal. It's a handy spot for them and it's just far enough to one side to shield us from anyone using the footpath.' He gave a satisfied nod. 'Nice touch, mate. Nice touch.'

Colin looked at his watch. 'We've got almost two hours before we have to be in position. Plenty of time for breakfast and to pick up the other motor.'

By ten to ten the changeover car had been left in a nearby sidestreet and Colin was dropping the others off before carrying on to position himself in the car park. His body was a knot of nerves as he slid his stolen motor into place. Two minutes later he

41

watched the others enter the car park and make their way to the Cortina. Stillness settled over the parked vehicles and, dry-mouthed, stomach fluttering, he checked his watch. Five to ten.

The car park was quiet. In five minutes only one vehicle entered, its elderly woman driver hurrying off to the shops. At eight minutes past ten a dark blue Rover entered the car park and cruised slowly along the line of waiting vehicles, searching for a space. Colin saw the Cortina pull out as the Rover approached and, just as he had predicted, their quarry surged into the empty slot. A moment later two men, one of them carrying a heavy leather satchel, left the car and strode briskly along the path towards busy Kilburn High Road. Two minutes later the Cortina slipped back into the car park and took up its ambush position.

Outwardly everything seemed to be going like clockwork, yet an insidious feeling of unease disturbed Colin. At first he made excuses, telling himself it was natural to feel edgy. After all, he reasoned, four years in prison would affect anyone's performance. But something just wasn't right. He could feel it in his bones, and goosepimples rose as the prickling sense of danger conjured up a vision of Wandsworth. Angrily he shook his head in an effort to dismiss this train of thought. *There's no danger here,* he told himself for the third or fourth time. *I'm only a lookout.* But still the feeling of danger persisted.

Trust your own instincts, he recalled advice passed on by an old villain. *When your concentration is targeted in one direction, your survival instincts take over. So, when you feel that fear, stop and take a good look round.*

His eyes swept the car park again, letting them come to rest on the Cortina, noticing its windows had steamed up from the body heat of the men inside. As he looked, a hand wiped condensation from the car's windscreen and he felt a sudden coldness in his stomach as the penny dropped. His eyes darted to a dark-coloured Vauxhall squatting two rows ahead of him, its windows also opaque with condensation. Peering hard, he could just make out some movement on its front seat. Then a dark shadow leant forward from the rear; at least three bodies in the car.

A stake-out team! Watching . . . waiting . . . They had to be cops! Somehow the law must have got wind of the job – maybe the cashier had caved in; perhaps the Cortina had been sussed. Whatever it was, the game was a bogey now. A movement on the footpath caught his eye and he focused on the two clerks as they returned, the satchel heavy between them.

43

Suddenly sweating, Colin tightened his grip on the steering wheel, trying to squeeze out the vivid visions of prison that were piling on his mind. His world was shrinking into a bare twelve-by-eight cell again. He could practically *smell* the place.

Groaning inwardly, he cursed himself. *Stupid bastard! Should've had them spotted the minute I drove in.* He pounded his fist on the steering wheel, but recognised the beginnings of panic and made an effort to collect himself. Reasonably certain that his own presence had gone unnoticed, there was no denying the initial temptation to simply drive away to safety. But he was part of the firm and knew he had no alternative.

The two clerks were nearing the end of the footpath.

Colin looked at the Vauxhall and saw pale, staring faces pressed against its windows. Any hope of a mistake gone, he twisted the ignition key and, nerves at breaking point, moved out onto the perimeter road.

The two clerks had reached the end of the footpath and entered the car park when the Cortina began to roll forward, both nearside doors inching open in readiness. The doors opened wider. The heads and shoulders of two masked men began to emerge. Colin saw a blast of exhaust fumes belch from the Vauxhall and floored his accelerator. Burning rubber, he scorched towards the Cortina, pounding his horn and pointing at the suddenly accelerating Vauxhall. He saw the look of shocked comprehension on Doc's face, the widening eyes behind the masks of Bert and Eddie. There was nothing more he could do and duty done, he crashed down a gear and raced for the exit.

Too late! There was no mistaking the appearance or intention of the fast-moving police support vehicle careering into the car park, its doors already swinging wide. Another police vehicle swung across the entrance and blocked his path.

Colin stood on the brakes, wrenched his car through a sharp turn and headed deeper into the parked vehicles, sideswiping one car then another as he gunned the engine, feeling the rear end skid and fighting to keep control. A police car loomed large in his rear-view mirror and his side vision caught the impression of running figures as the car park exploded into frenzied action.

Fear lent Colin a desperate recklessness and he battered his way past yet another car, heading straight for the only way out; the footpath. He smashed into a concrete bollard that divided the path and felt it explode under the impact of his racing car, the bonnet folding like tinfoil as shattered stonework chewed into the grille, forced metal into the fanwheel and ruptured the radiator. A jagged piece of concrete flew across the bonnet, whipping the windscreen into a blank white mask and his fist lashed out to clear a gap, giving him a limited view of the path ahead. But in a few yards, barely halfway along the path, blinding steam spewed from mangled metal and the staggering car lurched to a halt.

Colin leapt from the crumpled vehicle, almost falling as he sprang round the open door and sprinted along the footpath, screaming klaxons and loud, excited yells spurring him on. People had begun to gather at the head of the footpath, staring towards the source of noise and excitement. In a moment he was among them, lashing out at one man who seemed to deliberately step in his way. Then he was through the gathering crowd and onto the broad pavement of the shopping area, spinning left and sprinting on a few yards to get out of his pursuers' line of sight.

No one had emerged from the footpath yet but he knew they could only be seconds behind him, delayed a little by the abandoned car. Desperately, he lunged into the stream of traffic, ignoring the hooting of angry drivers, almost going under the wheels of a huge red bus as he crossed the crown of the road. He felt a thump on his hip, then he was staggering onto the pavement, going down on one knee as he stumbled over the high kerb. An elderly gentleman, censoriously tut-tutting, helped him to his feet, his sober warning hanging in the air as Colin pulled himself free and hurried on, the broad stream of traffic isolating him from the confusion across the road.

Heart pounding, he forced himself to keep to a steady stride as he turned one corner then another; distancing himself from the activity, his mind racing as he considered his situation. The police wouldn't be far behind; too many pedestrians had witnessed his reckless scramble across the busy road, and they would have little difficulty in picking up his trail. He could hear the demanding klaxon of another squad car and it underlined the urgency of his situation. Striding hard, but not wanting to break into an attention-drawing run, he rounded another corner. His heart sank. A long straight street, devoid of intersections, lay ahead of him and on either side the long rows of terraced houses showed uniformly closed doors. A siren sounded from another direction. Pursuit was close. *Too close.*

Abruptly he turned towards the nearest doorway, his fingers reaching out to press the recessed bell-push. For a few impatient seconds nothing happened and he pressed urgently again. Thankfully a flicker of movement showed through the opaque glass panel as an interior door opened and light spilled into the hallway.

Come on! Come on! He willed the blurred figure to hurry, acutely aware of the rising sound of a speeding car closing down on him. A dim outline showed through the thick discoloured glass and, with a quiet smoothness, the door swung open.

He began speaking the moment the gap appeared, hoping to gain entry without having to resort to force.

'Good morning, Madam,' Colin switched on his most disarming smile with all the charm he could muster as a flickering blue light appeared on the edge of his vision. Still smiling, he stepped into the hallway and pushed the door shut just as the police car went prowling by.

The plain-looking woman he addressed was flustered; a little frightened at his intrusion. 'Wha . . . What do you want? Who are you looking for?' she asked nervously.

'I'm the Daz man, madam,' Colin quickly improvised. 'The Daz Challenge! You know? From the TV adverts?' His boyish smile made him look inoffensive and the woman visibly relaxed.

'The Daz Challenge?' The woman cocked her head.

48

Colin sighed with relief; she was going for it. He would be okay.

'Correct!' His smile broadened. 'Yes, madam, the Daz Challenge. Daz washes whiter brighter!' He pulled a twenty pound note from his pocket. 'If you can show me a packet of Daz you win twenty pounds. If you have one in use, plus an unopened packet you win' . . . he pulled out another note. 'Two Daz Challenge twenty pound notes! Now, madam,' he held the money out temptingly. 'Do you qualify for none, one, or two of these lovely twenty pound notes?'

A pleased smile lit up the woman's face. 'Oh! I use Daz,' she exclaimed. 'I always use Daz.'

'I have to see it,' he grinned at her. 'You must produce the goods.'

'Oh yes, yes. In the kitchen . . .' she gestured and started towards the rear of the narrow hallway. 'I've got one out just now as a matter of fact.'

Breathing a heartfelt sigh of relief, he followed her into a small cluttered kitchen.

'There you are!' she pointed triumphantly at the large coloured packet on her sink-top. 'Giant size too!'

'And in your cupboard?' Colin raised his eyebrows.

Her face fell. 'I've just opened that packet. The

empty one is still in the bin.' She pedalled it open to expose an empty Daz packet. 'I usually keep one spare. In fact I'll be buying another when I go out shopping.'

'Oh, well . . . I think I can stretch a point,' Colin conceded, smiling. 'After all, you do have two packets, even if one is empty.' He held out the money. 'Madam, you are a winner!'

The pleased woman happily accepted her 'prize'. 'That's wonderful,' she enthused. 'I've never won anything like this before.'

'Is that coffee I smell?' he distracted her again. 'I could do with a break. I've been tramping the street all morning trying to give these twenties away.'

For over an hour he regaled the woman with fictitious tales of his door-to-door adventures, killing time, knowing every minute that passed reduced police activity outside. Finally, when the woman hinted that she had some shopping to do, he asked if he could phone for a mini-cab. 'Have to get back to the office,' he explained. 'If you get your coat on I'll drop you off at the shops.' Ten minutes later they heard the toot-tooting of a car from outside and, using the housewife for cover, jacket casually slung over his shoulder, Colin escorted her across the pavement and into the waiting mini-cab.

A few minutes later the happy housewife got out

of the cab outside a supermarket, leaving Colin with a cheery wave. He sagged against the cab's upholstery, utterly drained. He had felt the walls of Wandsworth closing in; heard the clanging doors and echoing shouts of the long prison wings. It had been close – too close.

Carefully he weighed up his situation. At least he was clear of the police. He had about fifty pounds on him, a wristwatch, a handkerchief and a comb. Like all good villains he carried nothing to identify himself on a job – just a few pounds for emergencies. He thought things over, trying to figure out a plan. There would still be time to get his gear from the flat, even if Bert had been nicked. He would be using the old *'false name, no fixed abode, no comment'* ploy as a delaying tactic to gain time for friends and accomplices to get clear, dump anything incriminating and prepare a tale. He looked at his watch – eleven thirty-five – and made up his mind. 'Make that Eustace Road, driver,' he instructed. 'Eustace Road, Fulham.'

Less than an hour later, Colin had packed a bag, picked up his passport and exited Bert's flat, anxious to avoid any confrontation should any unwelcome visitors come calling. Later on, settled into the safe haven of a small hotel in Paddington, he scoured the late editions of the *Kilburn Times*. There was a small article about the robbery attempt at the foot of the front page and Colin felt a wave of relief at the concluding sentence, 'As yet, no arrests have been made.'

Good news! But still too dangerous to hang about; the cops would be working on solving the case and who could tell what they knew? Colin felt for his passport. He wouldn't be around if the cops came calling.

4

'Good afternoon, may I help you, sir?' The attractive counter assistant in the British Airways shop in Regent Street flashed perfect teeth at the young man in front of her, noting the stylishly cut lightweight coat casually unbuttoned over a smart blue suit and well-chosen tie. And although he was pale, he looked fit – blue eyes clear, skin taut over broad cheekbones, lean, his squared jaw lending him an angular, athletic appearance.

The States . . . New York or Los Angeles. She played her usual guessing game with herself.

'I'd like to book a flight to Accra, Miss.'

'Accra? Accra, Ghana?' the girl asked, a little surprised at her misjudgement.

'Accra, Ghana. That's right,' Colin confirmed, looking on as she referred to a thick air schedules book.

'Here we are, sir. British Airways have three flights weekly. Any particular day you wish to travel?'

Colin looked out onto Regent Street. It was a

bleak January scene; people outside scurrying by, heads tucked low as streaks of grey sleet lashed at them and splattered the pavement outside.

'Tomorrow,' he smiled.

The girl smiled back in sympathy and pressed buttons on her computer keyboard. 'Yes. We have a flight tomorrow – BA231. Accra direct, leaving Heathrow 10.35 in the morning.'

'That will suit me fine.'

'Return ticket, sir?'

'One way, Miss. I don't know when I'll be coming back.'

'In that case, I have to ask if you have an entry visa?'

Colin's eyes screwed up in consternation. 'Entry visa?'

'I'm sorry.' The girl recognised his bewilderment. 'It's airline regulations, sir. They won't carry you on a one-way ticket unless you have an entry visa. You see,' she explained, 'if the airline carries you to your destination and you are refused entry, then the airline is responsible for getting you back again.'

Shit! Colin cursed to himself. *Something like this would have to happen.* Aloud he asked: 'And where do I get a visa, Miss?'

'You'll have to go round to the Ghanaian embassy,

sir.' She scribbled down the address. 'You shouldn't have any difficulty.'

He took the paper with a sigh. 'All right, Miss. I'll be back as soon as I get this sorted out.'

★

'Excuse me,' Colin addressed the girl behind the reception desk in the foyer of the Ghanaian Embassy. 'I'd like to apply for a visa, please. Who do I see?'

'I have the application forms here.' The receptionist handed him the paper. 'You can fill it out over there,' she indicated a desk against a wall of the foyer.

'Thank you.' He accepted a form from her and moved over to a chair beside the small writing desk.

The reception area was quiet as he worked away at filling in the form. At one point three laughing Africans entered the hallway, looking over curiously when they spotted him sitting at the desk. Five minutes later he was handing the girl the completed document.

'Thank you,' she smiled at him and slipped the form into her 'in' tray.

'Well,' Colin waited. 'What about the visa?'

'We will write to you soon.'

'But . . . I need the visa now,' he explained. 'I want to travel to Ghana tomorrow.'

'I'm sorry,' the girl told him. 'Your application has to be processed. We will write to you within a day or two and you can come down with your passport.'

'But I'm buying a ticket today. I've got my passport here and I want to fly out as soon as possible,' Colin explained.

'I'm sorry, sir. Your application must be processed.'

'Is there anyone here I can speak to?' he finally asked in exasperation.

'I'm sorry,' she said again. 'But this is the way it is done.'

Jesus Christ! Colin tried to maintain his composure. 'Miss,' he enunciated the words slowly, 'can I please see someone in authority?'

'Excuse me . . .' Colin felt a hand on his arm. 'Can I be of any assistance?'

He turned to see one of the three young black men who had entered earlier standing beside him.

'I'm trying to get a visa,' he explained. 'But the girl here tells me I have to wait. Do you think you could help me?'

'Well, normally visa applications do take a few days to process. Are you in any particular hurry to travel?'

'I thought I just had to buy a ticket,' Colin

56

explained. 'I didn't know anything about a visa and I want to travel out tomorrow. Is there any way you can help me?'

'Please come with me,' the man said in a pleasantly soft tone. 'I'll see what I can do.' He led Colin through a door leading off the hall and showed him to a chair. The man took the seat facing him and held out his hand.

'I'm Yarty Okufu,' he introduced himself.

'Colin Grant.' He extended his hand. 'Pleased to meet you.'

'Actually, we have met before, you know,' Yarty smiled.

'I don't think so,' Colin cocked his head and looked closer at the black man facing him.

Yarty looked at the room's other occupants and lowered his voice. 'About four years ago in the Central Criminal Court – The Old Bailey, as it is better known. I had just begun my law studies and your case was my first experience there. I believe the result was a long term of imprisonment?'

Colin could see no point in denial; the man obviously knew what he was talking about and he didn't appear to be very concerned.

'Aye,' the native Scots surfaced in his voice. 'You're right enough,' he admitted. 'S'matter of fact, I only got out last week.'

'You have my sympathies,' Yarty told him. 'I would hate to be locked away behind bars like that.'

'That's how I feel myself,' Colin answered. 'And that's the reason I want to get to Ghana. There's too much *business* going about just now and I don't want to become involved. If I'm out of it for a while, maybe I can stay clear.' He could see no reason not to lay it on a little.

'*Stay clear?*' Yarty smiled grimly. 'In my country you would be in more than serious trouble if you did not, as you put it, 'stay clear'. And the prisons . . .' He spread a slim hand and shrugged. 'You would not survive four years in a Ghanaian prison as well as you seem to have survived Her Majesty's hostelry here.'

'Believe me,' Colin spoke sincerely. 'I'm only going for a holiday. All I want to do is lie in the sun and relax.'

'Are you quite sure a holiday is all that you have in mind?'

Colin smiled. The possibility of '*earning*' had occurred to him. But he spread his arms. 'What else?' he appealed.

'*Business*,' Yarty employed the same inflection Colin had used. 'If nothing else, my experience at the Old Bailey instilled in me a great respect for the ambition, willingness and sheer audacity of the London criminal.'

'What possible *business* could I get involved in out there?' Colin asked. 'I'm not even certain where the place is.'

'H'mm . . .' Yarty gave him a calculating look. 'Then why bother to go? My country could hardly be described as a holiday resort.'

'I've an uncle there – manager in a cocoa mill. He invited me out for a holiday to help me get over . . .'

'I understand,' Yarty interrupted him. 'So you're definitely not going to Ghana to seek employment then?'

'No way.' Colin assured him. 'It's a holiday I'm after. I need a break.'

'There's not much work in my country for Europeans, you know. Hardly enough work for my own people.'

'You don't have to worry about me doing anyone out of a job,' Colin assured him, seeing the way Yarty's mind was working. 'The less I have to do the better.'

'You have a passport with you?' Yarty held out his hand as he came to a decision.

Colin handed over his passport and watched him leave the room. Five minutes later Yarty was handing his passport back to him, a visitor's visa taking up almost a full page. 'Permitted to enter Ghana for the purpose of . . . .' The blank space had the word 'VACATION' stamped on it. Another endorsement stipulated: 'Valid for twenty-eight days'.

'Twenty-eight days! I'll be there a bit longer that that,' he said.

'It's all right,' Yarty assured him. 'A tourist visa is the easiest type to get. Once you're in Ghana you can simply keep renewing it at the Government Office in Accra. You'll be able to stay on as long as you like, as long as you don't start working.'

'Thanks again, Yarty. I'm obliged to you.' Colin gave the helpful African a wave as he went down the steps to the pavement, fingering his passport through the cloth of his coat pocket, anxious to get back to the British Airways office and finalise the details of his flight.

5

The 'No Smoking' and 'Fasten Seat Belts' signs lit up on board the British Airways 707 as it headed downwind, parallel with the main runway of Accra International Airport.

From his window-seat, Colin could see the runway lights, bright orange against the pitch-black of the countryside below. Further away, coming into view as the aircraft banked into its final turn, a myriad of lights picked out the city of Accra and his stomach churned with excitement as the big jet slid down the dark sky. There was a sudden glare of light, a flash of black and white striped tarmac, then the wingtips were ripping past orange runway markers as the giant plane touched down.

A large crowd waited behind the railings of the single-storey arrivals building to greet the passengers. Colin tried to pick out his Uncle George, hoping he would be able to recognise him after a gap of almost ten years. He had no problem.

In fact it was his uncle who looked uncertain, until Colin caught his eye and smiled.

'My God! Colin!' George's voice was full of surprise. 'What a difference in you.'

'It's been a long time,' Colin smiled, pleased at his welcome.

'And you've certainly changed,' George told him as they shook hands and walked the short distance to immigration control with the steel crush barrier between them. 'I'll see you once the formalities are done with. You shouldn't be held up for too long.'

He was waiting outside when Colin emerged and stepped forward, hand outstretched for his suitcase. 'Come on,' he said, 'I've got a friend waiting with a car; we'll soon be away from here.'

Once his cases were stowed in the boot of the car Colin was introduced to Brian Smithers, the cocoa buyer for the same company George worked for. A lean six-footer, with a dry, laconic air about him, Brian was younger than George's forty-six years, but the African sun had dried him out and he had the mien of a much older man as he shook hands with Colin. Two minutes later they were leaving the lights of the airport behind as they headed in towards Accra.

Colin was fascinated by the sights, sounds and scents he was picking up as the car traversed the outer edge of the city. Their route took them between long lines of single-storey whitewashed cottages, the black openings of unlit doors and windows giving them the appearance of a long domino set. He could see the locals outside on the broad packed-earth pavements, sitting round candlelit tables and engaged in a loud, vociferous, hand-banging card game. Now and again their excited voices reached inside the car. Other groups of men and women sat at street corners, socialising under the yellow glow of street lights, talking, laughing and singing as small children crawled over them or lay curled contentedly fast asleep at their parents' feet. He found the whole throbbing scene enormously exciting.

The humid night heat had a muffling effect which enhanced the peaceful mood, and too soon for him the car turned off onto a quieter road, coming to a halt in the driveway of a large villa set in the residential suburb of Ikeyi, on the northern outskirts of Accra.

'We'll be here for the night,' George explained as they entered a spacious lounge.

Brian broke in. 'This is a company house, Colin, and there's always a place here for you when you visit Accra. If I'm away on business Koffi, the houseboy, will be here to look after you.' He waved a hand at a smiling African who stepped forward to be introduced.

Sighing with contentment, Colin relaxed into an armchair, inspecting his palatial surroundings as Koffi poured him a very welcome ice-cold beer. *Sure beats a cell in Wandsworth*, he caught himself thinking with a smile. *I'm going to enjoy myself here all right. Fuck me! They've even got servants!*

'And once you're settled in at Takoradi . . .', he realised his uncle was speaking to him, '. . . you'll find plenty to do with yourself. There's the Volta Dam Scheme, the diamond fields at Tarkwa, bauxite mines at Kumasi and the goldmines at Obuasi. Plenty to keep you interested.'

Colin's ears pricked up. 'Diamond fields, goldmines? I didn't know they had things like that here. I thought it was all cocoa beans.'

'Cocoa beans, yes,' Brian spoke out. 'But there is also the timber industry, vast mineral deposits, a good yield of industrial diamonds and the richest gold mine in West Africa.' He raised his glass. 'There's lots for you to see here, Colin.' He drained off his beer as he finished speaking. 'Well, I'm off to bed. Got an early start in the morning. George will show you to your room. There's a shower and toilet en-suite, so you should have everything you need.' He rose to his full height and stretched himself before bidding them goodnight, his 'See you in the morning' floating over his shoulder as he mounted the open stairway.

George turned to Colin when they had the lounge to themselves. 'Well, Colin, I hope you enjoy your stay here. It'll certainly be a change from the other place, eh? And, by the way, no one here knows anything about you, except that you're my nephew here on a prolonged vacation.'

'That's fine, Uncle George.'

'And you can cut out the "Uncle" bit, m'lad. What are you trying to do, put years on me?'

Colin smiled. 'Anyway, I'd like to say thanks, George. I appreciate you putting me up and I'm glad to get away from that London scene for a spell.'

'Well, you'll have no difficulty in keeping out of trouble here, son. There's very little in Takoradi to get involved in, so we'll say no more on that aspect of things. And now, I think it's time for bed. Come on, I'll show you your room – Koffi will have the bed turned down by now.'

After a welcome shower Colin lay back on the large, comfortable bed, listening to the hum of the air-conditioner as it blew cold air into the room. *Diamond fields! Goldmines!* He couldn't put them from his mind and was still considering their absorbing possibilities when he drifted off to sleep.

6

Cruising through bright sunlit air at 3,000 feet enhanced Colin's view of the exotic scenery sliding by below. Absorbed, he watched the turquoise blue waters of the South Atlantic foam into white lines of surf as invisible waves tumbled onto mile after mile of golden beach. He changed seats to get an inland view and was surprised at the richness of colour the rolling coastal hills afforded.

George pointed out the university township of Cape Coast and its neighbouring Cape Coast Castle, an old fortress that had in the past held captured natives before they were shipped off to the West Indies as slaves in the diabolical conditions of the 'Triangular Trade'. Ironically, this ancient fortress that had once witnessed so much human suffering now served as a police training barracks, although a small section of it had been set aside as a museum; a grisly reminder of days gone by.

'Sekondi,' George nodded downwards as some larger stone buildings slid under the aircraft's wing.

'Five miles east of Takoradi. We'll be landing in a minute or two.'

As he spoke, there was a whine of hydraulics and the undercarriage reached out from the underside of the wings, the flaps dropped and suddenly the ground seemed to leap towards them. Then the wheels touched down, spinning into furious motion as they bit greedily into the tarmac of Takoradi.

Being a domestic flight there were no landing formalities and in minutes a waiting car was whisking them through the dusty streets of Takoradi towards the cocoa mill, three miles east of town on the road to Sekondi.

It was the sight and sound of monkeys capering high in the trees that brought it home to Colin that he really had shifted continents; that he had finally left the cold and the danger of London thousands of miles behind. A wide smile spread across his face and he craned his neck to keep the cavorting animals in sight as a tremendous feeling of freedom and adventure surged through his entire body, an exciting, exhilarating feeling that he had never experienced in the streets of London or his native Glasgow.

The car slowed to negotiate a right turn, a roughly painted sign simply nailed to a convenient tree trunk indicating that the Ghana Cocoa Company lay ahead. Half a mile on they passed through a large gateway and turned up a short, steep hill that took them past the cocoa mill and on to the living quarters of the European workers.

'Here we are,' George said as the car turned into a short drive and came to a halt in front of an elegant, whitewashed bungalow.

Colin had guessed his uncle enjoyed good accommodation, but the beautiful stone bungalow went well beyond his expectations. Twin flights of steps curved on either side of the long, low building to open onto a wide, flower-bedecked verandah that was furnished with white garden lounge chairs surrounding a large, glass topped, wrought iron table. Above the flowers an exotic parrot squawked a welcome as it danced excitedly from foot to foot on its open perch. Suitably impressed, Colin was still admiring the scene when a young African man appeared from inside the house and George introduced him to Sam, his houseboy. In moments Sam had led them inside and produced two iced Heineken beers before returning to the car and bringing in their luggage. *Yes*, Colin told himself, sipping at his drink, *I really am going to like it here*.

*

The first days passed quickly as Colin settled in. A

cup of tea and a biscuit from the attentive Sam prepared him for a mid-morning breakfast before he began his daily dawdling tour of the factory. He was content to remain within the cocoa mill's boundaries these first few days. The novelty of meeting the various characters as he wandered about kept him thoroughly interested. In the evenings, as cooling breezes brushed the verandah, he sat with George, nursing sweating glasses of Heineken and looking down over the tangled vegetation of the hillside to the crashing waves of the South Atlantic as they rolled in from the broad Gulf of Guinea. Often a ship would be in sight as sea traffic steamed along the coast or headed directly for the port of Takoradi itself. It seemed an idyllic existence to Colin, recent memories of Wandsworth only serving to emphasise his appreciation.

As the days grew into weeks, Colin settled into life in Takoradi. George had introduced him to Takoradi Sports Club, the hub of social activity for the local European population, and it soon became a focal point for him. And there was a girl there too, Lesley Farrell, the blonde-haired, twenty-two-year-old daughter of the manager. They had been introduced and he had spoken to her several times, but it was difficult to get her full attention, especially with her father always hovering in the background. Still, he nursed the hope of getting to know Lesley better as time went on. A spare set of golf clubs was found for him and he spent most afternoons hacking happily over the nine-hole golf course, often joining his uncle for a round in the early evening when he had finished at the cocoa mill. Altogether he was having a great time and the use of an elderly but reliable company car solved his transport problem, giving him some extra independence.

7

Colin's drive hooked deep into the rough to the accompaniment of George's stifled laughter.

'You'll have to do better than that when you get to Obuasi,' he said, preparing to drive off from the third tee of a late afternoon round of golf.

'Obuasi?' Colin spoke out on George's downs-wing, and laughed as the white ball disappeared deep into the rough.

'Damn!' George turned on him with a bad-tempered look. 'You know you're not supposed to do that!'

'Sorry,' Colin grinned unrepentantly. 'You mentioned something about Obuasi?'

George sent his caddy into the long grass after his ball. 'I'm teeing-off again. You deliberately distracted me,' he accused.

'C'mon, it's only a game. You can tee-off all day as far as I'm concerned. Now what's this about Obuasi?'

'You'll have to start taking your golf more

seriously,' an admonishing finger waved under his nose. 'Only a game indeed!'

'C'mon, George . . .' Colin appealed.

'I've arranged a long weekend for us up there. You did say you wanted to see a gold mine, didn't you?'

'Oh aye,' Colin tried to sound off-hand, belying the sudden interest George's news had generated in him. 'Is it far then?'

'It's in the Kumasi region of the Ashanti Tribal Lands. The mine itself is at Obuasi, about twenty miles south of Kumasi city. I've been in touch with John Ogilvie, the general manager up there. He's an old friend of mine and we're invited for the weekend. You can tour the mine and we'll be able to fit in a round or two of golf. That is . . .' his face turned stern. 'As long as you are prepared to treat the game seriously.'

'When are we leaving?' Colin hid his rising excitement.

'We leave on Friday evening. We'll have the full Saturday and Sunday there and return on the Monday morning train.'

'We can't drive there?'

'We could, but not direct from here. Driving would mean going via Accra to get on the Kumasi road and that would more than double the mileage. On top of that, the road is pretty poor once you get a few miles out of the city. So driving is not really an option.'

'It's a fair distance then?'

'Not really; it's only about 120 miles from here to Obuasi as the crow flies, but the roads north of Takoradi are nothing more than dirt tracks.'

'Aye,' Colin nodded agreement. 'I've noticed that myself. Went for a drive the other day and nearly wrecked the old car's suspension.'

'Exactly! That's why we're taking the train. It leaves Friday night and I've already booked the tickets.'

'That's good.' Colin abandoned his first drive and teed up another shot, driving his ball a good 200 yards. 'That's really good.'

★

It was midnight when the old narrow-gauge steam engine gasped to a wheezing standstill at the small, wooden-platformed station of Obuasi, where George and Colin were met by a driver from the goldmine. Less than ten minutes later, they were settling into one of the Ashanti Goldfield Corporation's guest-houses where, weary after the hot, rackety train journey, the cool-looking beds were a welcome sight for both of them.

★

73

The following morning John Ogilvie, a dark, saturnine, lanky Aberdonian of about fifty years, collected them from their rooms. Looking like a scoutmaster in freshly laundered khaki shorts and long woollen socks, he led them to the mining company's clubhouse and social centre for a late breakfast.

'So you wanted to see a goldmine, eh?' He turned dark eyes on Colin as they sat at a table overlooking the mine-head workings.

'Well . . . seeing as I'm here.' Colin smiled.

'Aye. And nae doubt ye'll be expecting to see lumps of gold lying about, or sticking out of the walls like rocks, eh?' He grabbed up the pepper pot from the table and held it tight in his fist. 'Like this?' He stared hard into Colin's eyes, a hint of amusement tugging at the corners of his mouth.

Colin shrugged, wondering if this strange man understood more than he was letting on. It was obvious to him that George and John Ogilvie were old friends; they seemed to communicate easily without saying very much. He couldn't quite put his finger on it, but something was definitely amusing the two older men and their Scottish accents became more and more exaggerated as they talked on.

'Aye . . . The loon here will be doon the mine looking for the gold. Aye, like thoosands afore him.'

74

Ogilvie grinned knowingly. 'Gold fever!' he added, his Aberdonian accent almost destroying the words. 'They all come lusting after the bonny Ashanti Gold.' He looked into Colin's eyes. 'Well, m'loon, you'll ha'e your chance wi' the gold, same as a'body else. You'll ha'e your chance.'

Puzzled by his host's enigmatic statement, Colin peered down at the dust-covered work-sheds, feeling a familiar quiver as he eyed the activity below. He was keen now to get down into the mine and see the gold for himself, totally unaware of his hands rubbing together in the universal language of greedy anticipation. A younger man dressed in a carefully pressed, one-piece, white boiler suit came across to their table.

'Ah! Good morning, Gareth.' Ogilvie waved the newcomer to an empty chair. 'You'll be having a bite with us?'

'Thank you, Mr. Ogilvie,' the man replied in a quiet, lilting voice. 'But I'll just have a coffee, thanks – I've already eaten.'

Colin identified the accent as Welsh. 'You married men,' Ogilvie raised thick eyebrows and smiled. 'Mollycoddled day and night you are.' He turned to Colin. 'Gareth Davies,' he said, introducing them to each other. 'Assistant Mine Manager – Operations.' He turned back to Gareth, the slightly amused tone entering his voice again. 'He's come to see the mine; that's the reason I asked you to meet me here this morning. Give him the usual tour and see he doesn't collect too many free samples.' His voice broke off in a smothered laugh as the three men looked at Colin, grinning knowingly.

★

'This is the deepest mine in West Africa,' Gareth informed Colin as the metal cage plummeted underground. 'We're mining now at 4500 feet – that's not far off a mile straight down, boyo.'

'Amazing.' Colin looked at the raw rock through the mesh of the cage as the lift descended. He was twin now to Gareth – wearing an identical white boiler suit, a white safety helmet with its miner's lamp, and a heavy battery-pack slung on his hip. Not normally the nervous type, Colin had to admit to a certain apprehensiveness as the flimsy-looking lift rattled and clanked downwards to level twelve, the temperature dropping along with them as they moved further away from the heat of the mid-morning sun above.

There was little sensation of being deep underground when they left the lift. A long, smoothly cut tunnel stretched ahead of them, illuminated by alternate pools of light and dark, the curved concrete props of the tunnel gleaming white, like the ribcage of a whale, in the reflected glow of a string of naked light bulbs. A faint rumbling sound was gradually growing louder as they progressed along the underground passage.

'Be at the working face in a minute,' Gareth volunteered, breaking a longish silence. 'There's always lots of dust and stones flying about, so be careful,' he warned as rumbling sounds increased where the tunnel reached a T-junction.

A conveyer belt moved steadily along against the far wall of the new tunnel and Colin could see the dim shapes of men through flying dust as they went about their work. One of the men looked up, raising an arm in greeting as he moved towards them.

'That's Kwakko, overseer on this level,' Gareth told him. 'Good man. The Africans need one of their own to get the best out of them.'

'Good morning, sah,' Kwakko pulled a neckerchief from his face as he approached them and addressed Gareth. 'All work is ahead.'

Gareth showed his teeth in a smile and nodded. 'Kwakko, this is Mr Grant.' He introduced them, pleased to see Colin extend his hand to the black overseer. 'We'll show him the new face. You should be well into it by now.'

'Yes, sah.' Kwakko turned to Colin. 'You come?'

he said, lifting his mask back over his mouth and turning towards the sound of heavy machinery.

Gareth produced two rectangles of cloth from a pocket in the leg of his boiler suit, handing one to Colin and demonstrating its use as a mask before nodding in the direction of the noise and flying dust.

The machine was operated by three African workers. One man sat at main controls, his thin black hands moving skilfully over the shiny knobs and wheels, while two assistants operated levers at either end of the cutting blades.

Colin scrutinised the walls of the tunnel for the gleam of gold and saw nothing. He looked at the area where the cutters were chewing, peering through flying chips as he leant closer.

'Where's the gold?' he shouted at Gareth, who pointed at the wall in front of them and held up his thumb. Puzzled, Colin stared hard and shook his head. He still couldn't see any of the precious metal.

Kwakko was pointing at the revolving blades of the machine, evidently explaining their function and proudly indicating the operator, who threw himself into the spirit of things by making several adjustments to his knobs and switches in an exaggerated exhibition of efficiency. After a few minutes Gareth touched Colin on the shoulder and jerked his head back along the tunnel.

'Where's the gold?' Colin asked again with a distinct tone of disappointment when he removed his mask. 'I didn't see any gold.'

The Welshman smiled and drew him over to the rumbling conveyer belt. 'There's your gold, boyo,' he pointed to the moving detritus on the conveyer belt. 'Everyone expects to see chunks of the stuff sticking out of the walls,' he said, shaking his head in amusement. 'It gives us a laugh watching their expressions, but it's not like that at all.' He lifted a handful of dust from the belt.

'Two and a half ounces to the ton, that's the average yield down here – and that's good! But you've got to get it out of this stuff,' he said as he spilled the dust from his hand. 'Come on, we'll head back up now and I'll show you the furnaces.'

*

It was hot inside the smelting shed, its corrugated iron roof absorbing and magnifying the power of the noon-high sun. But even this heat was overpowered by the incandescent blast emanating from three oil-fired furnaces which 'cooked' the excavated earth in massive pots held hard in their mountings against the cherry redness of flames.

African workers, wearing only ragged shorts and worn sweatbands round their glistening foreheads, stood at the base of the number three furnace as the overhead crane manoeuvred to hook on to brackets on either side of the huge pot.

Gareth nudged him. 'Now you'll see the stuff, boyo! Now you'll see the gold!'

The crane succeeded in hooking on and the huge pot, accompanied by a thermometer-bursting blast of heat, swung high through the shed to be tipped on to a loading chute for the travelling skips.

'The furnace heats the ore until the particles filter through the drain holes into the base tray,' Gareth explained. 'Once the gold is collected, it's ready for pouring. There you go; they're pushing the mould in now.'

Sure enough, two men were manoeuvring a flat trolley into position under the lip of the base-tray. Another figure, a white man, approached the small knot of men.

'That's Fred O'Hara,' Gareth told him. 'He's the shift supervisor and he's got to be present at every pour. I'll introduce you.'

Wild blue eyes stared into Colin's face as he shook hands with Fred. At close quarters the man had a crazed look about him.

'Heard we had a visitor,' Fred inspected Colin, blinking slowly as though trying to squeeze moisture from dry eyes. 'Right on time to catch a pour too. Just stand back a bit, it can spit when it hits the cold tray.' He warned Colin, waving him off a pace.

'Right?' Fred looked at a sweating worker who stood by a large metal wheel.

'Yes, sah!'

'Okay.' Fred inserted a key in a lock to release the wheel. 'Slowly then,' he instructed.

The man turned the wheel and the tray began to tilt, sending its glowing contents rippling towards the vee-shaped spout.

'Steady! Steady!' Fred fluttered his fingers delicately. 'That's it, you beauty!' The liquid metal radiated light as it bled from the spout in a heavy, golden stream.

Colin stared, hypnotised. Gold! Raw gold, fresh from mother earth. It was all he had ever imagined. In a few moments the base-tray was vertical, the last blob of richness sliding heavily into the mould, melding like quicksand into the glowing coalescence of the pool.

'Good pour!' Fred opened his eyes wide at the wheelman in appreciation, receiving a broad, pink-gummed smile in return.

Colin had been too engrossed to notice the arrival of the two soldiers who stepped forward to take command of the trolley, one of them pulling it forward a few feet to allow the second soldier to take up position at the rear.

'Right then?' Fred addressed the towing soldier, receiving a nod of acknowledgement before the three of them moved off towards a door at the end of the shed where another soldier stood guard.

'Weighing room and vault,' Gareth explained as they followed behind the trolley. 'The gold is made up into 400-ounce ingots in here and locked away in the vault.'

'Why all the soldiers?' Colin asked, although he was pretty certain he already knew their purpose.

'Security,' Gareth confirmed his suspicions. 'We had a bad scare about six months ago. A team from some political group tried to finance themselves by dynamiting the safe and liberating the gold – damn near done it too! They had to install a new vault and now they've got a permanent army unit practically living in the place.'

'What happened to them?'

'Huh?' Gareth looked puzzled.

'The men who tried to steal the gold? What happened to them?'

Gareth shook his head. 'No mercy where their gold's concerned. Fellow in charge of security, Major Judas Akaba, had the poor bastards shot where they stood.'

'Just like that?'

'Judas Akaba's well named. He'd shoot his own grandmother if she as much as touched a pennyweight of his precious gold.'

Colin looked away and swallowed before speaking again. 'Didn't look much in that last pour.'

'I'd estimate 250, 270 ounces there, boyo,' Gareth told him. 'We're into rich ground just now. Averaging 2.8 ounces to the ton, we are.'

'How much gold do they get in a shift?'

'Government's ordered us to increase production to at least two pours from each furnace every day.'

Colin tried to work out the totals in his head, but the effort was too much and he merely nodded, impressed by the figures.

'Come on, boyo.' Gareth led him up to the door that had just let the gold trolley pass through. 'You'll have your chance to get rich now.' He beckoned to a puzzled Colin and led him through the door.

Air conditioning made it almost cold in the well-lit office they entered and for a moment Colin thought they were in a bank, as he took in the broad counter and thick security screens rising to meet the ceiling. There were two soldiers lounging on a bench facing the counter and as he looked a door opened behind them to allow two other squaddies into the office. The four soldiers exchanged desultory words before the first two left, allowing the new men to commandeer the bench where they made a show of inspecting their weapons.

Colin could see Fred O'Hara eyeing a set of scales as two white-coated Africans busied themselves with the fresh delivery. Fred looked round and came over to let them behind the counter. Suddenly his hands went out to squeeze Colin's biceps, making him jerk in surprise.

'Don't think we've got too much to worry about here,' he said, grinning inanely at a mystified Colin. 'I've seen more muscle in a piccaninny's pecker!' He gave Colin's arms another squeeze and turned back to the scales.

Colin watched the weighing operation, keen to learn as much as he could about this fascinating business. One of the white-coated Africans smiled at him.

'We are making up a standard 400-ounce ingot,' he explained, eyeing the quivering indicator on the sensitive scales. 'That's . . . it!' The needle steadied precisely on the 400 ounce mark.

'What about that?' Colin pointed to the excess gold remaining in the mould the man had poured from.

'Next pour go on top till 400 ounces. Make one ingot.' The smooth cheeks of the man rounded as he smiled. 'Now all gold go for vault.' He inclined his head towards the rear of the office.

A huge steel door stared balefully at Colin. It covered almost half the rear wall, highlights glinting forbiddingly on the massive steel portal.

The door opened silently, allowing the two workers to carry both the new ingot and the remains of the last pour over the metal step and into the strongroom.

'Come on then,' Fred beckoned Colin. 'You wanted to see the gold, didn't you?' He made a courtly little bow and held his hand out in invitation.

A surge of excitement gripped Colin as he entered the interior of the Ashanti Goldfield Corporation's gold store. Barely the size of his cell in Wandsworth Prison, with heavy steel shelving lining three walls, there was little room for the four men who crowded inside. Colin didn't mind, he could have stood beside the gold forever. He held his breath without realising it, drinking in the sight of the gold bars and swallowing as they reflected opalescent waves of soft-hued, reddish light. It was all he could have hoped for, the intrinsic richness of the gold bringing a lump to his throat as, like thousands before him, he became mesmerised by the gleaming bars of Ashanti gold.

Fred's voice broke into his almost hypnotic trance.

'Come on now . . . Let's be having a bit of space. Let the dog see the rabbit.' He strained to lift a bar of gold onto a low wooden stool. 'Now's your chance.' He grinned wildly at Colin and pointed at the gleaming ingot. 'Go on,' Fred insisted. 'Have a go.'

Colin looked round at the faces of the others, seeing only eyes widened in expectancy. There was a movement at his back and a grinning Gareth squeezed in beside them.

'Pick it up with one hand and it's yours,' Fred told him.

'What?' Face screwed up in perplexity, Colin looked into Fred's staring eyes. *Maybe the man is mad!* The thought leapt into his mind, but it was Gareth who helped him out.

'It's an old custom,' he told Colin. 'Everyone gets a chance at being rich. If you can pick up the gold with one hand, you can keep it.'

'Really? Keep it?' His every syllable dripped doubt.

The two Africans grinned widely at him, both nodding in concert. Gareth nodded too, trying to keep his face straight as Fred clapped his hands impatiently and pointed to the gleaming bar. 'Come on then. Give it a go.'

Colin looked at the gleaming ingot thinking: *Lift it and it's mine? Must be a catch in it somewhere.* He studied the bar more closely. *Doesn't look too heavy. What was its weight again? Four hundred ounces, they had said.* His brain worked on the problem while the others looked on silently.

'If I lift it, I can keep it?'

'Lift it – it's yours!' Fred's reply was emphatic.

'Right.' Colin blew on his hand and flexed his fingers. 'I know there must be a catch in it, but I'll have a go anyway.' He stood astride the stool and adjusted his position until the gold was directly under his face. Rubbing his right hand dry on his thigh in a final nervous movement, he held it over the golden treasure, seeing it flush his palm yellow, like a buttercup held against a child's chin. He took a deep breath and with as much strength as he could muster closed his fingers on the ingot.

At first Colin thought he had a good grip and the bar was actually lifting, but as he slowly raised his hand he found that the gold sat solidly on the stool. He tried again. Trying to force his fingers hard under the bottom edge – but no. Again his hand slipped over the silken surface. The steep taper of the ingot's sides, coupled with the smooth, oily sheen of the gold, meant that the harder he squeezed, the easier his fingers slid over the gleaming surface. Frustrated, he watched helplessly as 400 ounces of pure Ashanti gold literally slipped through his fingers.

'Can't be done!' He breathed harshly, stepping back from the stool. 'It's impossible. The harder you grip the easier it slides. It can't be done.'

'And if anyone ever does manage the impossible . . .' A cold, humourless voice hacked like sharp ice into the joviality of the moment, '. . . they still have me to pass before they can enjoy their good fortune.'

Colin felt nervous, as if he had been caught with his hands in the till. He turned to see who had spoken. An army officer, a major, stared unnervingly at him, eyes as black as the deepest pit peering out from a narrow, sharp-featured face. He was a blend of cruel jungle and sophisticated coastal native, and his face showed it. High cheekbones framed a thin, aquiline nose above narrow lips that looked scarcely capable of smiling. Right now they were parted in a devil's grimace as his left forefinger lightly stroked on a deep scar just over his left eye. At the same time his free hand brushed against the heavy automatic weapon hanging from his belt, drawing everyone's attention.

'Only a game, Major Akaba,' Fred was the only one not intimidated by the major's sinister presence. 'Got to amuse the visitors, you know how it is?'

'Yes, Mister O'Hara.' The thin lips moved only slightly. 'It is only a game. But be sure it remains *only a game*.' He stared bleakly at each individual in the vault, as if imprinting their images in his mind, before turning to go.

'Should've known,' Colin grunted, removing his eyes from the malevolent figure. 'There's no way anyone is going to get walking out of here with a bar of gold. I should have known better. I must have been off my head.'

'Not the first time gold's done that, boyo,' Gareth observed. 'And not the last time either. Get people near raw gold and they can become very irrational. It wouldn't be the first time we've had a perfectly respectable visitor trying to snaffle a gold bar out of here. The sight of the gold seems to drive their principles clean away.'

'And bring all their vices to the surface,' Fred intoned, leaning forward to lift the gold in both hands and replace it on the shelf.

As they left the security area the lounging soldiers rose to their feet and moved towards them. Gareth stepped forward, holding his hands out from his sides to allow a perfunctory rub-down. Memories of prison searches vivid in his mind, Colin stepped in front of the soldier and slipped naturally into the 'rub-down' position, receiving a more intensive search than the familiar Gareth had. In the short passage beyond the door the sound of squabbling drew his attention, and he caught a glimpse of more uniformed soldiers noisily playing cards in a side room. Then he was past and stepping out into the heat of the sun.

'Are the soldiers here all the time?' he asked Gareth as they walked uphill towards the administration buildings.

'Twenty-four hours a day,' Gareth agreed. 'It's all part of the new security arrangements. The gold is under heavy guard from the moment it's poured until they lock it away in the treasury vaults in Accra.'

'And how do they get it down to Accra from here?' Colin asked casually. 'There's hardly a road worth talking about.'

'Oh, the army boyos have it all sorted out. Once a week they lay on an armed convoy to Kumasi and it gets flown down from there; they've been doing it for years.' He stopped and looked at his watch. 'Well, you've seen all that's worth seeing. What say we both go for a shower and have a pint in the clubhouse later on?'

'That'll be fine,' Colin gave a relieved sigh. 'I'm just about knackered anyway.'

★

His Uncle George and John Ogilvie were waiting for him in the bar of the social club.

'Well?' Ogilvie's dark eyebrows rose questioningly. 'Did you get your chance at the gold, laddie? Are we looking at a wealthy man?'

Colin waved in dismissal. 'Chance at the gold!' he scoffed. 'You'd need to be built like King Kong to lift that gold.'

'Aye,' the grinning Ogilvie admitted. 'We're no' as daft as we look, eh? Anyway . . . did you enjoy your tour?'

'It was . . . eh . . . different from what I had expected,' he admitted. 'I always thought a goldmine had seams of gold running through it.'

'In some countries you can find gold in seams and nuggets, but not out here. It's the way it was originally deposited that makes the difference.' Ogilvie seemed ready to deliver a lecture on gold deposits when George interrupted.

'We're teeing-off at two o'clock, John. I think it's time we had our lunch; the course will be busy today.'

'Aye. You're right enough.' Ogilvie turned back to Colin.

'You play, I take it?'

'Plays at it, is more like it!' George sniffed. ' *"Just a game"*, he says.'

A look of alarm filled Ogilvie's eyes. 'Oh! "Just a game", m'lad, is it? Well,' he humphed. 'I sincerely hope ye're no planning tae interfere wi' oor game the day, laddie?' His eyebrows bristled like thistles, as thick and Scottish as his accent.

'I'll leave you to it,' Colin assured the relieved man. 'I'll just wander about here; probably take a dip in the pool. Maybe tomorrow I'll have a quick knock-round.'

'My heavens!' Ogilvie's voice despaired. 'A quick knock-round! What kind of Scot are they breeding nowadays?'

*

Diamond fields ... Goldmines ... 'H'mph!' Colin snorted, nursing a cold beer on the club's shaded verandah. He looked down on the smelting shed, scowling at the squat security block attached to it like a greedy suckling pig, and watched a squad of soldiers arrive by truck. Mentally ticking off their numbers he counted twelve men, a full platoon; plus Akaba in a skipped cap, giving out orders. Eventually things settled down and the truck lumbered away with the off-duty guard platoon, leaving two men on view outside the bank-like building.

He shook his head: *No chance!* The gold was as safe here as it would be in the Bank of England. He felt a pang of disappointment; there was no gold here for him; no chance of earning. Time now to settle down and get on with his holiday. Concentrate on having a bit of fun. His thoughts turned to Lesley – maybe it was time to try and get closer to her.

8

Two weeks after his disappointing visit to the goldmine, Colin was sitting on the verandah having his usual evening 'sundowner' drink with George when he broached a subject he had been turning over in his mind for the past few days.

'When you mentioned the goldmine, George . . .' he said, keeping his voice casual. 'Remember? When I first arrived? You said something about diamond mines as well, and you said I would be able to see them.'

'Aye,' George nodded absently. 'Aye, that's right, or half right anyway,' he chuckled. 'There's the goldmine all right, but there are no diamond *mines* in Ghana. It's diamond *fields* out here – surface diamonds. Alluvial diamonds, to give them their proper title. The natives dig for them in the ground. Oh, they might dig a fairly deep hole or two, but mostly it's just shallow digging and hard sifting for the stones.'

'What? They just dig about and find diamonds?' Colin straightened unconsciously in his seat.

'Well, it's a wee bit more sophisticated than that,' George admitted. 'There's a lot of mechanisation in the diamond fields nowadays. But basically, that's it. You just go out and dig.'

'Can anyone do it? Could I have a go?'

'No, no, no,' laughed George. 'It's all government-controlled – part of national resources. Anyway, they're not diamonds you'd recognise. They don't sparkle and shine, if that's what you think.'

'But I can go and see all this?'

'Certainly you can see it. The nearest fields are up Tarkwa way, about forty miles north of here. Mind you, the road is a bit rough once you get away from the coast, so it's not just as handy as it sounds.'

Colin could barely contain his excitement, but he kept his voice casual. 'You know, I'd really like to see these diamond fields, George. D'you think I could get there on my own?'

'Och! You're a big laddie, Colin – you'd manage fine. Why don't you make a day of it? Get Sam to pack you a meal and a few bottles of beer.'

'That's a good idea,' Colin spoke quietly, his mind already considering the tantalising possibilities. *Sure, the goldmine hadn't played out, but diamonds – industrial or otherwise – just lying about! Surely there had to be an earner there for him.*

9

Colin hummed to himself as he drove past the outlying houses of Takoradi, heading north. *No bother!* He smiled to himself, almost quivering with anticipation. *Lovely weather, good road, car running well and diamond fields just forty miles away. What a life!* The only faint cloud on his horizon was his relationship with Lesley. True, he had managed a drink or two with her, but only in the club under the watchful eye of her father. Not that he blamed him for being protective; attractive, single white girls were in very short supply out here and Lesley, with her lithe, beautifully tanned figure, sun-bleached hair and eyes the colour of tropical seas, was always the centre of attraction. He sighed out loud, wishing he could find a way to get to know her better.

The car's nearside wheel thumped into a deep pothole, almost wrenching the steering wheel from his hands. He had been driving automatically, lost in his reverie. Now Colin looked ahead and was surprised to see how narrow the road had become.

He was barely a mile from Takoradi and already the township's tarmac had given way to the ubiquitous red dust of the bush. Another huge crater made him jerk in his seat, forcing him to ease off the pedal. With his speed reduced to less than fifteen miles an hour, he realised what George had meant about it being a long trip.

It was almost noon before a straggling line of tin-roofed huts told Colin that he had finally reached his destination. He came to a halt and looked around for a watering place where he could stop for some refreshment and find out where the diamond fields were.

'Good!' He spoke the word aloud on seeing the familiar sight of a Coca-Cola sign and pulled up behind the first private car he had seen in more than twenty dust-tossed miles. He was pleased to see the car, assuming it must belong to one of the local Europeans and hoping he would be able to get directions to the diamond fields.

He entered the cool interior of the bar, the shadowy dimness a welcome relief after driving in glaring sunlight for three hours or more. At first he thought he had misjudged the ownership of the car when he spotted a dark-skinned man sitting at a zinc-topped table. But a closer look identified distinctive Caucasian features, sunburned almost to the point of blackness. The man raised his tumbler to Colin and shoved a chair out with his foot.

'Thanks,' Colin accepted the invitation and sat down with a grateful sigh. 'I'm dying for a pint,' he said. 'You ready for another one yourself?' he offered, raising his hand to the barman.

'Just get one and we'll split it. They get less time to warm up that way,' he was advised in a strong Lancashire accent. 'By the way, I'm Walter Ellis. Watty to my drinking pals.' He smiled crookedly and extended a bony, work-worn hand. 'Haven't seen you around before?' He cocked his head, waiting for a reply.

'Colin Grant.' Colin gripped the outstretched hand, immediately conscious of work-hardened calluses. 'I've just come up from Takoradi to see the place,' he explained.

'A tourist!' Watty exclaimed, jerking upright in genuine astonishment. 'A fucking tourist! For Christ's sake! I mean . . . well . . .' He was stuck for words.

'I suppose you could call me a kind of tourist,' Colin admitted. 'I'm on an extended holiday, staying with an uncle in Takoradi. I just fancied seeing this place; it looked quite interesting on the map.'

His explanation was accepted with a calculating nod.

'I guess it's all right down on the coast for a bit of

a holiday. You've got the sports club there; golf, tennis courts, even horse-riding. You won't find anything like that here. As for being interesting . . . Well, that's a new one on me.'

'What do you do yourself? Out here, I mean?'

'Plant engineer.' Watty gave a wry grin. 'Glorified mechanic would be a more accurate description, I suppose.'

'There's surely not a lot of motors out here?' Colin said, faintly puzzled.

'Oh aye,' Watty assured him. 'There's the lorries and the dump-trucks at the diamond fields. Then there's the plant itself – conveyer belts, riddler and all the other bits and pieces; they're always needing attention. Even the hand tools, shovels and the like.'

'You work at the diamond fields?' Colin kept his voice casual and hid his excitement at Watty's offhand nod. 'I've heard about the diamond fields,' he said. 'As a matter of fact it's one of the reasons I decided to come here. D'you think I might be able to get a look at them?'

'You want to see the diamond fields?' Watty looked surprised, then he laughed. 'Imagine coming all the way up here just to see a bunch of black fellas digging holes.' He slapped his thigh in appreciation. 'I'll buy you another beer for that one.'

'But I can see them?' Colin persisted.

'Take you out there myself,' Watty looked at his watch. 'I'm due back at the workshop about now anyway. You can come along with me and I'll show you round the diggings. Your car will be safe enough outside here, providing you dash one of the local lads to mind it.' He rose to his feet and showed himself inches taller than Colin; a long, lean-faced man, wiry arms showing every muscle and tendon where hard work in the sweating, hothouse conditions of the Equator had burned off any superfluous fat.

*

Watty's car bumped and rattled its way along a rough track, heading deep into the bush. After a mile of bone-shaking travel a tall, wire-mesh fence appeared alongside the track. Beyond the fence Colin could see yellow dump trucks in the distance, bright against the dark, rough-textured earth which had replaced the usual arid, red laterite soil.

'The diggings!' Watty spoke in jerks as the helter-skelter surface tortured the car's suspension. 'They fence . . . off . . . the area . . . Jesus Christ!' The front wheels plunged into a deep depression. 'I forgot about that bugger.' It was impossible to carry on a proper conversation, but despite the car's erratic progress and Watty's jerky commentary, Colin managed to piece together the set-up.

100

As each area was worked out, the security fence was extended on to fresh ground and the necessary equipment moved into place. Workers would bulldoze the diamond-bearing soil then scoop it into dump trucks that tipped it on to a seemingly endless conveyer belt. From there it was carried to the processing centre where the diamonds were extracted, graded, weighed and locked away in the diamond company's safe before being taken to the trade centre in Accra. It all seemed very simple and straightforward to Colin as they walked alongside the rattling line of a conveyer belt that seemed to stretch for miles. He felt Watty pulling on his arm and they stopped a few feet away from a raised inspection platform. 'Snakes,' Watty warned him. 'They often sun themselves on the metal treads.'

'Snakes!' Colin grimaced and took an involuntary step backwards. 'I hate the fucking things!'

'They won't bother you if you don't bother them,' Watty said nonchalantly, checking the stairs and underneath the platform. 'But they are deadly poisonous and don't like people invading their space, so we don't want to go treading on one of them, do we?' He grinned at Colin's horrified expression. 'Don't look so worried, it's all clear.'

A minute later they were standing on the inspection platform, watching the conveyer belt sliding past at a comfortable waist-high position. Watty picked up a small hand shovel and held it against the flow of soil. It quickly filled and he presented its contents for Colin's inspection. 'There you are! This is the stuff the diamonds come from. Here, have a poke about in it. See if you can spot one.'

A disappointed Colin looked down at the dross. 'Are there any diamonds in it?' he finally asked.

'Could be lucky,' Watty admitted. 'But they've got to sift through tons of this stuff to get any results.'

'But they do get results?' Colin persisted. 'I mean, all this gear,' he waved a hand that took in the conveyer system, the dump trucks and the distant clutch of buildings. 'They must find it profitable.'

'Highest quality industrial diamonds in the world,' Watty told him. 'It's profitable all right; high yield, low overheads. We're doing 100 carats a ton just now, and that's pretty good.'

'What's that in normal weight?'

Watty seemed pleased to talk about it. 'Diamonds are weighed by the carat, Colin, and there are just five carats to the gramme. Right now we're getting just over three carats to the ton.'

'Is that all?'

'It's enough when you're processing 500 tons of soil a day.'

'And how much is a gramme worth?'

'Around fifty pounds sterling.' Watty's reply was succinct.

'More than a hundred and fifty pounds per ton, and you do five hundred tons a day? Jesus!' Colin gasped, his mind trying to compute the totals. 'That's nearly eighty grand a day!'

'About that,' Watty agreed, stepping down from the platform. 'C'mon, I'll show you the finished product.' He attracted the attention of a dumper driver and they hitched a ride to the diamond company's permanent buildings.

*

'This is the security room,' Watty explained as they entered a brightly lit chamber where half a dozen white-coated African workers were busy sorting and weighing what looked like fine gravel to Colin.

'The diamonds are graded here before being put into the safe. Then once a week they are taken to Accra where the government agent handles their sale and distribution.'

'And is there much in the vault just now?' Ideas, possibilities, were already forming in Colin's fertile mind.

Watty seemed to weigh the question, and for a worrying moment Colin thought he had been too forward.

'What day is it?' Watty finally asked.

'Wednesday,' Colin breathed in relief. He too had difficulty remembering the days.

'Three days' production. That'll be about two hundred and fifty thousand pounds worth,' Watty finally said. 'And that's to us. The retail price is much higher that that.'

'And they ship them out fairly quickly?'

'Weekly basis.'

'I expect they're well protected,' Colin continued to sound offhand. 'Armed guards and that sort of thing?'

For the first time Watty hesitated, tilting his head a little to look into Colin's eyes. 'Not really,' he finally answered. 'Armoured car once a week to Accra. And we keep them here in the vault until it comes.' He pushed open a door as he spoke. 'They're safe enough.'

Colin's eyes automatically covered the doorframe for wires or contact studs before he looked across at the safe. 'It's a monster of a thing.' He heard Watty's voice as his mouth fell open.

An ancient, double-doored safe, about seven feet tall and four feet wide, dominated the small windowless room.

'Safe as the Bank of England.' Watty stepped forward and patted it.

Colin nodded, not trusting himself to speak. He knew the safe – or at least some of its close relatives. A Samuel Withers, circa 1920. Inch-thick sheet metal riveted onto an angle-iron frame, four inches of fireproof packing and a thin inner skin of twelve-gauge metal protecting the inside cavity. *A ripper* in any cracksman's language. He let his knuckles rap casually on its side. *Yes!* The distinctive dull, slightly hollow sound confirmed his suspicions.

'Any cold beer in your office?' he turned to Watty. 'I'm drying out in this heat.'

An hour later he was heading back to Takoradi, the familiar quiver of excitement and challenge once again coursing urgently through his body.

10

It took Colin one week to convince himself he could do it, another to prepare. There would be no need to carry any tools; Watty had all the equipment he needed in his workshop and a second reconnaissance trip had familiarised him with the area around the diamond field. One hour after dusk, exactly two weeks since his first visit, he was bumping his car off-road and into the bush a mile south of the diamond field's security fence.

Working quickly, he stripped off his light-coloured clothes and donned a dark tracksuit, exchanged his sandals for black trainers and rolled a makeshift balaclava down over his face. Then, taking a pair of wire cutters and a torch from the glove compartment, he was ready.

There was no moon, but the clear African sky gleamed with stars, providing more than enough light to guide him through the night. At first he felt strange, as though he was walking in a tunnel of silence, the insects and small animals near him falling silent as he passed, whilst those further away continued to screech, croak and cry undisturbed.

The perimeter fence was no obstacle and with the fields deserted he was soon lowering himself into a shallow depression overlooking the diamond company's buildings. The office block and work-shops were deserted, but there were signs of life coming from the living quarters beyond them, where Colin could see a knot of chattering natives squatting round the entrance of their barracks. Only the distant throb of their music carried to him as he dug himself in and settled down to wait, every sense alert, silent, sweating, watching.

A few minutes after nine o'clock one of the squatting men rose to his feet, flicked on a torch and began making his way round the buildings. Colin realised that this was the night watchman and was pleased to see him making only perfunctory checks as he punched time clocks at the offices and on the wall of the workshop before returning to rejoin the men outside the barracks. At ten o'clock the man began a second ambling circuit and when he set off again at eleven Colin knew he had the timing right and would know when to expect him.

The men around the doorway had disappeared inside and all was quiet when the watchman began his midnight round. Fifteen minutes later he returned to the barracks and went inside. Colin rose to his feet as the door slammed and slid towards the buildings. Making an entry to Watty's workshop was easy, simply pushing a window slat aside and slipping an arm through the gap to turn the handle of the lock. Once inside, working as fast as the judicial use of his torch allowed, he collected the tools he would need and stockpiled them near the door: oxygen and acetylene bottles, along with their pressure gauges and tubes, a burning nozzle, a selection of small tools and a keen-edged knife. It was enough. Sweating profusely, he sat with his back against the door and waited, head slumped between his knees. Suddenly the doorknob rattled and his eyes flew open in alarm. For a split second he almost panicked, then he realised he was safe and breathed easy again. Quickly he rose to his feet and stood back from the window to observe the watchman wend his way to the office block to complete his hourly round. In another five minutes he would be safely back in the barracks.

Colin gave the man a few extra minutes to settle down before easing open the workshop door. A line of parked trucks provided cover from the barracks and after a careful scan of the area he moved, darting from shadow to shadow until he crouched under a box-like construction of mosquito netting that protected the window of the sorting room. Quickly Colin cut out the wire from the base of the frame, the sharp knife making short work of the fine mesh, and in seconds he had reached inside and forced the window open.

It took him four sweating, nerve-racking trips to transfer his chosen equipment to the window, but by two o'clock he was pushing a large oxygen bottle under the frame of the mosquito netting. It stuck – the gap was too neat. Cursing, he lowered the heavy metal bottle to the ground and glared at the offending woodwork. It was slight enough to break. He could even cut a hole directly in front of the netting and feed the bottles straight in through the window, but either of these ploys would leave visible signs of entry; a dead giveaway to the patrolling watchman.

Christ! He sank wearily to the ground. He had been certain there was enough room. Suddenly he spotted a wavering beam of torchlight setting off from the barracks and flashed a look at his watch. *Almost two o'clock! What had happened to the time?*

Disgusted, he rose to his feet and thumped the wooden framework with his fist – and felt it move. Bending quickly he checked its underside. Only two metal brackets held it to the wall and standing back he saw their twins on the upper strut; only two screws to each bracket. It took as many minutes to free the bottom pair then he stood up and pulled at the frame, gasping in relief when it moved easily outwards. The extra inches were enough and moving quickly he threw the torch, gauges, tools and rubber tubes through the window, hurrying to follow through with the heavy metal bottles before time ran out.

The bottles weighed over 120 pounds apiece, and it took all of Colin's strength to push the first one up into the gap, tilting it up until it slid through the open window to land with a dull thump on the coils of tubing already inside. The second bottle went more quickly, but he heard the sharp *'ping'* of a time clock being used. Urgently he scrambled up and through the window, using precious seconds to reach out and pull the wooden frame tight again. A beam of light turned the corner and he eased the window shut, holding his breath as the watchman sauntered unsuspectingly by.

Colin's sigh of relief was audible as he sank to the floor, utterly drained. But time was on his side now and he rested a full fifteen minutes before dragging his equipment into the room that held the safe.

With the interior door closed, the windowless room allowed Colin free use of the torch and he began setting up his equipment. He tackled the side of the safe, aiming the blue spearhead of flame at a point six inches in from the front edge. The thick skin of many layers of paint blistered and burnt, giving out an acrid stench as the lancing flame incinerated it and cut through the metal underneath. No work at all for an ex-shipyard worker.

For fifteen minutes he worked at cutting a large section from the side of the safe, coughing and spluttering as the smoke inside the room thickened. Engrossed in his task, he failed to notice a gentle updraught teasing the smoke towards an almost invisible ventilator grille.

★

Inside the barracks Joseph Udi crossed and re-crossed his legs, trying to defy the demands of his swollen bladder. But he had taken too much Tomba and suddenly he could wait no more. It was a long dark walk to the latrines at the rear of the sleeping quarters and Joseph, bladder at bursting point, staggered from his cot towards the front door.

'Ahhh . . .' Relief washed over him as he urinated luxuriously onto the ground in front of the barracks. Finished and still sleepy-eyed, Joseph breathed in the balmy night air, stretching his arms and arching his back in a prodigious, mouth-gaping yawn. Suddenly he was wide awake, staring at a pale column of smoke rising from the roof of the office building. At first he thought it was a night spirit and was afraid. Then a puff of wind moved it and he knew it was smoke.

'Adawa! Adawa!' He dashed inside the dormitory shouting for the watchman. 'Adawa! There is fire! Come!' he screamed, drawing mumbles of reproof from some of the beds. Then Joseph remembered his fire drill.

★

The thin metal skin of the inner box offered little resistance to the searing oxyacetylene flame and in seconds Colin had breached the inner cabinet. Smiling through sweat and fatigue, he extinguished the burner.

Finished! He gloated. *What an earner!*

Then a clanging alarm, obscenely loud, shattered the silence.

Colin froze, paralysed with shock. He stood still for several seconds until self-preservation took over and galvanised him into action. Cursing, he flew to the window, the clamour increasing as he entered the sorting room. From the window he saw a string of half-naked Africans bursting from the barracks, some of them screaming at a man who was furiously clanging on a fire triangle and pointing with his free hand directly at the office building.

Jesus Christ! Colin exploded through the window and crashed to earth in a shamble of shattered wood and mosquito wire. The group outside the dormitory froze in a snapshot stillness. There was a stunned silence. Then a shout went up like a huntsman's tally-ho.

'T'iefman! T'iefman!' Their cries rose loud. Then, like hounds sighting a fox, they surged towards him.

Colin ran. He ran as he had never run before. With a bare fifty-yard start he knew he had to reach the cover of the diggings to stand any chance of escape from the baying mob behind. Slipping and slithering, he scaled the first steep slope and sprinted into darkness. Behind him he heard the coughing of engines and headlamps slashed the night.

You would not survive four years in a Ghanaian prison. Yarty Okufu's words echoed in his head as he changed direction, running now at right angles to his original course, his legs pumping out a steady rhythm. Two hundred yards on, he flung himself into a crater and looked behind. The chasing mob seemed to have gone straight on, following the headlights of the searching trucks. He breathed easier; he could still make it clear. Then he saw two dark shapes trotting along the route he had taken.

Bastards! He rose to his feet and broke into a run again, breathing hard, tasting blood in his throat as

113

he ran into the darkness. Suddenly something even darker loomed out of the night and he swerved quickly, but too late. Grunting painfully he crashed to the ground, head ringing as he bounced off the conveyer system. Gagging and coughing between heaving breaths, he strove to steady himself and saw his pursuers outlined against the stars. They were less than fifty yards away.

Unable to stand, Colin rolled forward under the conveyer belt and painfully pulled himself erect. The rapid *crunch crunch crunch* of approaching feet spurred him on as he used the heavy canvas of the belt to haul himself away.

The pursuers halted at the conveyer belt and began to jabber at one another as, less than twenty feet away, Colin strained to control his breathing. One of the men went down on his knees and crawled under the belt, making signs for the other man to follow. Colin watched the movement and slid in the opposite direction, putting the barrier between them again, and found himself crouching beside an inspection platform, its darker shadows inviting him to hide. His hunters seemed to be having an argument and he quietly slid into almost total darkness.

At first Colin was too exhausted to notice, but gradually, as his breathing settled, he became aware of a weight moving against his thigh and shifted slightly. But the weight seemed to follow him, leaning even harder. Then he felt it move, a long, sinuous, gliding motion that sent cold shivers down his spine, and he knew it was a snake. Then the weight slid upwards to settle on his thighs and his breath screeched inwards in a long silent scream. Down to his left his pursuers were coming again.

The approaching footsteps seemed to irritate the snake and he felt it stiffen, heard its low '*ssss . . .*' as it slid over his buttocks and moved onto his back. The footsteps drew closer and he felt a serpentine hump press against him as the snake slithered upwards.

Paralysed with fear, he stared straight ahead, cringing as the snake slid on to his shoulder. He wanted to scream, felt the need deep in his lungs and began to swallow convulsively to prevent any sound escaping his straining chest. A louder hiss sounded in his ear and the snake slowly slithered into view on the extreme edge of his vision, not six inches from his face.

'*If you see a snake, ignore it.*' George had repeated the warning to him a hundred times.

Not daring to blink, Colin stared fixedly ahead. *Concentrate!* he told himself. *Ignore it! Concentrate!* Sweat flooded his eyes and he blinked, bringing an immediate reaction from the snake. Twin pinpricks of light fixed on him and the black slit of the snake's mouth hissed wide, exposing long, needle-sharp fangs dripping viscous, poisonous venom. He felt and smelled its alien breath and cringed inside. Then the stalking Africans were on the other side. The serpent swung its head towards this latest intrusion and darted forward, its hissing suddenly loud and angry at this continued invasion of its territory.

The natives froze. Then suddenly their legs were pumping like pistons as they skittered and skidded in a frantic frenzy of escape. Colin lay motionless, still feeling the snake slither and slide over his shoulder as burning bile burst from his mouth, the nauseous, stinking mess sticking to his mask, forcing him to react again and again. It took a full two minutes for the racking convulsions to cease before he could start thinking clearly again.

Hurriedly he scurried from under the platform, worried about more snakes and anxious to take stock of his situation. For the moment at least he seemed to be safe. Far off to his left he could see figures outlined against a crescent of headlights focused accusingly on the gap he had cut in the boundary fence. Deciding to do what he thought would be the last thing they would expect, he headed back towards the office buildings.

★

Colin ducked his head as a car careered into the yard below. It disgorged two figures that hurried towards the door of the office block, where the night watchman stood guard. Hungrily, Colin eyed the parked car and began his approach, leopard crawling on knees and elbows until he was directly opposite the vehicle.

The group outside the office had disappeared inside and already the first disappointed pursuers were straggling back. He had to move swiftly. Slipping down the embankment, he covered the short distance to the car in a crouching run. The door handle moved and he breathed a heartfelt prayer of thanks as dangling keys winked at him from the dashboard. Slowly he eased the door open and raised his foot to climb into the car. Suddenly a wiry arm locked round his neck and he felt fingers tearing at his mask.

Gasping, Colin began to struggle, kicking out with his feet and punching back with his elbows in an effort to break the vice-like grip that threatened to cut the breath from his lungs. He felt the body behind him move, the arm flexing as its owner strove to obtain better purchase. Colin slumped forward, knees bent, forcing the man behind him off balance with his sudden dead weight. Quickly he thrust a hand over his head and entangled his fingers in a mop of hair, dropped on one knee and dragged the head down onto his shoulder, forcing the arm to loosen its grip on his neck. Suddenly he could breathe again, and using both hands he hauled the body over his shoulder, breaking the grip that threatened to strangle him. Desperately sucking air into tortured lungs, he flung his weight on top of the writhing body, hands seeking the mouth ... the throat ... his knee jabbing viciously as his pounding heart pumped adrenaline into his system.

Through a haze of near panic, Yarty's warning echoed in his head. The thought lent a desperate strength to his limbs and his hand caught an open mouth, straining to cry out. He tore at the lips, fingers clawing savagely to contain the shout that would attract assistance. Under his right hand the rough shape of a stone seemed to mould itself into his clawing fingers. Panting, he raised it high as flailing hands ripped the balaclava from his face. He heard a gasping voice – muffled, agonised. *Christ!* An English voice!

'Colin! No ... !'

Jesus Christ! The stone veered off target smashing into the ground millimetres from Watty's head. 'Watty!' Colin stared into the dark face, scarcely able to distinguish anything in the darkness but knowing it could be no one else. He rose silently to his feet and held his hand out to help him rise.

Watty clambered up and stood staring at him, breathing heavily. 'I should have guessed,' he panted. 'All those bloody questions.' There was a long pause. 'Well, what do we do now?'

'That's up to you,' Colin told him. 'But you surely don't think I would have tried to use that rock if I had known it was you I was fighting with?'

'Colin, you've stolen the diamonds!' Watty accused. 'I can't let that go.'

'But I didn't steal them, Watty. I was disturbed. I got nothing when I had to run.'

'The diamonds are still in the safe?'

'Yes.'

'Jesus Christ, man . . .' Walter shook his head. 'Don't you realise what they'll do to you for even *trying* to steal their diamonds?

'Nothing, if you'll help me,' Colin stared into his eyes. 'C'mon, Watty,' he pleaded. 'You have to help me. I could have battered your head in to get away and no one would have been any the wiser. They don't even know who they're looking for.'

'Come on, Colin. I'm a company man,' Watty told him. 'They pay my wages.'

'But nothing's been stolen,' Colin argued. 'And they think whoever done it got away through the fence.'

'You're certain you took nothing?' Watty weakened.

119

'My life on it!'

'But I don't want to be involved,' Watty cried, raising his eyes to the dark sky. 'Why me, for Christ's sake?'

'Please, Watty. I'm a white man. I couldn't do time out here.'

'Aww . . . Jesus!' Watty slapped the side of the car and threw his arms wide in a gesture of hopelessness. 'Quick! Into my office. I'll come and get you when the excitement dies down.'

'*Why me?*' Colin heard the plaintive wail as he darted towards the office door and let himself inside.

*

Some time later, a worried-looking Watty dropped Colin close to where he had hidden his old Peugeot.

'What can I say?' Colin bent by the window of Watty's car.

'Say nothing!' Watty held out a widespread palm and made vigorous pushing movements. 'Just get in your car and go back to Takoradi.' He engaged gear and began to move away. 'And for Christ's sake,' he implored, '*Don't come fucking back!*'

II

'You were out late last night,' George looked over at Colin as they sat on the verandah, enjoying their first sundowner beer of the evening. 'Or should I say, this morning?'

'Went a bit too far,' Colin gave a wry smile at his words. 'Ran into a bit of a problem.'

'Aye,' George nodded. 'That old motor is just about worn out.'

'H'mm,' Colin muttered, offering no further enlightenment. He was only too happy to be sitting with his uncle after his close call the night before. He sipped luxuriously at his beer, vastly relieved to be doing so. He had been disappointed there had been no gold, and the diamond job had been a close call, nothing closer in fact. But at least he had saved his skin. He sipped again at his beer. *Yes*, it did taste extra special this time.

'Out again tonight?' George queried, a trace of censorship in his voice.

'I'm taking a run down to the Princess,' Colin

named the local cinema. 'I fancy a picture for a change.'

'There's a video on at the club.'

'No. I fancy trying the local fleapit,' Colin insisted. 'I've never been there, but it's showing an old Clint Eastwood western tonight and I'd like to see it again.'

★

The antics of the native audience gave Colin almost as much pleasure as the ancient *Fistful of Dollars* epic. The locals certainly believed in audience participation: they rejoiced loudly at their hero's victories, hooted derisively at the baddies' blunders, shouted urgent warnings as their champion rode into an ambush and screamed in anguish when he was tortured by the bandits. Finally, their triumphant cheers of support and victory rang loud and long as the victorious nameless stranger rode into nowhere again.

Still chuckling at the boisterous audience reaction, Colin made his way to the bar where he bought a bottle of beer before wandering out to the open verandah of the building. Seated at a table, he looked round at the other people near him, his eyes meeting giggling smiles from a party of four young African girls who openly ogled him from their nearby table.

122

The sight of the girls held his attention and he returned their looks with an amused, friendly smile. At this the girls giggled even more and went into a huddle of intense conversation, their huge, warm brown eyes sneaking looks at him as he watched their carry-on.

There was no denying he missed the friendliness and intimacy of having a girlfriend and he eyed the four girls with a pang of loneliness. He had always welcomed the company of lively girls, liked to listen to the breathless, unimportant gossip, enjoyed parrying their constant feminine inquisitiveness, hearing their indignant complaints about this and that. He missed their gentleness and most of all he missed their essential sexuality. He knew that some of the sports-club members had girls in town and sometimes he had felt tempted himself. But his natural Scottish inhibitions, as well as an awareness that gossip about himself could harm his uncle's reputation, conspired to combat any desire he may have felt.

One of the girls smiled boldly at him and, seeing no signs of rejection, waved her fingers in a girlish gesture. He smiled, enjoying the moment, but shook his head in firm refusal.

'Don't you like the local girls?' He twisted in his seat as a soft voice sounded behind him, and rose quickly when he recognised Lesley Farrell.

'What are you doing here?' The question burst from his lips without thought.

'Could ask you that same question,' Lesley replied coolly, looking very attractive in a wide-skirted, white cotton dress that emphasised her deep tan and threw highlights into her already dazzling blonde hair. He gazed open-mouthed at her, drinking in her beauty, finding it difficult to raise his eyes from the low-cut bodice of her dress.

'Well, do you intend to strip me or buy me a drink?' she asked with a smile, pulling a chair out for herself.

'I . . . I . . .' He sank into his seat fumbling for words. 'I'm just surprised to see you here, that's all.' He almost dislocated his neck trying to see who she was with.

'Oh, don't bother yourself,' she said airily. 'I'm on my own. I am a big girl, you know. Over twenty-one and all that.'

Colin began to regain some of his self-control. 'You often come here on your own?' he asked curiously.

'Not normally,' she smiled. 'But I knew you were here and just had a crazy impulse to come and talk to you. We don't seem to get much time to get to know one another at the club.'

'How did you know I was here?' he asked her.

'You're not having me followed, are you?' He grinned to show he was joking.

'Nothing so mysterious,' she replied. 'We ran out of spirits at the club earlier on tonight and I drove over here to borrow a case of Scotch. I saw your car outside and looked for you. When I didn't see you I guessed you were inside the cinema and decided to come back at the end of the show. Just in the nick of time too it appears.' She looked over at the table where the four local girls were staring over.

He felt himself flushing. 'Hey! Wait a minute!' he began, 'I never . . .'

'Kidding, Colin. Only kidding.' She made a face at him, then smiled. 'I've already asked you . . . don't you like the local girls?'

'Well . . .' he searched for an answer. 'They're all right,' he finally said. 'I've spoken to one or two of them in the market. But I've never had anything to do with them, er . . . socially, if that's what you mean.' He was looking into her eyes as he spoke and felt sure he recognised the shine of approval. Then the waiter was taking their order and the moment was past.

It was beautifully cool on the verandah as they chatted, both of them relaxed, feeling comfortably at ease with each other. But Colin was aware of a subtle change in the atmosphere, as if somehow they had

125

become closer and he listened attentively as she began to tell him about herself.

He was sensitive enough to recognise that, for her, sharing her story was some sort of release and he settled back to listen without interruption.

She told him that her home was in Guildford, Surrey, where she lived with her mother. Her parents had divorced amicably five years earlier and after being alone for a while her father had opted for the sunshine of Africa. He had finally settled in Ghana, a country where he had served during his army service, and accepted the job of manager at the sports club in Takoradi. She had been old enough to see the sense – even the need – of their divorce, and she remained very fond of both her parents. Leaving school at seventeen with three A levels, she had gone on to secretarial college in London, where she had earned her Diploma in Business Studies. There had been a number of boyfriends while she had been at college, but none of them serious. She smiled a little at this and his hand stole across the table to cover hers, giving it an encouraging squeeze.

Lesley seemed happy enough to feel his touch and continued to talk softly. Sometimes meeting his gaze, but mostly looking out over the veranda at the scene below, she described how she had met her first real boyfriend, Derek, and fallen hopelessly in love with him. They had become engaged and set a date to be married. She couldn't have been happier. Then three weeks before the wedding Derek had been killed in a motorway pile-up. On the day the wedding should have taken place she had flown out to her father for a long break, trying to escape the memories.

Colin saw that her cheeks were wet with tears and he felt an unfamiliar tenderness envelop him. He had had several girlfriends, loads of casual affairs, but no really close emotional relationship with any woman other than his mother. He remembered the feeling of utter desolation he had suffered at his loss. Remembered, too, his own running away from the memories and how his life had changed course. He thought he knew a little of how Lesley felt, and he ached in sympathy.

They sat in silence for a while then he rose, still holding her hand, bringing her to her feet along with him. 'Come on,' he whispered. 'I'll take you home.'

She followed him silently and he wondered if she regretted revealing her secrets to him. But by the time they reached the car park Lesley had recovered her composure and most of her natural cheerfulness.

They both had cars. Colin stared at the problem, reluctant to part from her until he had seen her safely home. 'I'll drive yours,' he said, holding out his hand for her keys. 'Someone from the club will give me a lift back.'

'Thank you, Colin,' her hand reached out to touch him. 'Thank you for listening. I've kept it bottled up for over a year now but the dam just gave way tonight. I'm glad it was you.'

He had intended taking her straight back to the club, but the feeling between them was too close, too emotional to end so soon. He turned on to a broad track that ran down through the golf course to the beach and parked the car.

'Let's walk,' he said.

He told her about himself as they walked on the soft sand – his life in Glasgow, the disillusionment of redundancy, running away from the death of his mother. Then, feeling uncharacteristically guilty, he gave her a slightly edited version of his introduction to crime and how he had gradually become more deeply involved. Finally, without going into detail, he told her about his prison sentence, admitting that he had been released just over a month before. He considered it prudent to omit any mention of the robbery attempt that had precipitated his departure from London, and totally ignored his intentions at the goldmine or the abortive raid on the diamond company. He felt an unexpected pang of conscience when she squeezed his hand encouragingly.

'So I'm here to get away from my past as well, I suppose,' he said, turning to place his hands on her shoulders. They stood still for a moment, then his arms were around her, moulding her body to his.

'Oh, Colin,' she sighed. 'The past has gone for both of us. It's time to start thinking about the future.' She raised her head and crushed her lips against his mouth.

Arms round each other, they drifted to the sand dunes on the edge of the golf course and he drew her close, feeling her body tremble against him as she tilted her head in offering. They kissed long and hard, Lesley sighing as Colin gently lowered her to the ground and began to unbutton her dress. She felt his passion and did not protest, lifting her buttocks a little as he removed her panties and helping him off with his own clothes. Then, naked, with cool evening air wafting over them, they made passionate love, clinging to one another afterwards. Later, they made love again; slowly this time, both of them relishing the excitement and beginning of a new love.

12

Colin looked at his watch as the venerable DC-3 of Ghana Airways touched down at Kumasi airport. It was 3.20. Ten minutes on the ground and they should be off on the Accra leg of the journey. He settled back to read a magazine and was surprised when the pilot made an announcement requesting all passengers to disembark and wait in the airport departure lounge for re-boarding instructions.

The trip to Accra was necessary so he could have his visitor's visa extended. It was the second time he had made the journey for this purpose but as Yarty Okufu had told him, as long as the extension was for only twenty-eight days it was a 'rubber stamp' procedure. He had been looking forward to another flight over the Ghanaian countryside and his discovery that the afternoon, midweek flight took the longer route, via Kumasi, was an added bonus to him.

He carried coffee over to one of the lounge chairs that overlooked the aircraft parking area, wondering why the passengers had been asked to disembark. *Probably a minor mechanical problem,* he thought to himself, looking out at the aircraft. Sure enough, a group of overall-clad men approached the plane and disappeared inside the passenger cabin. Minutes later he was surprised to see them emerge, manoeuvring a pair of seats through the aircraft's narrow exit. Eventually four sets of seats were removed from the plane and carried off, leaving him to wonder what was going on. The mystery deepened when a three-vehicle military convoy rolled into view, drawing up alongside the DC-3.

The convoy was led by a Land Rover fitted with a machine-gun, its crew sitting alertly at their station. The rear vehicle was an eight-man personnel carrier with its full complement of armed soldiers. But it was the centre vehicle that really grabbed his attention and he looked on interestedly as a small armoured van backed up to the door of the plane.

There was a shouted command and the armed soldiers leapt from the troop carrier to take up defensive positions round the plane. At the same time the Land Rover swung round to face outwards, its gun covering the main approach road and terminal building. When the tableau had settled down an officer strode towards the rear of the van, imperiously rapping his swagger stick against its side as he marched past. The van's rear doors opened and Colin's view was restricted to shuffling feet and the straining backs of uniformed men as they mounted the steps of the plane. Five minutes later the van pulled away and the Tannoy requested the passengers for flight GA 670 to Accra to re-embark the aircraft.

When he entered the cabin Colin saw that two rows of seats had been removed, leaving a space in the middle of the aircraft. His own seat had been one of those removed but he settled into an aisle seat that gave him an unobstructed view of what was going on. He counted twenty-two rope-handled ammunition boxes spread evenly across the deck where the seats had been.

'Bit dangerous that, eh?' he nudged the man beside him.

'Dangerous?' The other passenger, a prissy-looking man in a business suit, looked puzzled.

'Well . . .' Colin pointed at the boxes. 'Ammunition on a passenger plane? I'd certainly call that dangerous.'

'Oh, I see!' The man gave Colin a superior smile and touched the knot of his tie. 'The soldiers . . . the boxes . . . ergo – explosives! A natural but totally erroneous assumption.' He smirked, obviously pleased to be able to display his knowledge. 'Gold.'

132

He pointed at the boxes and tapped the side of his nose. 'Gold bullion.'

Colin was taken aback. 'Gold bullion! All those boxes?'

'Weekly shipment from the Ashanti Goldfield Corporation,' the man confirmed. 'It's being transferred to the treasury in Accra.'

'They do this *every week*?' He tried to keep his voice calm.

'Every Wednesday, yes. It's a convenient flight for them I suppose.' His two-day-old *Financial Times* rustled as he went back to his reading, leaving Colin to gape at the green-painted boxes.

Of course! He recalled Gareth telling him that the army transported the gold by road from Obuasi and then onward by air to Accra. But he had assumed a military aircraft. Yet here it was, sitting on the deck of a scheduled passenger flight. And they did it every week too! He blew his cheeks out in a silent whistle. *It must be worth millions*, he told himself.

The plane's captain was counting the boxes, the army officer paying careful attention to every metal seal. At last the pilot nodded his satisfaction and signed a receipt for the gold.

With a smart salute the army officer turned and Colin found himself looking into the obsidian, cruel eyes of Major Judas Akaba. For a moment their eyes met, Akaba's narrowing at first, then widening slightly as recognition came, but he permitted no smile to breach the thin line of his lips before the pilot ushered him out of the plane. Two soldiers remained aboard, settling into seats facing the gold, old-fashioned Lee-Enfield rifles held carefully erect between their knees. The aircraft's steps were drawn in and the door thudded tight. In another minute they were thundering down the runway, en route for Accra.

Colin's appreciation of the scenery was forgotten as he stared at the twenty-two boxes – twenty-two bars of gold! He peered down the length of the cabin looking for more soldiers. None. Casually he turned his head and looked behind. No sign of uniforms there either. Almost against his will, he felt familiar feelings creep over him. *What an earner this could be!* Then he shook his head, as if to chase the thoughts from his mind. If he wanted to keep Lesley he couldn't afford to take any more chances. Besides, he consoled himself, the gold was as safe here as in the Bank of England. Nevertheless, his eyes remained fixed on the bullion and he was still daydreaming about it when the stewardess asked him to fasten his seat belt for landing in Accra.

On the ground he watched an identical convoy remove the gold from the plane and, sirens blaring, disappear along the airport exit road. Despite his earlier good intentions, Colin stared thoughtfully down the road the convoy had taken and, almost against his will, found himself thinking that *maybe . . . just maybe . . .* a way could be found to get at the gold.

13

Fascinated by his discovery, and telling himself that he was only playing mental games, Colin invented reasons to visit Accra. Telling George that the immigration office was closed allowed him to make the trip the following week. *An action replay.* Twenty boxes this time.

He had finally worked out a price for the twenty-two boxes of gold he had seen on his previous trip. At the current world price of over £350 an ounce it came to a staggering three million pounds. Each individual gold bar was worth over £140,000. Even one of them would set him up for life, and life was beginning to look rosy to him, especially as far as his relationship with Lesley was concerned. The only fly in the ointment was his awareness that he had no security to offer her, and because of this he was reluctant to discuss marriage knowing that he would be relying on villainy to pay his way. He had seen too many weeping women to risk putting Lesley through the pain of loneliness and prison visits. But if he could get his hands on the gold it would set them up for life and villainy would be firmly in the past.

The gold drew him like a magnet. Three weeks later, he took an excited Lesley on a shopping trip to Accra and saw it all again – no change. It haunted him. He sat for hours thinking about it, trying to come up with an idea. Finally he was forced to recognise that he would have to lay to rest the spectre of the gold – either work out a feasible plan to steal it, or satisfy himself once and for all that it was an impossible dream.

It was during a visit with Lesley to the museum in the ancient Cape Coast Castle that an idea exploded in his mind. They were on the battlements of the old fort when a shadow swept over the sand and drew his attention upwards. Just out over the water the afternoon Accra-to-Takoradi flight was droning lazily westwards, following the coastline, the fat underbelly of the DC-3 bulky and black against the blue-white glare of a cloudless sky. In his mind's eye he saw black dots detach themselves from the cruising plane and the swelling bloom of silk as parachutes deployed. He felt a tingle run through his entire body as every nerve came suddenly alive.

Parachutes! Of course! He recalled a case in the United States some years earlier. D. B. Cooper, the name sprang into his head, an American airborne veteran, had hijacked a jetliner, demanded a ransom be put on board, jumped, and hadn't been seen or heard of since. An almost uncontrollable excitement gripped Colin and he drew puzzled looks and mild protests from Lesley as he began hustling her through their visit. Suddenly he was anxious to get back to Takoradi.

*

He sat on the edge of his bed with a Ghana Airways map spread across the coverlet, staring at it in thoughtful silence, not really knowing what it was he was looking for. The airline's routes: Accra to Takoradi to Kumasi then back to Accra again made a neat, almost equilateral triangle. He thickened the line between Kumasi and Accra and continued to stare, tapping the pencil thoughtfully against his teeth. After a few minutes he folded the airways map and went out to his car, returning a few minutes later with a large-scale Michelin road map and began to study it, paying particular attention to the coastal area between Takoradi and Accra. For almost an hour he peered and poked at the map as if trying to rearrange the landscape. Finally he lay back, his mind clear on one thing. The Ashanti Gold could be 'got at' and 'got at' with every chance of success. All it needed was an idea; a twist, and he just *knew* the gold could be his.

Suddenly he sat up, eyes narrowed in concentration, trying to recall something George had mentioned one night on the verandah. Something about a boxing match. He remembered George had been reading from an air-mail edition of the *Daily Express* at the time and rose from the bed to pad into the living room, searching under the coffee table and through the magazine rack for the newspaper. When he found it he turned to the sports page, too impatient even to sit down.

The report was on the inside of the back page:

COOPER FIGHT DATE FIXED

K.O. specialist, Big Lloyd Cooper, East London's world heavyweight contender, has signed to meet Ghanaian heavyweight Azumah Alloteh, in an eliminator fight that could earn him the right to a fight with undisputed World Champion, Mighty Mike Honeywell.

The venue for the fight is the People's Stadium, Accra, West Africa. The date: May 11th

Tingling with a strong sense of déjà-vu, Colin turned to a calendar, knowing even before he looked that May 11th would be a Wednesday.

14

Colin's old Peugeot bumped along the neglected red earth road, every spring protesting as the wheels took another severe jolt. He was about six miles north of Cape Coast, edging his way through the low rolling hills that protected the coast, heading deeper inland towards the worked-out diamond fields of Uturri. He swerved to avoid another axle-breaking pothole and grinned happily, knowing that the road must be practically unused. The total absence of either tyre marks or footprints endorsed this opinion and with mounting confidence he saw the trees start to thin until eventually he ran out on to a flat plains area where the colour of the earth changed from usual red laterite dust to the same dark, rough textured soil he had seen at Tarkwa. He stopped to check his map, fingers tracing his route from the main highway. He was about twelve miles inland from Cape Coast.

Further north, stretching out from either side of the disused road, the ground lay flat and bare of all but the meanest scrub-bush, the sterile earth offering little sustenance to encourage life. He turned to the map again. The road he was using was marked all right, but the red line ended in the centre of a shaded area at the village of Uturri, just four miles ahead.

Uturri was a ghost town of tattered, long-abandoned shacks, its single stone building once substantial but now a roofless shell. A walk round the eerily empty village showed no signs of recent habitation and a haunting animal cry sent him scurrying back to the safety of his car. But he was pleased. Already the first definite steps of his plan were forming.

15

'You've been keeping yourself gey busy this weather,' George remarked at dinner one evening. 'Seems as if you're always on the go at one thing or another.'

'Aye,' Colin agreed conversationally. 'I've been finding out a bit more about the country . . . doing a bit of sightseeing.'

'As long as the wee job's not interfering with you and your, er, romance,' George smiled. He was pleased that Colin was getting on so well with Lesley.

'No, no,' Colin laughed at his uncle's reticence. 'I enjoy going on board the ships and meeting the men. It makes a change for me. Besides, Lesley's quite busy herself doing voluntary teaching at the High School.'

'As long as you don't mind.'

'Once or twice a week down the harbour suits me, George. It's not really work, is it?'

A while back, George had asked him to carry out a simple task in the dockyards. Several firms had recently complained that their deliveries of cocoa butter had suffered some damage in transit. The fault had been traced to loading officers jam-packing the cartons ceiling-high in the ship's hold, even though the cocoa company had paid for the empty space above to prevent this damage from occurring. Colin's task was simply to make sure that the boxes were stacked no more than seven high, and although the job only involved checking up, it gave him satisfaction to feel that he was in some small way repaying his uncle's generous hospitality.

'I'm getting on well enough,' Colin assured him. 'There's plenty to do to keep me busy.'

It was no understatement. As well as romancing Lesley, the past two weeks had seen him covering the coast road several times, timing the runs from the abandoned village to both Accra and Takoradi. Paradoxically, he saw the theft of the gold as a way out of villainy. The money the gold would fetch would be more than enough to establish him and secure a future for Lesley and himself. He was prepared to take the gamble, to risk everything in one fell swoop. The fact that he was planning to commit a serious crime with consequences too horrendous to contemplate if it went wrong did not enter his mind. He saw only the prize – the new life ahead of him when the job was over.

He had made three trips on the bullion flight by now and the job had become more attractive with each journey. He had plotted the plane's course and knew every landmark along the flight path to Accra, the increasing familiarity giving him a real feel for the job. But he knew that he couldn't do the job alone and realised he would have to go back to London. A face-to-face confrontation with his old 'firm' would be the only way he could present his idea properly and persuade them to have a go. However, returning to London posed problems. There was no reasonable excuse he could offer either Lesley or his uncle for a prolonged absence and simply to disappear for a week or two was out of the question. *Or was it?* An idea occurred to him.

Since he had begun checking the loading of the cocoa butter he had received many invitations to take a cruise along the coast. Most of the ships that called at Takoradi continued along the coast in short hops, discharging here and there and picking up cargo for the return trip to Europe. It was fairly common for a ship to discharge some of its cargo at Takoradi then take on a load and carry on along the coast to Tema – Ghana's main port, Lagos in Nigeria, and on again to the river ports of Sapele, Warri, Burutu and Port Harcourt before returning to Takoradi to pick up a deck cargo of logs to top off its tonnage before returning to the United Kingdom.

Colin had studied each ship's itinerary as it passed through Takoradi. Most of them were not due back for three or four weeks, but the *Nasia River*, one of the Ghanaian National Black Star Line's vessels, had only three calls to make before she returned this time: Lagos, Port Harcourt, back to Lagos again, then back to Takoradi. Today was March 21st, and the ship was due to take on a deck cargo of logs on April 2nd – just twelve days ahead. It suited him perfectly and he had prepared his plan around this ship.

*

The arrangement the cocoa mill had with the shipping companies was that any empty space above the seven-high cartons would be paid for and kept clear, to prevent excess weight damaging the lower cases. On board the Black Star Line ship, *Nasia River*, Colin could see that the cartons had been stowed the correct seven high, but the gap above could easily accommodate three more layers.

'Go ahead, stack it up,' he smiled at the loading officer, knowing he was on a tonnage bonus.

The officer looked at him shrewdly, assuming he was looking for something more tangible than a polite 'Thank you' for the extra tonnage he could accommodate. 'Would you like a drink, Mister Grant?' He indicated the ship's living quarters, hoping it wouldn't cost him too much, and wasn't surprised when his first tentative offer of £100 was refused. He was calculating how much higher he could go when Colin took the initiative.

'I don't want any payment over the cargo space,' he said. 'What I fancy is a trip to Lagos. Is there any chance you could give me a lift?'

'You just want to go to Lagos?'

'That's right. Drop me off at Lagos and pick me up again on your way back, that's all.'

'It'll be a pleasure to have you on board.' The pleased officer smiled and held out his hand.

*

'You want to take a ship down to Nigeria?' Lesley raised her eyebrows at him. 'When did you decide this?'

'I've wanted to take a trip along the coast for a while, Lesley,' he told her, surprised at how difficult he found it to spin the lie. 'But usually the ships take over a month to get back here and that's too long for me. However, the *Nasia River* is due back in Takoradi in less than two weeks. The offer only cropped up today and I don't want to miss it.'

'Well there's certainly nothing to stop you,' Lesley agreed. 'But I haven't seen very much of you these last two or three weeks, have I? You always seem to be disappearing in that old car of yours; God knows what you are up to.'

Up to? He felt a spasm of nerves at her words, but he ran his hand through her luxuriant blonde hair and drew her head onto his shoulder. 'I'm just trying to see as much of the country and the people as I can before I go home.' He lifted her chin with his finger so he could look into her face and added in a low voice, 'Before *we* go home. And now I've got the chance of a quick visit to Nigeria I'd like to take it.' He bent his head and kissed her full lips, feeling her body mould into him as her arms slipped around his neck.

'Oh, Colin, I do love you so much,' she murmured.

'You don't mind then if I go?' He took full advantage of the moment.

'Of course not, darling. I only wish I could go with you.' She kissed him again, oblivious to the guilty feelings she had stirred in him.

George offered no objections either. 'Enjoy yourself, Colin,' he enthused. 'If you want to gallivant about the coast for a couple of weeks, just you go ahead and do so. But be careful,' he warned.

'Some of these West African ports can be very dangerous.'

★

At midday, eighteen hours after leaving Takoradi, the *Nasia River* dropped anchor in Lagos Lagoon, outside the entrance of the main harbour.

'How long will we be here?' Colin asked a deck officer, as the anchor chain clattered through its scuttle.

'We have to wait for berth twelve. It should be free by early evening.'

'What!' Colin exclaimed. 'I've got a plane to catch. I can't wait that long.'

'Then you've got a problem.' The deck officer shrugged. 'We can't dock until the berth is free.'

'But I've got to get ashore,' Colin grabbed his arm. 'My flight leaves at 2.25. There must be a way for me to get ashore.'

'If you have said earlier you could have gone off with the pilot.'

'How did *he* get ashore?' Colin demanded.

'Pilot's launch. But they won't come back for a passenger. Mind you . . .' he hesitated. 'There are the native canoes if you're *really* desperate.'

'Canoes?' Colin mimed paddling. 'That kind of canoe?'

'Yes. They operate an illegal ship-to-shore taxi service – fifty pence will get you there. But we advise against them. They are, to put it mildly, unsafe, especially for a European. You make an attractive target even in the clothes you stand up in.'

Colin looked at his watch: almost 12.30. 'Where do I get one of these canoes?' he demanded.

★

He almost changed his mind when he saw the flimsy craft that had been summoned for him. Showing just an inch or two of freeboard, it looked as though he was taking his life in his hands when he stepped gingerly into the barely floating craft. Balancing as well as he could on its narrow wooden seat, he signalled the boatman to shove off, holding on to the sides of the canoe as it drifted away from the shelter of the ship and turned towards the shore.

He sensed the antagonism immediately. The oarsman in front of him was too stiff, too quiet; his belligerent stabs at the swirling, muddy water telegraphing his mood. Halfway to the shore Colin heard the low, insinuating voice of the steersman addressing him from behind.

'Ten pounds, Johnny. We take you for shore – you pay ten pounds.' It was a demand not a question.

'I pay one pound,' Colin decided to be generous.

'Take me for shore.' But his generosity was mistaken for weakness and the steersman became bold.

'You have plenty money, *Bruni*.' He used the native word for white man which, literally translated, meant white bastard.

'Take me for shore!' Colin disguised his misgivings by using what he hoped was an authoritative voice.

The canoe's prow swung away from the bank until it was pointing upriver.

'Take me for shore!' Colin turned, his sudden movement causing the canoe to ship water. 'You take me for shore – Now! You bastard!' His venom showed and the man's eyes shifted uncertainly.

'You no dash me money, you go for river.' The steersman made a deliberate rocking motion, allowing a wave of river water to slop inboard.

Christ! Colin thought. *It would be worth a tenner to get ashore, but any weakness now would be a bad mistake, leading only to higher demands.* He knew they would hesitate from drastic measures; the ship's officer had seen them. But they could make things difficult – drop him miles away, or on the wrong side of the river. He could miss his plane.

The steersman took his silence for fear and became bolder. 'You dash me ten pounds, we take you for shore.' The canoe rocked harder, shipping more water into the wallowing canoe. 'You no dash me, you go for river.'

The man in front turned his head to look coldly at Colin. 'You no pay, you go swim for shore.'

Colin knew they were both wound up as tight as watch-springs. London or Lagos, the mentality of the petty crook was the same – hoping against hope that their victim would give no trouble. Colin made up his mind to force their hand. Suddenly he rose in a crouch, his hands gripping both sides of the canoe. 'Then we all go for river!' he yelled, violently rocking the boat, allowing gallons of brown river water to rush over the low gunwales. *We all go for fucking river!*

Suddenly paddles were churning the water into foam as the terrified boatmen sculled for the shore, the whites of their eyes bulging like hen's eggs. Colin kept up the crazy rocking motion, threatening to totally swamp the flimsy craft. The canoe was awash, on the very point of sinking, when it grounded on a sandy beach just below a main road. The two boatmen leapt ashore, running fifty yards before stopping to glare back at the mad *Bruni*. Grinning at them, Colin squelched ashore. He knew that his clothes would soon dry, and one of the yellow-winged taxis already pulling up on the road above would take him to the airport.

He had ten days to persuade his old firm to take on the job. Ten days to finalise his plan to steal the Ashanti gold.

16

With only hand baggage to carry, Colin strode through the green customs gate ahead of the other passengers. The duty men gave him the eye but let him pass unchallenged. One of the people waiting in the arrivals hall raised a hand and he saw the jaunty, leather-jacketed figure of Doc grinning at him in welcome.

The two of them shook hands warmly, then Doc broke his grip and stepped back, eyes scanning Colin in approval.

'Christ! You're looking well,' he finally said. 'Brown as a fucking berry!'

'Aye! And not from a lamp either,' Colin grinned back at him.

Doc waved a carefree dismissal. 'That's right – Ghana!' he said. 'We wondered where you'd got to after that cock-up in Kilburn.'

'Aye, Doc. I got a bit of a fright there all right. Just out the nick and almost back in again, within a matter of days. I just took time to grab my gear from

Bert's and disappear. The evening paper said that no arrests had been made so I knew you'd all got away. But I was really pissed off, just out the jail and nearly back in again. Ghana suddenly seemed like a good place to be, so I took off running.'

'You might have taken off running, Colin, but if you hadn't spotted that stakeout team we'd all have been done bang to rights. As it was, you gave us just enough time to make a break. Anyway, you're back now and ready for work, I'll bet?'

Colin nodded his head. 'I'm ready for work all right, but not at the old blagging game. I've latched on to something that will set us up for life.'

'Sounds interesting.' Doc gave him a cavalier grin as they walked towards the car park. 'Tell me about it in the car.'

Doc's casual demeanour deserted him and his car attracted angry horn blasts as it suddenly swerved across his lane. 'Hi-fucking-jack a plane! Come on!' He regained control of his driving and turned startled eyes on Colin. 'You've got to be fucking joking!'

'No joke. I'm serious.' Colin spoke confidently. 'You, me and the rest of the old firm – we're going to hijack a plane. I've got it all worked out.'

'C'mon, Colin. Who're you kidding? That's not our game. Besides, the old firm's split up. Eddie's chucked it. That cashier turned him in and he's looking at a five-stretch. He's out on bail and set himself up in the taxi business, trying to make it look good for when he goes to court. There's only me and Bert now; that's the reason we were so chuffed to get your telegram.'

'Only the two of you?' Colin turned to him. 'That means I'll have to find another man. Might even be a good thing; give us a chance to find the sort of man we need.'

'It's hard to find good men,' Doc went on. 'And we've been quiet since Eddie got nicked.'

'Never had any bother yourself? After they got Eddie I mean?'

'Bit of hassle,' Doc admitted. 'That bastard, Detective Inspector Lambert, gave me and Bert heavy spins; section two'd us as well and held us for the whole six hours trying to break our alibis. Even now he's still lurking about trying to get something against us. He's a snooping bastard!'

'My name crop up at all?'

'Nah. He didn't even know you were out.'

'What happened? I mean ... How *did* you get away? It looked bang-to-rights to me.'

'We all got away at the time! When they charged after you we went over a wall and through the service door at the rear of the supermarket. Eddie only got done later on because the cashier caved in under questioning. The coppers guessed it was an inside job, and once they found out about his gambling debts they dragged him in. Just as well he didn't know any of us or our names.'

'Aye, lucky there,' Colin acknowledged. 'Eddie kept schtum?' It was more of a statement than a question.

'Took it like a man,' Doc said nodding in appreciation. 'No comment right down the line. Denied everything! Even denied knowing the cashier.'

'Did they swallow it?'

'Course not!' Doc gave a guffaw. 'But a jury might.'

'Well, good luck to him. I wouldn't like to see him ending up in Wandsworth. I was never so glad to get out of anywhere in my life.'

'And now you want to go hijacking a plane!'

'It *can* be done,' Colin spoke seriously. 'Not easy, mind you. But with the right preparation and a good team on the job, it *definitely* can be done.'

'I'll believe that when I see it.'

'I'm telling you, Doc. It can be done!'

'You couldn't get a team out there?'

'You must be joking! I want the old firm on this one, so here I am.'

Doc shook his head. 'Hijacking?' He sucked air

156

into his lungs and released it in a long, thoughtful whoosh. 'I can't see Bert going for that.'

★

Bert was there to meet them at his flat in Eustace Road and greeted Colin with a strong handshake. 'The disappearing man, eh?' he joked. 'Come on in and have a drink.'

Eddie was reported as '*doing well*' with the minicab business he had started up. Getting charged with the Kilburn job, spending a month on remand in grimy Brixton prison before being released on bail, followed by continuous hassling by the Robbery Squad, had finally persuaded him to go straight. With up to two years to wait before his trial, he was busy building up the image of an honest, hardworking businessman. Bert was still operating four tipper lorries from a small office in the North End Road and Doc was having trouble with 'cowboy' window cleaners encroaching on his territory. Very little had changed.

'And now you're back.' Bert brought him completely up to date and got down to business, looking at Colin with his lugubrious, bulldog expression. 'You back on the firm now, or what?'

Colin stared into his glass, drinking in the atmosphere of the room; the furniture, the wallpaper, the carpets, even the ubiquitous 'Crying Child' looking tearfully down on them. This was civilisation – his civilisation. This was the real world. Suddenly, even to himself, his vision seemed preposterous.

'Aye,' he nodded his head, trying to rekindle enthusiasm. 'I'm back on the firm.'

'Good!' Bert leant forward, his chubby grocer's face taking on a calculating look. 'That gives us a working team again, and we've been looking at a nice little earner over . . .'

'I've found an earner,' Colin interrupted, putting his real world aside for the chance at a better future. 'How would you like to steal three million pounds' worth of gold bullion?'

'What did you say?' Bert's mouth fell open.

'Three million in gold – just waiting to be plucked.' Colin committed himself to his plan.

Doc shot his cuffs, flashing a gold bracelet, and moved to the edge of his seat. He hadn't heard this part of the story. 'Set us up for life, that would,' he agreed. 'Hey, Bert, old son. D'you want into three million quid?'

'I think we better listen a bit more,' Bert cautioned. 'Three million pounds' worth of gold doesn't grow on trees, you know.'

'It's in gold bullion, and it's in transit,' Colin told them. 'All we've got to do is take it away from them.'

'Been done often enough before,' Bert agreed, wrinkling his eyes in consideration. 'Van job, is it?'

'Plane job,' Colin stated quietly. 'The gold's on an aeroplane.'

Bert's interested expression changed to one of astonishment. 'On a fucking aeroplane!'

'That's right. A plane with three million pounds' worth of gold bullion on board, just begging for someone to come along and take it.' Colin sat back, knowing what was coming.

'Hijack a plane?' Bert spoke carefully, as if to be certain he had not misunderstood. 'I suppose you mean in this Ghana place you've been to?'

'That's right. You see . . .'

'Forget it!' Bert growled. 'You've been out in the sun too long, mate. Hijack a plane? What d'you take us for?'

'I want you to listen to me, Bert. You too, Doc. I know it sounds fantastic – I couldn't believe it myself at first. But I've seen it with my own eyes. Sat next to the stuff. Practically touched it.'

'C'mon,' Doc shook his head. 'I told you it wasn't our sort of thing.'

'You both know me,' Colin appealed. 'I've always been able to sort them out. Remember the Goodyear job? I set that up all right, didn't I?'

'That was *here*,' Bert threw up a hand in

exasperation. 'And it was on the fucking pavement, not miles high in the sky!' But Colin spoke through his interruption.

'I wouldn't come all the way back here and lay a load of nonsense on you – you know that,' he argued.

'Well . . . okay,' Bert agreed. 'I'll admit you've always done well in the past. But that was mainly fiddles, scams, the old credit card game and even the odd blag. And when we did go on a blag it was always a set-up, with a good inside man helping out. But hijacking a plane!' His cheeks swelled and he grunted dismissively. 'Nah,' he said. 'You're talking guns here . . . maybe even shooting people! C'mon, Colin, you know we're not into that sort of stuff.' He looked at Doc for agreement.

'I'm with Bert on that, Colin,' Doc spoke out. 'I mean, I might be tempted on a heavy blag as long as everything was set up, no danger of hurting anyone. But shooters? Hijacking a plane? That's a bit over the top for our little firm.'

'We're just not into that sort of stuff,' Bert broke in again. 'Not here, and definitely not in fucking Africa! And we're not taking the chance of shooting anyone, not even for a load of gold. You should know that yourself by now, old son.'

'Of course I know that,' Colin answered. 'But there's no danger of anyone being shot. That's why I want you to hear me out on this. Believe me, you'll have a different opinion once you've heard the tale.'

Bert glanced at Doc, who simply shrugged and said, 'Don't suppose it'd do any harm to listen. We can always knock it back if we don't like it.'

'Okay,' Bert agreed, 'we'll listen. As long as you're not talking shooters, we'll give you a hearing. But don't go holding your breath on us.'

'Look, if I'd come along in sixty-three and suggested holding up the Glasgow-to-London mail train you'd have been in stitches – remember that one?' he asked them.

'I remember they got thirty years apiece,' Bert observed. 'And that was in this country.'

'But they still pulled it off,' Colin argued. 'They were let down afterwards by other people. Just listen to the tale,' he went on. 'It's not perfect yet, but you'll see the potential.'

Sitting on the edge of his chair he related his experience at the mine and his stumbling across the gold shipment at Kumasi. 'Once the plane lands at Accra the gold is taken away under military escort again. But in the air, anyone could take it.'

'Yeah!' Bert's voice was derisive. 'With armed soldiers guarding it?'

'I'd bet my share their guns aren't even loaded,' Colin stated soberly.

161

'Not loaded?'

'They were 303s, Bert. Old British Army rifles, far too powerful to discharge in an aircraft. They've got specially designed weapons for that nowadays – powerful enough to kill someone without risking structural damage to the plane.'

Bert gave careful consideration to this information. 'Makes sense,' he admitted. 'What d'you think, Doc?'

'He's right. If they were really expecting to fire guns on board they'd have the proper weapons.'

'Okay, so the guards are unarmed,' Bert agreed. 'But we're still stuck in a plane miles high in the sky. What do we do now?'

'We take over the plane. There'll be no opposition, just a matter of producing shooters and . . .'

'Hey, hey, hey . . .' Bert's hand went up like a policeman stopping traffic. 'I've just told you; we don't go in for the shooting business.'

'Not *real* shooters,' Colin retorted. 'Replicas. That's all we'd need on a job like this. Once you pull a gun on a plane, you're in charge. Believe me, people on board a plane will do exactly what they're told when they see a gun. Any kind of gun! Fuck me, planes have been hijacked with a match and a bottle of petrol before now.'

'And supposing we do hijack a planeload of gold,'

Bert butted in, derisively. 'Where the fuck do we go with it? Cuba?'

'We don't go anywhere.' Colin took a deep breath. 'We off-load the gold and follow it down by parachute. Wait! Wait!' He motioned a rapidly rising Bert back to his seat. 'You've got old age pensioners leaping out of aeroplanes for charity nowadays. It's not as crazy as it sounds.'

'Nah,' Bert shook his head. 'C'mon Colin. Hijacking! It's just not on. There's plenty of work in London for us. Why should we take on a job in Ghana? Christ! We don't even know where the place is. I can think of hundreds of reasons against it.'

'Give them to me,' Colin demanded. 'You raise objections and I'll try and overcome them. That way we'll end up with a plan.'

'Well, in the first place, you're talking about Ghana,' Doc said. 'We can't just stroll over there, hijack a plane and simply disappear. We'd stick out like a zack on a Zulu's arse!'

'And what would we do with the gold, supposing we did get it?' demanded Bert. 'It would be hard enough to get rid of it here, never mind bloody Ghana!'

'And I'm willing to bet this Ghana place is no Costa Del Sol,' Doc cut in. 'I mean, there can't be that many tourists arriving there that they can't keep tabs on them.'

'Is that all?' Colin disconcerted them with his question.

'No, it's not!' Bert finally found his voice. 'We're not some kind of high-flying terrorists. We're blaggers . . . pavement artists. We work best at ground level. And besides, this parachuting business? I don't know the first thing about it. How about you, Doc?'

'Not me,' Doc shook his head. 'I've never even seen a parachute, except in the movies.'

'Least of your problems,' Colin insisted. 'It's a big sport nowadays. Clubs all over the place.'

'Well . . . I suppose you're right about that.' Bert reluctantly agreed. 'But what about getting into Ghana? And then getting rid of the gold, supposing we did get it?'

'You don't need to worry about the gold. I can handle that. Once we get the gold off the plane you can forget about it until I get it to London.'

'You could handle that?' Bert queried, the first faint flicker of interest showing on his face.

'I've got the perfect set-up. And as for getting into Ghana,' Colin drew a newspaper cutting from his pocket. 'We use this as cover.'

'You mean . . . go in with the supporters?' Bert read the boxing announcement and passed the cutting to Doc.

'That's it! Cooper has a fantastic following in

London and they're already offering package deals at some travel agents. You go with the crowd – in and out. They've even waived visa requirements for the fight fans.'

'How does the fight date fit in with the gold movement?'

'Same day,' Colin enthused. 'That's what makes it perfect. Everything fits into place like a *Cluedo* set. It's almost as if it was meant to happen.'

'At least it's beginning to sound a bit more practical,' Bert grudgingly acknowledged, his spectacles glinting across at Colin.

'It's all a matter of mind adjustment,' Colin said. 'Put the idea of it being thousands of miles away out of your head. We've travelled to some work before, haven't we? This job could be in Wales or Yorkshire for all the difference it makes.'

'What about a team?' Doc asked. 'It would take more than three of us to pull off a job like this.'

'Four,' Colin said without hesitation. 'It would take four to be safe.'

'Hold up! Hold up!' Bert broke in. 'You two are talking as if it's all been settled.'

Doc stared into his tumbler. 'I'm not saying it's settled, but I am interested in hearing more about earning three million pounds.'

'And so am I, Doc, so am I. But all we've got so far

is a rough idea of the work. What about the details? How much would it cost? It's not like grafting in London, you know.'

Colin spoke earnestly. 'I've got the whole thing in my head – it just needs sorting out. I reckon five . . . ten grand, would cover expenses.'

'And where do we get that?' Bert asked. 'Every penny I've got is tied up right now. And I know Doc's got problems.'

'And we haven't had an earner in months,' Doc added.

Colin felt deflated. This was one obstacle he had not anticipated. 'It would only take about two and a half grand apiece,' he said.

'Look,' Bert leant forward. 'Supposing we got the money? We would be in a position to talk about this gold business in more detail without committing ourselves. See how it shapes up.'

'*Got the money?*' Colin had caught the inflection in Bert's words.

Bert turned to Doc. 'Patterson's?'

'Seems like a good time for it.' Doc slapped his hands together and rubbed them in anticipation.

Colin looked on, knowing something was cooking.

'You're really keen on this job?' Bert came on again.

'It can be done!'

'And you agree that there's no point in us even considering it if we don't have the expenses?'

Colin nodded slowly, as if trying to put off what he knew was coming.

'I'm not making any promises,' Bert warned. 'But if this job is as good as you say it is, you wouldn't mind doing a little blag to finance it, would you?'

'Patterson's?' Colin stared at him.

'Patterson's,' Bert confirmed. 'It's a pick-up. Money bagged and the guy knows we're coming. Only comes to about fifteen grand; that's the reason we've left it out so far. But it's enough to get us talking about this plane of yours. The job's tomorrow. You in?'

17

'That bastard's been blocking the pavement for twenty minutes now.' Doc spoke over his shoulder at Bert and Colin as they crouched behind him in the rear of a Luton-type Ford Transit van.

'Drivers!' Bert growled. 'Park any-fucking-where they want these days. Don't care who they mess up.'

They were waiting in a side street, looking across a main road at the entrance of a small cash and carry warehouse.

'The collection's about due. If we don't get in there in the next five minutes, it'll be too late.' Colin tapped anxiously at his wristwatch.

'Don't panic,' Doc said, airily. 'They often run late. Hold it!' His voice took on an edge. 'Someone's getting into the car.'

'Thank Christ!' Bert pulled a black balaclava down over his face. 'About fucking time too!'

Colin pressed gloved hands together and felt for his sledgehammer. 'Whenever you like, Doc. We're ready.' He pulled his mask down and moved back to stand alongside Bert at the roll-up door, raising it an inch or two so they could get their fingers firmly underneath it.

The blue Transit emerged from the side street normally enough, until startled motorists saw it suddenly swerve across the centre-line and screech to a halt, forcing oncoming traffic to brake. Ignoring angry horn blasts from indignant motorists, Doc coolly leant from the window and backed the van over the kerb, reversing directly towards the office window of Patterson's Cash and Carry as blaring horns from impatient drivers forced the stalled traffic on.

George Lombard, chief cashier at Patterson's, was filling out his pay-in book when his office window darkened. For a moment he thought the van was going to come crashing through on top of him, but it stopped inches short and he breathed a sigh of relief. Then his world went suddenly crazy as the plate-glass window exploded inwards to reveal two terrifying figures in dark boiler suits wildly swinging sledge-hammers behind the hail of flying glass. Lombard knew the raid was coming, but not how or when, and he sat paralysed with genuine shock as the masked men leapt from the back of the van right into his office. One of the men grabbed the cash bag sitting on his desk while the other screamed obscenities at him and destroyed a chair with one wild swipe of his sledgehammer. Then the bag was flying through the air into the rear of the van, followed immediately by the raiders as they scrambled over his desk and leapt back on board the vehicle.

Bert pounded the side of the van three times and it accelerated away, throwing him heavily to the floor. Colin just managed to stay erect and thought at first that Bert had injured himself. Then he realised that the sound he was hearing was not screaming – it was hysterical laughter.

'Did you see his face?' Bert hooted, going into another paroxysm. 'Did you see Lombard's fucking face?'

The van swung round a corner and roared away.

*

'That's it,' Bert pulled the last bundle of notes from a Co-op carrier bag. 'Fifteen thousand three hundred quid. Not bad for a ten-second quickie!' he grinned at the others, who had left him to count the money while they enjoyed a can of beer.

'But nothing like three million,' Colin pointed out. 'So what do we do now? Split it or use it?'

'We haven't decided that yet,' Bert reminded him. 'You've proved that you've still got plenty of bottle, but this gold business is another matter.'

'You said that if we got the finance you'd talk about it.'

'Yeah,' Bert agreed. 'We'll talk about it all right. But it will have to be fucking good to convince me.'

The heavy thumping at the door was unmistakable and the three of them froze.

'Christ!' Bert leapt to the curtains. 'It's the fucking coppers!'

Doc grabbed the money and began stuffing it back into the carrier bag. 'It's that fucking Lambert!' Bert wailed.

The pounding on the door increased.

'Stash it somewhere!' Bert mouthed at Doc as he moved towards the hallway. 'I'll stall them as long as I can.' Doc was already in the kitchen.

'Yeah?' Bert's voice could be heard in the hallway. 'Who? Police! Oh, it's you, Inspector Lambert. What is it? Something wrong?'

'You're wrong,' the unmistakable voice of Detective Inspector Lambert gravelled out, getting louder as he marched into the house.

'Hey!' Bert backed up and spread his arms across the width of the narrow hall. 'You got a warrant?'

'If I had a warrant I wouldn't be wasting my time talking to dirt like you, Maddren. Now, come on. You inviting us in, or do we have to do this the hard way?'

171

'Never give a man a bit of peace, do you?' Bert grumbled. 'What is it this time?'

'We'll just come in and talk about it,' Lambert's voice grew loud as he and Detective Sergeant Colon pushed past Bert and entered the living room.

'Grant!' He raised his eyebrows. 'You could be a bonus.'

'What the hell do you want?' Colin asked. 'We're just having a quiet drink.'

'Champagne?'

'Brown ale,' Colin waved his can.

'Too good for the likes of you,' Lambert knocked it from his hand, letting its contents froth out onto the carpet.

'Okay. You're in,' Bert snapped, 'Invited. So we'll have no fucking mess. What is it you're after, Lambert?'

'Earlier this evening,' Lambert made a show of looking at his watch. 'About four hours ago . . . Nice little blag – Patterson's Cash and Carry in Acton. You were suggested. You too,' he looked at Doc. 'And chummy here,' he stared at Colin, 'makes it even better.'

'He's visiting. Doc's just dropped by and I was working all day,' Bert bristled.

'And a dozen witnesses to vouch for it,' Lambert sneered.

'And the rest!' Bert snapped. 'Check it out.'

'Sooner check your house.' Lambert indicated upstairs to Colon, who had been standing quietly in the background. 'On your way, sergeant. I'll handle things down here.'

'You don't mind?' He grinned sardonically as he spilled cushions from the settee and felt around the seams before kneeling to peer underneath.

'Be my guest,' Bert said sarcastically, picking up the beer can.

Lambert spent ten minutes prying and poking in both the living room and kitchen, growing less and less enthusiastic – even less so when Colon came downstairs with equally negative results.

'I'll admit this one wasn't your usual style,' Lambert grudgingly acknowledged. 'Then again, you've been a bit too quiet lately. And now he's back on the manor.' He turned to Colin.

'They don't even tell us when they're letting you vermin loose,' he complained. 'How long have you been out?'

'Not long enough!' Colin glared at him.

'And not for much longer, chummy. Not if I've got anything to do with it.' Lambert's stubby finger jabbed belligerently under Colin's nose as he spoke. 'Right!' He tided the front of his coat, fastidiously smoothing the lapels and squaring the knot of his tie.

'You seem to be clear this time. But I'll be keeping my eye on you lot. And if there is any blagging on my manor, you're IT! Understood?'

'Don't know what you're talking about, Inspector.' Bert answered. 'All we're trying to do is make an honest living these days.'

'Don't make me fucking laugh,' Lambert retorted as he led Colon towards the door. 'Remember! I'll be keeping a very close eye on you.'

'Pheww!' Bert flopped into a chair when the two policemen had gone. 'That bastard! He's trouble.'

'Didn't think he'd suss us for that one,' Doc moaned.

'He didn't suss anyone,' Colin told him. 'He was shooting in the dark. Hoping for a lucky strike.'

'Where'd you hide it?' Bert asked.

'Didn't.' Doc's voice was cool. 'I emptied your vegetable box into the bag and left it on the table.'

'You what!'

'It's still there,' Doc shrugged. 'That Lambert always did miss the obvious. He thinks we like to hide things.'

'Jesus, a psychologist!' Bert raised a hand to his forehead. 'I was shitting bricks when he was in there.'

Doc extended his hand. 'And I was making the mortar.'

★

174

The success of the robbery at Patterson's had rekindled Colin's enthusiasm and he talked eagerly about the gold job. 'I handle the preparations,' he said, 'do all the preliminary work in Ghana and take charge of the gold once it's on the ground. All you have to do is turn up on the plane and even at that late stage you can still scrub it if you don't fancy it.'

'You make it sound easy,' Bert admitted.

'It is easy!' Colin declared vehemently. 'And when it's all over we'll never need to put ourselves on offer again.'

'It definitely sounds as if it's got possibilities,' Bert admitted. 'But there's still a lot to be worked out before I'll be convinced. How about you, Doc? You struck on it, are you?'

'Well ... we know Colin, and he knows the strength. Knows what to look for. He wouldn't come all the way back here unless it was something special.'

'Right!' Colin took the initiative. 'And now we've got the expenses I can begin making preparations at this end.'

'We're not committed to anything yet,' Bert reminded him. 'There's a lot we'll need to get sorted out before I make a final decision.'

'Look,' Colin addressed both of them. 'I'll be here

for a week yet. Talk it over. Ask me anything. Think about what you could do with three million pounds.'

'Okay?' Bert looked at Doc and received a nod. 'We'll give it a real chewing over.'

'That's good,' Colin smiled. 'I can't ask more than that. Now, who's going to drive me round so's I can begin setting things up?'

Bert's head swung quickly round, ready to mouth an objection, but Colin raised his hand. 'Just a precaution,' he told him. 'My arrangements can always be cancelled, but I don't have time to leave things while you make up your minds.'

18

Doc eased the car into the kerb just beyond the underground station on Goldhawk Road, near Shepherd's Bush roundabout. Across from them an estate agent's red and white board advertised a shop to let.

'All right?' He nodded at the building.

Colin shook his head. 'No good.' He pointed to the curtained windows of a flat directly above the empty shop. 'People who live above shops tend to be nosey about what's going on in them. We need empty premises above us, or better still, a shop in a single-storey building.'

They stopped three times to check empty premises, two 'probables' making it into Colin's notebook. Then a parade of single-storeyed shops appeared on the left-hand pavement with several estate agents' boards projecting untidily over the pavement.

'Looks better,' Colin muttered. 'Now if we can only find one for rent.'

'TO LET'. A well-weathered sign jutted from the

flaking paintwork of a double-fronted shop. Colin peered into the premises through grime-covered windows and, although the interior was dirty and obviously long neglected, it was ideal for his purpose. He wrote down the details of the estate agent and returned to the car, directing Doc to head for W1. An hour later they were back and letting themselves into the shop, having signed a short-term agreement and paid a relieved estate agent a deposit and three months' rent in advance.

*

'Looks a bit rough,' Doc muttered as he followed Colin inside their newly acquired shop. 'Suit you, does it?'

'The inside isn't important.' Colin told him, poking about the neglected interior. 'As long as the outside can be tarted up, we'll be in business.' He pushed at the door leading to the back shop.

'Bit of a camel's,' Doc grimaced at the dust-covered ruins of a table, two broken chairs and a heavily stained sink. 'Think it's all right?' he asked, taking care not to get too close to anything.

'It's perfect,' Colin replied. 'It just needs cleaning up.' He opened a small cupboard and gave a grunt of satisfaction on seeing the battered electrical fusebox and meter. The lever moved stiffly, but the flick of a switch showed the power was still connected. Pleased, as though this was an omen of good luck, he slapped his hands together in satisfaction. 'Aye. We'll soon have a good wee business going on here.'

Doc looked at him with some perplexity. 'Business?' he queried. 'I thought you were after a load of gold. What sort of business are we going into in this dump?'

'Could be anything,' Colin stated enigmatically. 'Anything from chocolates to contraceptives,' he added, leaving Doc looking even more puzzled. 'Now come on. There's still a bit of running about to do.'

'Pull over!' Detective Inspector Lambert snapped at Colon, twisting round in his seat as he caught sight of Colin and Doc locking the door of the empty store. 'Now what the hell are those two up to?' he muttered, watching as they entered their car and drove off.

*

They sat in a small café as Colin pored over the business section of the *London Weekly Advertiser*, nodding to himself now and again before jotting down a phone number. He left Doc at the table while he went to the public phone and dialled a number, speaking only briefly before returning to his seat.

'That's it, Doc. First time lucky. I'll be nipping off

on my own now. Got a bit of business over Islington way.'

'I'm spare,' Doc offered. 'Got nothing else on today.'

'You've got plenty on!' Colin slid the keys to the shop across the table. 'Get on to a venetian blind company and get the shop fitted out. It's the easiest way to make the place look good and the blinds will stop nosey bastards looking in. And get the windows cleaned too, while you're at it,' he grinned. 'That is your line of business, isn't it?'

'Big time!' Doc grinned as he took the keys. 'Soon get that sorted out. What about the blower?'

'All in good time, Doc, all in good time. We don't even know the name of the business yet. But one thing to remember is that this is all on the level. Except for moody names this little business is all on the up and up.'

★

Colin was ushered into the offices of Greenberg, Greenberg and Perris by an attractive secretary.

'Mr Thompson.' She announced him by the name he had given at her desk, before letting the door close on them.

'Ah, yes, Mr Thompson. You phoned earlier,' Perris acknowledged as he leant over to shake hands.

'That's correct.' Colin sat down facing the solicitor and smiled.

'And you are interested in purchasing one of our "ready-made" companies, Mr Thompson?'

'That's right,' Colin agreed. 'I saw your advertisement in the *London Weekly*.'

'Well, we have ready-made packages for most types of business. I'm sure we'll be able to accommodate you satisfactorily. What type of business is it you wish to engage in?'

'Confectionery.' Colin's reply had no embroidery. Perris was here to sell his packages and he was here to buy. There would be few formalities.

Perris pressed a switch on his desk intercom. 'Rachel, would you be good enough to bring me the Bakers and Confectioners file?'

'Wholesale or retail?' He looked at Colin as the door closed behind his secretary.

'I'd like the articles to include a bit of both.'

'Of course. Very wise.' He received an approving nod. 'Always better to be prepared for any contingencies. Ah, here we are.' Perris produced a folder from the thick file his secretary had brought him. 'The "Articles of Memorandum and Association" of this company cover every aspect of the confectionery trade. Would you like to read them in full?'

'That won't be necessary,' Colin told him. 'As

long as they cover wholesaling, retailing, import and export I'll be satisfied.'

'Yes, of course. Well, this company,' Perris glanced at the name on the folder, "Hansel", was registered a month ago with myself and Miss Loomis as nominal directors, so if you could just give me your business address we can have the necessary transfer documents signed immediately.'

Ten minutes later, Colin was back in Goldhawk Road, £150 poorer, but now the director of Hansel, a registered limited company. He was up and running.

All I've got to do now is get Bert and Doc to commit themselves and we'll be well away. His smile widened at the prospect and the knowledge that he had successfully completed a vital step in his plans to seize the Ashanti gold.

19

'So what do you think?' Colin addressed Bert and Doc in the living room at Eustace Road.

'Speaking for myself,' Bert opened up, 'I admit the job has possibilities. But I'll need to know an awful lot more before I make any decision. I like the idea of getting into Ghana with the boxing crowd though. Checked with some of the chaps and the word is that Sports Tours is laying on a package deal and they say that the tickets are selling well. It's your plans for afterwards I'm worried about. They'd have to be 100 per cent.'

'That's it for me too,' Doc added. 'We can travel out there easily enough, but it won't be the same getting back. The place will be jumping with law.'

'There'll be some scream goes up,' Colin agreed. 'But there's no Flying Squad out there. In fact, I'm willing to bet that the army will be left to deal with it.'

'Fuck taking on the army!' Bert snorted. 'They'll be out shooting.'

'No danger!' Colin waved him down. 'By the time

they begin to suspect anything is wrong, you'll be back in Accra, just another couple of fans at the big fight.'

'I admit I'm beginning to like the idea of taking it off the plane,' Doc said. 'But how would we know where we were? And how would we move the gold once we're on the ground?'

'I've already found an ideal spot for dropping the gold,' Colin told him. 'And I'm still working on the problem of making sure we get the plane to the right place at the right time. I'll have to talk to someone who knows a bit about flying and something about parachute jumping.'

'Could be lucky there,' said Doc. 'I went round to Eddie's place after I left you this morning. He's got a guy working casual with him – just out the army. From the way he looks and talks, Eddie reckons he was in some special unit, maybe even the SAS.'

'Did you see the guy yourself?'

'Nah. But he's on shift at eight o'clock tonight and Eddie said he'd send him round here, like he was on a job.'

'Sounds all right,' Colin added. 'Did Eddie say anything about the guy? I mean . . . does he think he would entertain a bit of villainy?'

'Eddie says he thinks he's all right. Got turfed out of the army for some reason or other.'

'Could be just the man we need,' Colin nodded. 'If Eddie's right, and this guy is sensible enough, we could be in luck.'

'Supposing he is all right?' It was Bert again. 'You still haven't mentioned how you plan to handle the gold if we do manage to get it on the ground.'

'I've got that all sorted out. Anyway, it's my problem. You hit the deck, get into the car and head straight for Accra. You'd be carrying nothing more incriminating than tickets for the fight.'

'You think you can arrange it that way?' Bert stared him straight in the eye.

'It can be done!' Colin's voice left no room for doubt. 'All we need is someone with experience in parachuting and we're in business.'

At five past eight a car horn sounded outside Bert's window. With a nod to the others he went to the front door and beckoned the driver of the mini-cab inside. In a few moments a heavily built, fresh-complexioned young man of about twenty-five came striding into the room. He was fair-haired, tallish – around the five foot ten mark – but broad, sloping shoulders and a bulging chest made him look shorter. The turned-back cuffs of his shirt exposed strong wrists tapering to hands that were sturdy and workmanlike. A closer look would have shown his right hand roundly clenched, ready, moving a little as it squeezed and unsqueezed in a tight pumping motion.

'Eddie sent you round?' Bert's voice relieved the tension.

The man's eyes seemed to lighten in his ruggedly handsome face and he relaxed a little, moving his lips in a faint natural smile. 'Yeah . . . Maddren, 26 Eustace Road – 8pm. That's the message I got.' His voice was calm, even casual. 'I am at the right address?'

'You're all right,' Bert spoke again. 'Did Eddie mention anything to you about coming round here?'

'No. But he gave me the address himself and that's usually the dispatcher's job. Made me wonder.'

Bert motioned towards a chair. 'Take a seat, er . . . ?' He raised his eyebrows.

The young man looked at him through coolly calculating eyes, then down on Doc and Colin who had both sat silently through the exchange. His brow wrinkled as if he was making up his mind, then he stuck out his hand.

'Ray . . . Ray Quarry,' he introduced himself.

'I'm Bert Maddren. This is Joey Docherty – call him Doc, and Colin Grant. Two of my, er . . . associates.'

'Pleased to meet you.' Ray's handshake was firm

186

with each of them before he sank into the indicated chair, curious at his unusual reception.

'Whisky?' Bert held out a glass.

'Not right now, thanks,' he smiled easily. 'Working tonight.'

Bert didn't press his hospitality, but he left the glass on the table. 'Well, Ray, Eddie tells us you were in the army. That right, is it?'

'Yeah.' Ray was obviously puzzled at the enquiry but answered readily enough. 'I was in the SAS, B Company.' He shot out his wrist to look at his watch, reminding them he was working.

'Don't worry about the time,' Doc spoke out. 'I've had a word with Eddie.'

'What is this then, a job interview?' Ray came right to the point. 'It's pretty obvious you don't want a taxi,' he grinned good-humouredly at them.

'Eddie tells me you were chucked out of the army?' Bert brushed his question aside.

'Uh-huh,' Ray grunted, then realised more was expected. 'Had a difference of opinion with an officer and got carried away with myself.' He smiled grimly at the memory. 'He'll carry my mark for the rest of his days. They busted me to private, had me RTU'd and gave me twenty-eight days' chokey and a DD.'

'What's all that mean?' Colin spoke for the first time. 'RTU'd . . . DD?'

187

'Returned to Unit.' Ray's face hardened. 'Chucked out of the SAS and posted back to the Paras so that when they court-martialled me the SAS stayed clean.'

'And DD?'

'Dishonourable Discharge.' Ray seemed bitter at the admission. 'Bastards like to kick you when you're down.'

'You didn't like it then . . . the army, I mean?'

'Didn't like it? I loved it!' Ray declared passionately, his iron-grey eyes suddenly flashing points of fire. 'I signed up with the Paras for twelve years and enjoyed every minute of it. Transferred to the SAS after two years and liked it even better.' His fists clenched on his knees, knuckles white. 'Until some bastard of an officer acts well out of turn and *I* get kicked out! "Conduct prejudicial to military discipline," they called it.'

'Rank has its privileges,' Bert commiserated. 'Someone's got to carry the can.'

'You said you were in the paras?' Colin spoke up again. 'You'll have done a lot of jumps then?'

'Over 300.' There was a note of pride in Ray's voice. 'Low-level, high-altitude, freefall, static-line, day jumps and night jumps. I've done them all.'

Colin was impressed with his answer. 'You miss it then . . . the jumping I mean?'

188

'I've only been out a few months,' Ray answered. 'But I must admit that I'm beginning to miss it. What with shunting around in this taxi carry-on – dead boring.'

'You'd be interested in any other kind of *work*?' Colin put the question, laying stress on the word 'work'.

Ray looked directly into his eyes, his own gaze steady, unspoken strength in its coolness. 'I'm prepared to consider alternative work.'

'You know the sort of work we're talking about?' Bert spoke slowly, his eyes fixed on Ray.

'Well, seeing it was Eddie that sent me round and having heard a few tales from the other drivers about him, I don't suppose you're planning on opening a charity shop.' He stared at Bert with narrowed eyes. 'I'm interested. But I'm not getting involved in any real villainy – serious lawbreaking, that is.'

Colin's vibes had come good the moment Ray had been ushered into the room and he felt a pang of disappointment at his words. He believed in first impressions, and Ray had certainly made a good impression on him. With his military background, Colin knew he was ideal for the job. Knew too that they could work well together – make a good team – a winning team. In a world where first impressions and snap decisions could often mean the difference between success and failure, freedom or capture, he had that rare feeling of compatibility that told him: *This is the man.* He didn't want to lose him.

'You want to drive mini-cabs forever?'

'It'll do till something better comes along.'

'Listen, Ray. You've been in the army too long. Things don't just *come along* in real life. You've got to go out and grab the world by the throat and make your own opportunities come along,' Colin told him. 'You've got to take risks. People like us . . . we've got to make our own silver spoons.'

Grey eyes bored into Colin. 'Thanks for the offer, Colin, but no thanks.' Ray started to rise to his feet. 'I guess I'm just a law-abiding citizen at heart. Sorry chaps.' Standing, he seemed to tower over them, the very image of strength and dependability. 'I could recommend one or two guys, ex-SAS like myself, who might be interested,' he offered. 'But you'd have to take your chances with them.'

'You definitely won't change your mind?'

'Who can say that about anything?' Ray smiled easily. 'Things get bad, or there's reason enough . . . who knows what a man will do?'

'By the time they get bad enough it could be too late to do anything,' Colin pointed out.

'I've been through bad times before,' Ray turned towards the door.

190

'I thought you SAS guys liked a bit of action?' Bert sat back, his expression more bulldog than man as he looked quizzically up at Ray.

'I've seen my share of action,' Ray snapped, his eyes suddenly hard chips of flint as he looked back on a memory. 'And seen things and done things I'd rather not.' He hesitated at the door. 'You don't have a lot of choice in the army, you know.'

'You'd have a choice with us,' Colin pointed out. 'You wouldn't be forced into anything.'

'Honest, Colin, I really do appreciate the offer, but . . .' Ray shook his head and flashed a look at his wristwatch. 'Time I was moving.'

'You'd rather drive a taxi around London than take a crack at a load of gold in Ghana?' Doc ignored Colin's angry look.

Ray spun on his heel. 'Gold!'

Colin's anger at Doc was forgotten as he recognised the sudden animation on Ray's face. '*And brings all their vices to the surface,*' he heard Fred O'Hara's voice intoning in his head.

Ray turned back into the room. 'Gold!' he said. 'Gold in Ghana . . . the old Gold Coast?'

Doc looked at Colin and shrugged. He had never heard of the Gold Coast.

'That's right,' Colin replied for him. 'Ghana, West Africa.'

'The White Man's Graveyard.' Ray gave a smile. 'You're thinking of doing something out there?' He stared directly at Colin.

'I've just come from there, as a matter of fact.'

Ray nodded his understanding. 'Recce . . . and back now for the troops.'

'More or less,' Colin admitted. 'It's just something I stumbled across out there and it's too good to miss.'

'Join the villains and see the world,' Bert quipped, sensing a change in the atmosphere.

'You've heard more than you should have,' Colin threw a look at an unrepentant Doc. 'But it's right enough. We're planning on going to Ghana after a shipment of gold bullion.'

'It certainly sounds more interesting than all the cowboy carry-on we hear about nowadays,' Ray said. 'I could get interested in a load of gold bullion.'

'But it's villainy,' Colin added. 'I'm talking heavy stuff. It involves travelling and it involves shooters; replicas right enough, but it would still be considered armed robbery. I can't tell you any more than that until you declare yourself in or out. But if you're in, you're in at the deep end.' He willed Ray to commit himself.

Ray focused alert, intelligent eyes on each of them in turn. 'The other drivers say that's how Eddie got himself set up in business. He sent me round, so I presume he knows what's going on?'

'He only knows we need a man to make up the firm again,' Colin told him.

'And I'm to take his place,' Ray deduced aloud. 'Well, he seems to have done well enough out of it.' He stood in a thoughtful silence, letting his eyes dwell on each of them in turn before speaking again.

'I spent nearly five years carrying a gun for my country. I took risks then for army pay and look what it got me – court-martialled and chucked in the glasshouse. Now look at me . . . hacking about London in a mini-cab.' He clenched his fist, and made a pumping motion. 'I've changed my mind. If there's room for me, I'd definitely like to be in on this gold business.' He encompassed them with an intense, hard-eyed look, chin jutting aggressively.

Colin felt a surge of relief and stuck out his hand. 'Welcome to the firm, Ray. I'm sure you'll fit in well with us.'

Bert satisfied himself with a firm handshake accompanied with a stiff nod of acceptance. When he sat down again he pushed the still untouched whisky over to Ray and topped up the other glasses. He picked up his own measure and held it out.

'Here's to the new firm. May it reign successfully.'

Bert nodded his glass at each of them, receiving the same salute in return, before downing the toast. Ray hesitated, looking into his glass for a thoughtful moment, then decisively threw his whisky back, almost as if he was swallowing his past.

'Well,' Colin addressed the new member. 'You can forget about taxi driving now, at least for the next few weeks or so.'

'I need the money,' Ray pointed out. 'I've still got to eat and pay the rent.'

'You're on the firm,' Colin replied. 'We'll keep you going till the first earner.'

Ray's face stiffened. 'No offence,' he said. 'But I don't take handouts. Anything I get, I'll earn.'

'Don't worry about that,' Colin assured him. 'You'll earn it all right. Why do you think we're so interested in your army career?'

'I suppose it's the SAS reputation.'

'There's more to it than that.' Colin looked speculatively at him. 'Over 300 jumps, you said?'

'Three hundred and seventeen, to be exact. Fifty-two with the army, the rest with parachute clubs. I've got an instructor's rating and we have to log every jump.'

'You'll have spent a lot of time in the air then, flying I mean?'

'Well,' Ray gave a hearty laugh. 'You've got to get

194

up before you can come down. Yeah, I've done my share of flying time.'

'Ever done any actual flying? Piloting a plane, I mean?'

Ray shook his head. 'I've been up a few times as dispatcher and the pilot's let me hold onto the controls for a few minutes now and again, but I've never actually flown a plane.'

'H'mm,' Colin nodded thoughtfully to himself and turned to Bert and Doc. 'So we can accept that Ray is an expert on parachuting.' He received nods of agreement. 'That means he'll be able to advise us and I'll be in a position to put forward a finalised plan for the job we're discussing.'

Ray broke into the conversation. 'If I'm going to be any help to you you'll have to put me fully in the picture. It's fairly obvious that parachutes are involved but you'll have to be more specific.'

Colin nodded his head. 'You're right. You'll have to be told.' He looked at the other two, waiting until he received nods of agreement before turning back to Ray.

'You're right enough,' he said. 'The job we're considering does involve parachutes. But there's more to it than that.' He took a deep breath before continuing. 'What we're thinking about is hijacking an aeroplane.' He saw Ray straighten in his chair, eyes widening in surprise. 'I know it sounds ambitious, but once you've heard the details I think you'll see the possibilities.'

Bert interrupted. 'We're still only considering the hijack business,' he reminded Colin, before turning back to Ray. 'We've got other work lined up, Ray. So even if we decide against this hijacking idea you'll still be on the firm for anything else we set up.'

Ray moved his shoulders in a shrug. 'Yeah, well thanks for that, Bert. But I've already told you I'm not really interested in er . . . general villainy. This gold's another matter. I could go for that all right. Mind you, there's not been much success in the hijacking business. I mean, has anyone ever actually pulled off a robbery in the sky?'

'D.B. Cooper.' Colin spoke softly, knowing Ray would recognise the name.

Bert and Doc assumed quizzical looks as Ray slowly nodded and broke into a smile. 'Yeah . . . I forgot about him. He's one all right.'

'One what?' queried Bert.

'A hijacker that got away with it,' Colin told him.

'How?' The question hung in the air.

'Joined as a passenger and pulled a gun,' Ray told him. 'He even got them to land the plane so he could pick up half a million dollars' ransom money. Then he let the passengers go and got the crew to take off again.'

'It happened in America,' Colin took up the story. 'Cooper jumped and neither him or the money have been heard of since. But the thing is,' Colin made his point, *'he never fired a shot.* For all anyone knows he could have had a water pistol.'

'There was another one,' Ray started to speak.

'I know about him,' Colin interrupted. 'But they found traces of blood on the tailplane fuselage and think he killed himself on the way out. No body was ever found though, so they never got to the bottom of the story.'

'That's true,' Ray agreed. 'If I remember correctly, it was a Boeing 707 he jumped from and you can't make a safe side exit from that type of aircraft. The speed is too high, and they think he got swept back and hit the tailplane.'

Colin jabbed the table with a stiff finger. 'The fact remains – *they both took over a plane and got out of it without even firing a shot!'*

Ray agreed with him. 'I don't think anyone's ever fired a shot during a hijack, at least not in the air anyway. Believe me, no one will argue with an armed man on board a plane.'

'So,' Colin emphasised, 'Even with replicas, no one will interfere with you. If the hijack's set up right

197

it'll be a walkover – just like the two guys in America.'

'You just said one of them got killed,' Bert objected.

'Nobody knows that for certain. And if he was killed it was because he didn't do his homework properly.' Colin argued. 'Not because he lost control in the plane. But we've got Ray and he can keep us right on the finer points of jumping. Once I've convinced you and Doc to go ahead with this, you'll be signing up with a parachute club. With what they'll teach you, and Ray to keep you right, the job will be a scoosh case.'

'There's no question about it,' Ray told them. 'Get on board an aircraft with a gun, or anything that even looks like a gun, and a hijack's a done deal. And from the way you're talking I gather you don't intend using genuine handguns?'

'We're not into shooting people, Ray,' Colin reminded him. 'And as you know yourself, guns are dangerous things. From what I've read and what you've just said, a dummy gun is just as effective as a real one in a hijack situation, except there's no chance of shooting anyone. That's the way we want it.'

'Yeah,' Bert's voice was becoming more positive. 'Yeah, that's the way it has to be. And judging from what I've heard, it sounds all right to me. Okay,

Colin. For three million quid, run it by us again, old son.'

Once again Colin ran through the broad outline of his plan. With each explanation he was becoming increasingly familiar and happy about it and now, with Ray on board, he knew the job was well within the firm's capabilities.

'As I see it,' he concluded, 'our biggest problem is getting the plane to the right spot for dropping the gold. That's the reason we need someone with experience. We need the extra information Ray can give us about jumping under conditions out there.' He sat back, knowing there would be questions.

'What type of aircraft are we talking about?' Ray asked. 'Some of them can be very awkward to jump from, you know. That's where the guy in the States came unstuck.'

'It's an old Dakota, a DC-3 I think they're called,' Colin told him. 'Twin engine, and the passenger door is well clear of the propellers. I took special note of that.'

'I know the plane – seen them on airfields. And you're right about the passenger door; the army always used DC-3s for the parachute regiment until the Hercules plane came in. It's a slow plane so there wouldn't be any difficulty in jumping.'

'Well, it's about a 140-mile flight and they do it in

just over the hour. So it must be averaging about 150 miles an hour, allowing for take-off and landing speeds,' Colin told him.

'You can jump at that speed if you've had experience, Colin. But you're not going to get that kind of experience in a parachute club – more like Cessnas at seventy-five knots.'

'We can't expect to have it all our own way,' Colin pointed out. 'As long as it's a reasonable risk we have to take it. You don't make three million quid sitting on your arse!'

'Well, even amateurs would be safe enough up to about 150 knots,' Ray admitted. 'But at higher speeds the risk of an accident increases.'

'How long does it take to learn to use a parachute?' Doc asked. 'I've never even seen one before except on the telly.'

'It's nothing,' Ray turned to him. 'I still do a bit of weekend instructing with a club over Aldershot way. We have people come along in the morning, they do a couple of tandem jumps in the morning and by the middle of the afternoon they are making their first static-line jump. Nothing to it. Some of them make two or three jumps on their first day.'

'It's as easy as that?'

'You'd skate it, Doc! You too, Bert,' Ray confirmed with a positive nod.

'Okay,' Bert turned to Colin. 'We'll agree that learning to parachute is easy enough, but there's a lot more to this job than just jumping with a parachute.' He stubbed out his cigarette and immediately lit another, a sure sign that he was thinking hard. 'We'd have to force the pilot to fly us to the spot where we want to dump the gold and that means he'd be able to pinpoint the area for the coppers. They'd be onto us in minutes.'

'No danger!' Colin argued. 'I've told you about the police out there, and they're not trained for anything like this. We'd be moving off within ten minutes of hitting the ground and be miles away before they could even begin to react. A jump ahead of them, so to speak.'

'When you say, "dump the gold",' Ray looked at Bert. 'D'you mean just sort of . . . toss it out the door?'

'Well, yes. I thought that was the idea. Get it into a couple of sacks, chuck it out and follow it down in parachutes.'

Ray shook his head. 'Couldn't be done,' he said. 'At a terminal velocity of over 120 miles an hour it would splatter all over the place. In the meantime you'd be floating about in the sky in your parachutes and landing miles away from the gold. You'd be lucky to ever see it again, and it would take hours to gather in even if you did find it. Believe me, Colin, just chucking it down is a no-no.'

'Well, we're here to discuss problems and ideas, aren't we?' Colin appealed. 'That's what this meeting is all about.' He turned to Ray. 'You're the expert. How would you handle the drop?'

'No options.' Ray's voice was confident. 'The gold would have to go down in 'chutes the same as us. That way it stays together on impact and we land right beside it. Which means we can clear the DZ – sorry, that's the drop zone – more quickly.'

'Good. Good.' Colin was nodding. 'That makes a lot of sense.'

'I'm still not happy about the time element,' Bert said doubtfully. 'I don't know much about Ghana, but I'm willing to bet that there's not a lot of roads out there. Once the pilot gets the word out it wouldn't take long to set up roadblocks, even if the police are crap. I'd feel a lot happier if we could keep the pilot from knowing where we jumped.'

Colin wagged a finger at him. 'I've got ideas about that.'

'So?' Three pairs of eyes focused on him.

'We supply our own pilot.'

'Fuck me!' Bert threw his arms in the air. 'Be

reasonable, Colin. First we have to learn to parachute. Now you want us to learn how to fly a fucking aeroplane!'

'*You* don't have to learn to fly anything,' Colin told him. 'Nor Doc. You two will be busy doing your stuff with the parachute jumping.' He sat back, pleased with himself. 'But Ray here, he's already an expert in the parachute department. He's the one that can learn to fly.' Colin clapped his hands together, almost in applause for himself. 'Fuck me,' he said, 'he's even got a bit of experience.'

Three pairs of eyes settled on Ray.

'What do you think about flying a plane?' Colin asked.

Ray took on a quizzical expression as he leant his head to one side. 'Learn to fly, you mean?'

'That's right,' Colin nodded.

'Well,' Ray rubbed his chin. 'I've seen enough of flying to know there's no big mystery about it; some of the private pilots I've met were as thick as two short planks. So yeah, I'm pretty sure I could learn to fly all right.'

'Good!' Colin turned to Bert and Doc. 'So that's it.' He was triumphant. 'You two get on with the parachute jumping and Ray joins a flying club.'

'I'm happy enough with that,' Ray agreed. 'But I'm not going to learn to fly a DC-3 at any old flying club. More like Cessnas and Pipers – small single-engine jobs.'

'You don't have to learn to *fly* a DC-3,' Colin told him. 'You only need to be able to hold a course and alter the speed. Most of the hard work in flying is done during take-off and landing and you wouldn't be doing any of that.'

Ray was smiling. 'Yeah,' his head nodded approval. 'I like it!' He leant forward enthusiastically. 'From what I've seen, I don't think I would have a problem holding a plane on course.'

'And since we'd have our own man at the controls, the pilot could be tied up in the passenger cabin. He'd have no idea where we dropped the stuff,' Colin pointed out.

Bert deflated the rising enthusiasm. 'And the minute he gets back into the cabin he just has to find a landmark and radio in our location.'

'Aye,' Colin tapped fingers against his glass. 'That's one of the problems we've got to get sorted out.'

'We could destroy his radio,' Ray suggested. 'Then he couldn't report anything until he landed at an airport.'

'And the nearest airport would be about fifty miles away,' Colin muttered.

'That would be about fifteen to twenty minutes' flying time,' Ray made the calculation for him.

'Not long enough!' Bert objected. 'Nowhere near long enough! Even if the cops are a bunch of geriatrics, they could have us surrounded within an hour. Remember,' he jabbed a warning finger in the air. 'We'd be heading in their direction.'

'As I see it,' the reasonable tones of Ray's voice cooled things, 'the longer we can control the plane, the more time we gain on the ground.' His observation was met by nods from the others. 'So we have to come up with an idea to keep the pilot out of the cabin after we jump.'

'But what about the plane?' Bert demanded. 'It can't fly itself, and there's no way I'm leaving it to crash. That's definitely not on!' He waved a hand in absolute dismissal.

'But the plane *can* fly itself,' Ray stated emphatically. 'Automatic pilot! I've seen some of the pilots setting them when I've been doing my dispatcher. I can make a point of finding out how they are operated. Even get on board a DC3 and see the real thing. If I can learn to set the automatic pilot . . .'

'Now you're talking!' Bert's voice sounded out encouragingly. 'That's the way we've got to think, otherwise the whole thing is just not on.'

'And what Ray says is the answer,' Colin came back at him. 'If we can keep the pilot out of the cabin for a specific length of time after the jump, we'll have all the time we need.'

'Get that and I'm happy,' Bert nodded. 'How do you feel about it, Doc?'

'I like it,' he replied. 'We get that extra time you're on about and it'll be a doddle.' He turned to Ray with a grin. 'You're a real bag of tricks, mate.'

'Initiative, they call it, Doc. Initiative.' Ray grinned back at him, pleased at his easy acceptance into the group.

'Okay then,' Colin addressed Bert and Doc. 'Ray here can put you in touch with a parachute club – the sooner the better. Get in as much practice as you can before the big event.'

'Yeah,' Ray agreed. 'Most of these clubs are weekend affairs and it can be difficult to accumulate jumps, but there's a full-time parachute school up Nottingham way at a place called Langer. They do top-class professional training seven days a week so you should be able get in plenty of jumps.' He turned to Colin. 'What about you, you signing up too?'

'Not me!' Colin laughed. 'You won't catch me leaping out of aeroplanes. No, seriously,' he sobered up. 'I'll be the man on the ground. I'll be spending the next few weeks setting things up at my end. But there's still a lot of details to be sorted out before I go back. And you'll have to make a list of what we'll need by way of equipment.'

'How long before you have to head back?' Ray asked.

'There's a ship picking me up at Lagos this coming Friday, so I've got four full days left here.'

'Let me think about it. I'll need to sort out the best type of 'chutes for us, and then there's the other odds and ends we'll need. I'll be able to give you a full list by tomorrow. Wednesday at the latest.'

'That'll be fine. Just as long as I know what you'll be sending to me.'

Ray made a vague gesture with his hand. 'About the flying lessons, Colin. I don't have the money for that myself.' He seemed slightly embarrassed at the admission.

Colin's hand went up. 'Sorry, Ray. We should have settled that earlier.' He turned to the other two. 'The flying lessons come out of the kitty.' He took their agreement for granted. 'And Ray can draw living expenses when he's off work.' He turned back to him. 'You can keep on with Eddie part-time if you like – that should throw you a few extra quid, okay?'

'Yeah, that will suit me fine, Colin. And guys,' he looked at each of them in turn. 'You can rely on me. I won't let you down.' His chin jutted defiantly, still a

207

little embarrassed at the open-handed treatment, but daring them to laugh at him for his little speech of affirmation.

★

On Wednesday they were once again settled in Bert's living room, listening as Ray referred to a notepad, reading out his requisitions.

'Okay, we'll need two twenty-four-foot emergency 'chutes to drop the gold. They're designed to take about 250 pounds weight, but that's for landing a body safely. They can handle a lot more if the load is equipment or,' Ray tilted his lean face to grin at them, 'gold bars. Then we'll need two twenty-six-foot 'chutes for Bert and Doc. The low-porosity double 'L' type are best. That's the basic model you'll be using when you join a club and you should be familiar with them by then. The other 'chute,' he looked up, 'the one I'll be using, is a more advanced Ram-Air type.'

'We don't want any scrimping on the gear,' Colin warned. 'Everything depends on us having good equipment.'

'This stuff is ideal for the job,' Ray insisted. 'The emergency 'chutes will take up less room than the standard type and are still more than adequate for the gold. On top of that, they'll fit into small duffle bags and we can pack our personal 'chutes into decent-sized hand-baggage.'

'What about crash helmets?' Colin asked. 'They're pretty massive, surely?'

'Yeah, they gave me a problem at first,' Ray agreed. 'But we can use the old-fashioned crash helmets track cyclists used to wear; they're made of leather and fold into nothing.'

'I told you you'd earn your money,' Colin grinned at him. 'What other ideas have you come up with?'

'Well, there's the problem of opening the emergency 'chutes. Static lines are the usual thing but they're too bulky for us. I decided on using KAP automatic openers – they're operated by a mechanical timer that throws out the canopy. Czech made – good stuff!' Ray appeared to have thought of everything. It was an impressive, confidence-building display of knowledge.

'So all you've got to do now is buy the gear and air-freight it out to the address I've left with you and we're in business,' Colin said when Ray had completed his report.

'I must admit,' Bert said, 'it's starting to look good.' He turned his pugnacious, bulldog look on Ray. 'I only hope this parachuting business is as easy as you're making out.'

'You'll love it Bert; you and Doc both. I bet you

keep it up for fun when this is all over!' Ray grinned back at him.

'We'll see,' Bert muttered.

'Now, what about yourself?' Colin turned to Ray. 'Made any enquires about flying lessons?'

'There's umpteen clubs, Colin. Some of the bigger ones put you through a full PPL – that's a Private Pilot's Licence – in just three weeks! I'll have no problems.'

'Well, you know what's wanted. Just stick in and learn all you can. We need all the aces we can get for this job. And remember,' he stressed, 'you've only got about five weeks to prepare.'

*

On Friday morning they met once again for a final discussion before Colin left for the airport. He addressed them as they settled into chairs.

'Everything's going smoothly and you're all booked for the fight trip.' He turned to Ray. 'It was a good idea of yours to make your own travel arrangements. Now there's nothing to tie the three of you together – good thinking.' He smiled, already appreciating Ray's contribution to the firm. 'Ray has the business of buying the gear well in hand and by the time you arrive in Ghana I'll have everything set up. All you've got to do is get there as unobtrusively as possible. Mix with the crowd, but don't let yourselves get too pally with anyone in case they miss you later on. As long as you don't get involved with a group you should be able to slip away without anyone noticing. And remember, from the moment you arrive in Accra you'll be run off your feet. You won't have a minute to spare until it's all over and you're sitting at the fight.'

Three heads nodded sober agreement.

'Your return flight leaves Accra the morning after the fight and they'll probably be giving everyone a good spin. But you'll be carrying nothing suspicious, no different from any of the other passengers. You should be safe as houses going through the airport.'

'Should be!' Bert gave a loud snort. 'Fucking well *better be*! I don't fancy supping porridge out there.'

'Don't worry about that,' Colin assured him. 'You wouldn't do too long in the nick anyway.'

'Is that right?' Bert looked into Colin's innocently smiling face. 'Don't they lob out the heavy porridge over there?'

'Nah,' Colin scoffed, straight-faced. 'You'd only do a few months.'

'What!' Bert stared incredulously at him. 'A few months?'

'Aye,' Colin smiled wickedly. 'Then they'd take you out and shoot you!'

20

'So it's all settled,' Colin addressed his three friends against the background noise of the cafeteria in Gatwick Airport. He turned to Bert. 'You and Doc are fixed up with the parachute club and Ray . . .' he turned his head, 'will be starting his flying lessons next week. That's right isn't it?'

'Southend Airport,' Ray confirmed. 'A Civil Aviation Authority-approved course. And they do a twin-engine rating there too.'

'You'll need to try and get into the cockpit of a DC-3. It's important that you're at least familiar with the layout and controls.'

The public address system announced the final call for Flight BA 220 for Rome, Accra and Lagos.

'That's me this time,' he told them. 'We'll need to wind up now.' He reached under the table for his hand-baggage, propping it on his knees. 'From now on it's all up to us. As long as we all stick in and do our bit, we'll pull this off all right.' He rose to his feet as the final call was repeated. 'I'll see you all in four weeks' time,' he smiled confidently. 'Right now I've got a plane to catch.'

'We won't hang about,' Bert acted as spokesman. 'If we hit the road now we can be back in town before lunch.' He pushed his hand out, giving Colin the villain's farewell: 'Be lucky, mate.' Doc and Ray followed suit, both giving him a firm, confident grip.

*

Colin looked at the plastic tags for his seat number as he moved along the 707's aisle. Row 28, Seat F was almost at the rear of the plane. He smiled at the sight of an old DC-3 parked over to his left as he bent into his window seat, unconsciously nodding, accepting its tacit challenge. A bustle of movement at his side drew his attention and a black passenger lowered himself into one of the empty seats beside him.

'You don't remember me then?' The well-dressed man looked at him and smiled.

Colin was surprised to be addressed in such a familiar manner. 'Sorry. Should I?'

The man smiled at Colin, mildly amused. Then he pushed out a slim black hand. 'Yarty. Yarty Okufu.'

'Christ!' Colin offered his hand. 'I should have recognised you. But the clothes . . .' he waved at Yarty's impeccable style. 'That's what put me off.'

213

'No, no,' Yarty shook his hand and grinned at him. 'Be honest . . .' He hesitated, trying to recall Colin's name. 'Grant! Colin Grant! That's it. Now be honest,' he repeated. 'We black men all look alike to you, don't we?'

Colin smiled back, a little embarrassed by his comment.

'I thought you were in a hurry to get to Ghana?' Yarty looked curiously at him. 'All that rushing about for a visa?'

'I was in a hurry. I flew out to Ghana the very next day.'

'Yet here you are now?' Yarty's eyes turned quizzical.

'I had to fly home unexpectedly. Family problems,' Colin improvised. 'But they're sorted out now. So . . .'

'So now you are going back,' Yarty finished for him. 'I am pleased that you find my country so attractive.'

'I like it,' Colin assured him. 'I like it very much.'

The sober-suited man sitting beside him appeared to be a very different person from the casually dressed Yarty that Colin remembered from the Embassy. An expensive Patek Philippe watch adorned his left wrist and the huge diamond that flashed from a chunky pinky ring was hard to miss.

214

There was obviously a lot more to Yarty Okufu that he had originally thought. Yarty looked like a man of some substance and his speech seemed to have lost many of its easy-going mannerisms.

'Are you going home then?' Colin ventured a question.

For a moment Yarty's face took on a happy expression, then a shadow clouded his eyes.

'Yes. I go home.' His speech slipped into the Africanese Colin had become used to. 'I have to go home.'

'Why *'have to'*?' Colin sensed a hint of reluctance behind the words.

'It is my father's wish.' Dark eyes turned on him, staring for a moment. 'No! I do not speak true.' He spat out the admission. 'It is not my father's wish. My father desires that I stay in England to complete my studies.' His voice turned cold. 'But it is impossible.'

'How's that?' Colin could feel frustration emanating from Yarty and noticed his hand move to caress a gold medallion that hung incongruously against an immaculate collar and tie.

'It is the fault of the government.' Yarty's voice was uncompromising. 'Their policies have brought my country to the very brink of ruin. Corrupt ministers and officials have undermined the economy. Illegal

215

trading is rife, forced upon the people by iniquitous price controls. The Ashanti people have become apathetic in the face of widespread corruption and the workers find their living standards, once the highest in black Africa, diminished; their wages purchase less and less each month.'

'That's the way it is everywhere,' Colin commiserated. 'It's called inflation.'

'Their policies have reduced my people to little more than serfs!' Yarty exclaimed. 'First the white man enslaved them, raping the very earth for gold, diamonds, timber and minerals in the process. But at least they put something back into the country. They built schools, hospitals, factories and roads. They provided services. Indeed, we prospered under colonial rule and became the first African country to achieve independence. Since then we have had a series of governments, both military and civil, each one more corrupt than the last.'

Colin felt a little uncomfortable in the heat of the man's bitterness and tried to lower the temperature. 'The people I met out there seemed pretty happy.'

'Pretty happy!' Yarty's eyes blazed at him. 'A proud race, Warrior Ashanti, reduced to smuggling cocoa beans across the border so they can afford to feed their families? Their tribal lands stripped of natural wealth; labouring in the bauxite mines; grubbing in the goldmines. Ashanti men, once the proudest, fiercest fighting men in the whole of Africa, having to stand aside as their ancient tribal lands are looted by their very own government. Pretty happy!'

'I'm sorry.' Yarty relaxed, leaning his head back against his seat. 'I did not mean to get angry, not with you anyway. You do not see what is going on away from the main townships. But it is because of those things that I must return to my people.' His voice had returned to normal, the virulence fading to a bitter resentfulness.

'At least you seem to have done all right.' Colin's eyes took in Yarty's clothes and looked pointedly at the display of jewellery.

Yarty caught the look.

'You are surprised I have such things?'

'Well, after that little speech? Forced to leave university . . . reduced to peasants and all that. Yes, I am a little surprised. And look at the tom you're wearing!' Colin flapped a hand at the expensive jewellery and looked pointedly at the medallion and its heavy gold chain. 'You've got enough gold on you to sink a ship!'

Yarty's hand rose to fondle the gleaming talisman. 'My people would not like to see me going about in rags.'

'Your people?'

217

'Yes.' Yarty turned to stare, almost arrogantly, at him. *'My people'*, he emphasised. 'I am the eldest son of the Asantehene of Kumasi – Keeper of the Golden Stool, Chief of all Ashanti tribes and lands. I must inspire confidence in my people. Make them proud of me and proud of my father whom I represent.' He fingered the medallion on his chest. 'One day I will lead my people to a greater freedom. I want to give my people back their pride. I want to help them build a nation free from dependence on outsiders. I want them to take a just pride in modern skills; to become engineers, doctors, skilled workers, learn to operate modern production machinery, to be farmers wise in the new technologies and, most of all, teachers in all of these things to educate our future generations. True independence is what I seek for my people. Proud independence.' His hand caressed the medallion as he spoke.

'The medal means something?' Colin guessed out loud.

Yarty folded the gleaming gold disc in his hand. 'This medal means everything to my people. It is said that the soul of Osei Tutu, the Great Spirit of all Ashantis, dwells within it.' His fingers moved to the reddish, almost copper-hued links of the chain. 'Along with its chain, the medal of Osei Tutu is the history of the Ashanti nation. It is handed down, always to the Asantehene's eldest son.' He twisted a link in his fingers, letting the light play on a tracery of finely etched lines on its surface. 'This link tells of our defeat of the Dagomba tribe and the annual tribute demanded thenceforth by the victorious Ashanti Nation. This one,' his voice hardened, 'tells of the great slave raids that decimated our nation. And this one . . .' He looked into Colin's eyes, 'tells how 20,000 Ashanti warriors led by King Prempeh, legendary war hero of the Ashanti Nation, defeated the British army led by Sir Charles McCarthy and took his head at the battle of McCarthy Hill. Whenever something of great importance happens, it is recorded on this chain. Two links are forged in pure Ashanti gold so that the deed is never forgotten.'

'Why two links?' Colin asked. 'Is there another chain . . . a sort of duplicate?'

'No, no,' Yarty laughed. 'One link is for the chain, the other for the tribe, or warrior whose deed is recorded. It remains a token for life. They are greatly cherished and pass from father to son, from chief to chief.'

'So only a chief can get a link?'

'Any warrior whose deeds warrant a link in our history becomes a chief. Men of great deeds make great chiefs.'

The 'No Smoking' and 'Fasten Seat Belts' signs winked on above their heads and they checked their seat belts as the huge airliner rolled into motion. A few minutes later flight BA 220 was thundering down the runway to thrust itself steeply into a clear blue sky, outbound for Rome, Accra and Lagos.

'You are staying at the cocoa mill?' Yarty asked after the stewardess had served them with coffee.

'Yes. With my uncle.'

'Will you be travelling on to Takoradi this evening?' Yarty raised eyebrows at him. 'If not, Accra has some excellent night clubs.'

'Actually, Yarty, I never thought to mention it, but I'm going on to Lagos.'

'Lagos?' Yarty looked at him in mild surprise.

'Business for my uncle. He asked me to collect some important documents from the company's agent there. Apparently they don't think the postal service is reliable enough.'

Yarty nodded. 'Yes ... I can understand that. Everything has deteriorated, even the postal service. Pity though. I'm sure I could have shown you a thing or two of our night life in Accra.'

'I'll bet!' Colin grinned at him. 'Mind you, Takoradi has its places too.'

'And its girls?' Yarty gave him a sly look.

'No bother,' Colin winked, deliberately neglecting

to mention Lesley's colour. 'Got a beautiful little chick stashed away. Really nice.'

'All the comforts of home,' Yarty smiled knowingly. 'Still . . . I'm sure a night out in Accra would open your eyes.'

'Some other time,' Colin promised. 'You could always look me up, or give me a ring sometime. If you're still in Ghana, that is.'

'Yes. We'll leave it like that, Colin. I have some official functions to attend to in Takoradi fairly soon. If time permits I will look you up.'

They settled back in their seats, allowing the muted thunder of four powerful Rolls-Royce engines to lull them to sleep as the plane sped towards Africa.

Later, after disembarking some passengers at Accra, flight BA 220 terminated at Murtala Mohammed Airport, Lagos. Less than forty-eight hours after that, Colin walked down the gangplank at Takoradi harbour to be met by a smiling Lesley, the 'cruise' over, his plans for the Ashanti gold well and truly underway.

21

'Aye, m'lad,' George spoke to Colin as they strode down the short steep hill to the factory. 'Keep working like this and we'll need to be thinking about making it official.'

'No, no,' Colin waved his hand. 'I like wandering about the factory and going down to the harbour with the cargo. But as long as it's unofficial I can take all the time off I want. I'm happy with things just the way they are.'

'You'll soon know as much about the factory as I do,' George laughed, 'the way you keep poking around.'

'Aye,' Colin replied. 'And today I think I'll poke around in here,' he turned off into the packing section. 'I noticed some of the packages were a bit loose the other day.'

'You better be careful or you'll be needing a union card,' George called over his shoulder as he walked on. 'See you at tea break then.'

In the packing section Colin made his way to the

weighing room where liquid cocoa butter was poured into stout, polythene-lined cardboard boxes. The workers greeted him with smiles, grinning good-naturedly as he practised pouring the butter himself until he had mastered the technique of cutting the flow at the precise weight. The African in charge gave him a look that said 'Well done' and took over again, showing off a little with the speed of his work. Eventually Colin made his way into a room behind a heavy canvas screen where two shivering workers were stacking the sealed cartons on to a trolley before wheeling them into a huge walk-in refrigerator. In less than an hour the cocoa butter would freeze as hard as candle-wax and be removed from the refrigerator to be sewn into hessian sacks – two cartons per sack – and stored in a massive cold-room to await transport to the docks, prior to shipment abroad.

Colin spent most of his morning studying the packaging process from start to finish. George was right – he would soon know as much about the business as him.

22

Three weeks had passed since his return from London and Colin had taken on the daily chore of collecting the mail from the town's post office, hopefully checking the dozen or so envelopes each day for the letter he was looking for. At last he recognised the British Airways logo on an envelope and impatiently extracted its contents. Inside he found notification that the airline's Accra freight services office had forwarded a crate to Takoradi for the Ghana Cocoa Company – to be collected by a Mr Colin Grant.

Anxious in case some zealous clerk at the airport telephoned the office, he drove straight to the cargo terminal. He had no difficulty, merely producing the letter to a clerk, who in return required him to sign a receipt for one wooden crate – Contents: Sports Equipment. Ten minutes later he was manhandling the crate into the garden shed behind his uncle's bungalow, where he cut away the plastic ties and worried at its top with a heavy screwdriver. In a few moments he was inspecting three small suitcases and two tartan duffle bags crammed, sardine-like, inside the crate. He slipped the rope loose from one of the duffle bags to expose a web of canvas straps wrapped tightly round an olive-green bundle. Smiling in satisfaction, he turned to a wall calendar and checked the date – April 22nd. Less than three weeks to the big event. Time was closing fast and he still had to complete his preparations at the drop zone.

*

For the next two weeks he drove out to the abandoned village every day, quite literally preparing the ground as he laid the foundations of his plan. Every afternoon he laboured at digging two long, back-breaking trenches in the awkward, gravelly soil and it took him two full days and over five gallons of paint – most of which went on the ground – to daub the gable end of the ruined building so that it stood out, sparkling white against the barren landscape. The finished job was a rough arrowhead, the trenches long barbs extending from the gleaming white gable pointing south towards the coast.

After a final tour of inspection he stood for a full minute, staring north at the line of hills rising out of the plain, his mind's eye seeing the aircraft make its approach. *Yes.* He nodded to himself. *Yes!* It was going to happen. He would make it happen. *They would steal the Ashanti gold.*

★

A week before the fight he flew the gold route one more time, tense with excitement as the old Dakota rolled to a standstill outside the small terminal building at Kumasi. This was his last chance to see the gold before it fell into his hands at Uturri and he was anxious to confirm the procedure remained unchanged. There was an audible click as the intercom switched on.

'This is the captain speaking,' the pilot's voice was smoothly professional. 'Will passengers for Kumasi please leave the aircraft and make their way to the terminal building. I hope you had a pleasant flight and thank you for flying Ghana Airways.'

The announcement was slightly different, but Colin felt no cause for concern and confidently waited to be told to leave the plane. He watched the Kumasi contingent of passengers disembark and disappear inside the building. Still the intercom remained silent. A feeling of unease crept over Colin and he anxiously eyed the speaker, urging it to break into sound. The stupid pilot must have forgotten to pass on disembarking instruction. He wanted to stand up and leave, as if by doing so he would influence things, but he remained seated, groaning silently to himself, squeezing his eyes tight as he willed the pilot to speak. He turned to look at the stewardess, hoping she would smile and usher everyone towards the door. Instead, he saw her switch on a professional smile of welcome as the first of the boarding passengers appeared at the top of the steps and entered the plane.

The gold! he wanted to scream. *You've forgotten the fucking gold!*

'Excuse me.' He heard a voice and looked up to see a businessman standing in the aisle, preparing to move into the empty seat beside him.

'Uh ... ? Oh yes ... The seat's vacant.' He gathered his scrambled thoughts as the passenger took his seat. *The gold? Where's the fucking gold?* Sick with disappointment, he sagged back in his seat staring at the space the gold should be occupying. Then the door of the plane thudded tight, the sound killing off any faint hope that the gold might still appear. The man beside him took a newspaper from his briefcase, crackled it open and fussily folded it at the shares price index. Colin recognised the *Financial Times* and the man who had first told him about the gold.

He spoke as casually as he could. 'No gold this trip, eh?'

'I beg your pardon?'

'You told me a few weeks ago, remember? I thought it was ammunition and you told me it was gold. You said they always carried it on this plane.'

The businessman tilted his head back to look at Colin, giving a slight nod to acknowledge recognition.

'And so they did, up until three weeks ago.' He answered with some asperity, as though he resented any implication that he might have been in error. 'But the military authorities have stationed a helicopter unit here now and they have taken over the responsibility.' He leant forward and looked past Colin to peer through the small window. 'There,' he said, stabbing with a vindicating finger.

Colin turned his head and followed the direction of the pointing digit. Up until this moment he had nurtured a faint hope that this week was an accident; a one-off occurrence and things would return to normal next time. But there was no mistaking the scene that greeted his gaze across the airfield apron. Eyes widened in shocked disbelief, he saw a protective ring of soldiers guarding the armoured van as its cargo of gold bullion was loaded into the aggressive, shark-shaped silhouette of a heavily armed Lynx attack helicopter.

23

The week dragged by for Colin. Plans ruined, he found himself sinking into a morass of despondency. His comfortable vision of a crime-free future, with Lesley by his side, ripped apart by some faceless military bureaucrats. *Bastards!* He cursed them again, resentment festering deep inside him, as if he had been deprived of something already rightfully his. And the firm was due to arrive today – what would they have to say?

'Come on,' he heard George's voice through a thick fog of thought. 'Your breakfast is getting cold.'

With a guilty start he became aware again, shrugging off his uncle's look with a muttered complaint of a bad night's sleep.

'You've been having too many late nights, m'lad,' George cautioned. 'You've been running yourself ragged these last few weeks.'

'I'm okay,' Colin forced a smile. 'Been travelling about a lot, that's all. I suppose it's more tiring than you realise out here . . . with the heat and humidity.'

'And you've not been playing any golf,' George accused. 'A relaxing round in the afternoon would do you the world of good.'

'Aye,' Colin agreed. 'As a matter of fact, I'm going off down the club this morning before it gets too hot. I'll just laze about down there today and spend some time with Lesley.'

'That's the stuff! A day by the pool will work wonders for you.'

As soon as George had left for the office, Colin took the suitcases from the shed, loaded them into the car and headed for town. Once there, he parked in a quiet side street and walked round to a garage to pick up a Ford Escort he had hired. He had decided to run through the day according to his original plan, if only to prove to the firm that he had carried out his part efficiently. There was also the possibility that they might manage to recoup some of the money spent on the parachutes in Accra, or else carry them back to London as baggage. It was a case now of salvaging what he could.

*

The flight information board at Accra International Airport told him the charter plane was on schedule and due to arrive in just over an hour. With time to kill, Colin drifted up to the observation deck on the roof of the single-storey terminal building. A Nigeria Airways Boeing 737 from Lagos had just landed and was taxi-ing towards its parking stand. Admiring the sleek jet liner, he watched the ramp lower from its door and looked on as the passengers slowly disembarked, giving a start of surprise when he saw Ray emerge into the bright sunlight. He recalled Ray saying he would make his own travel arrangements, but had imagined he would use the same agency as Bert and Doc, merely purchasing the ticket separately to achieve the appearance of non-association they sought. Quickly, he made his way downstairs to the arrivals hall.

*

'Thought it safer to travel by a different route altogether,' Ray explained as they sat over coffee in the arrivals lounge. 'I booked tickets via Lagos and I'll be travelling home by the same route a couple of days after the fight. That way we're well separated. It could be important after we've finished our business.'

'There isn't going to be any business.' Colin's statement was blunt. He had expected to have the three of them together when he broke his news about the job, but Ray's unexpected arrival had upset his plans, and he could see no reason for subtlety.

Ray straightened in his chair, grey eyes fixed

enquiringly on Colin's face. 'Say again?' he slipped easily into military jargon.

'There isn't going to be any business,' Colin repeated tersely. 'The job's a bummer.'

Tensing muscles squared Ray's chin. 'What happened?' he asked, disappointment clear in his voice. 'Someone rumble what you were up to?'

'Nothing like that,' Colin spoke sharply, annoyed that Ray could have jumped to such a conclusion. 'The fucking army brought in a helicopter, that's what.' He went on to explain the new set-up at Kumasi.

'You're certain of this?'

'I did a dry run last week as a final check and saw the helicopter myself. Even saw them loading the gold.' He shrugged. 'It's a bummer all right.' A long sigh escaped him. 'A real earner. Enough to set us all up for life. Jesus!' He thumped the table in disgust.

Ray's eyes turned flint as he thought. Elbows on the table, he put his thumbs under his chin and rubbed both index fingers up and down the sides of his nose. Colin watched him, wondering what was going on in his mind.

'How long has the helicopter been doing the run?' Ray finally asked.

'Three weeks now, according to the guy I spoke to.'

'No problems since it began?'

Colin looked at him curiously. 'No problems? I wouldn't know. What d'you mean exactly?'

'Just that. We used helicopters a lot in the SAS and they were right temperamental bastards, always acting up on us, especially in these climates. Even the fuel is unbelievable in places like this.'

'What are you saying?'

'Well . . .' Ray spread his hands. 'There's always the chance the chopper could be out of commission. It might even be assigned to some other duty.'

'Instead of carrying the gold, you mean?' Colin looked at him doubtfully. 'Why would they do that?'

'I'm an army man, Colin. I know they haven't stationed a valuable helicopter in Kumasi simply to operate a milk run to Accra once a week. The gold will be very much a secondary operation. If the chopper is unserviceable or otherwise engaged, the chances are they'll put the gold back on the DC-3.'

'You're clutching at straws.'

'Bit stronger than a straw,' Ray disagreed. 'You've already told me that you watched them load the gold into the helicopter last week, right?'

'Aye . . . When I made my last dry run.'

'And that didn't tell you anything?'

Colin began to get red in the face. 'What is this Ray, a fucking quiz show? Make your point.'

'It means that the gold runs to a schedule. Probably some deal with the Treasury. That gold's been getting delivered every Wednesday for years and it's become routine. If the helicopter's out of commission, the gold will go straight aboard the original plane. If I was still in the army I'd stake my tapes on it.'

'Out of commission on the one and only Wednesday we want to hijack it? C'mon, Ray. Straw! You're not even clutching air!'

'Maybe,' Ray's voice became firm. 'But no position's hopeless until it's been overrun. Even if there's only an odds-on chance of the gold being on that DC-3, we'd be stupid not to consider it. After all, everything is prepared on our side.'

'You want to go ahead with the plan?'

'Well . . . we're all set up, aren't we? And if the gold isn't on the plane we wouldn't be any worse off than we are right now, would we?'

Colin looked at him thoughtfully. 'It is all laid on,' he finally said. 'And I've got all the gear outside in my car.'

'So we go ahead and chance it!'

Colin looked at his wristwatch. 'Bert and Doc are due to land in half an hour. I'll put it to them and hear what they have to say about it.'

'No!' Ray emphatically shook his head. 'They're

234

edgy enough about this job as it is. Telling them about the helicopter could turn them off completely.'

'But they'll have to be told about the new set-up.'

'No they won't! They don't have to be told anything.' Ray's voice was firm as he took control of the conversation. 'As far as they know the job is still on. Let them keep thinking that. If the gold isn't on the plane they'll moan about their bad luck for ten minutes then sit back and enjoy the flight. Telling them achieves nothing. In fact, you could put them off completely.'

'But they should be told,' Colin's voice was uncertain. 'We've always been straight with one another about any job.'

'If the helicopter could give us problems I'd be the first to agree,' Ray said earnestly, forestalling Colin's arguments. 'But don't you see . . . If the gold isn't on the plane, the job's simply cancelled. It's not as if you're putting them at any risk by not telling them.'

Colin drummed his fingers against the hard surface of the table. He hadn't thought things out the way Ray had, but he realised that the strain of not knowing whether or not the job was on until literally the last minute could break the nerve of the staunchest man. Ray, with his military training, could cope with the uncertainty. *But Bert and Doc . . . ?* He gave the table a last decisive rap. *Ray was right.* If there was one chance in a hundred of the Dakota carrying the gold, he had to take it. 'Right,' he said. 'We'll play it your way.'

'Good man,' Ray's eyes lightened, as if a weight had been lifted from his mind. 'We'll give it our best shot. And remember,' he grinned wolfishly, his eyes sparkling with enthusiasm: 'Who dares wins.'

Twenty minutes later they watched the chartered 707 land and they waited until they spotted Bert and Doc leaving the plane. Satisfied that they had arrived safely, Colin led Ray to his car and headed towards Accra city centre.

It was almost an hour before the first coaches cleared the airport and bore the fight fans off to their hotels. Knowing in advance that Bert and Doc were booked into the four-star Ambassador, Colin waited in the hotel's car park where they had arranged to meet. Ray had already taken a taxi to his hotel in another part of the city and would make his way back as soon as he had checked in. Colin looked anxiously at his watch. It was well after midday and they had a lot of ground to cover.

Once again Ray was the first to arrive, his smaller hotel having sorted out its rooming arrangements more quickly than the larger and more sedately run Ambassador. Wearing faded military-style trousers, with cotton shirt open at the neck exposing his tanned chest, and his bronzed face healthy under an army-length haircut, he looked well, the very picture of fitness. His step had an athletic spring to it, pleasing Colin as he watched him approach.

'Checked in okay?' he asked as Ray settled into the seat beside him.

'No problem.' He got a thumbs-up from the smiling Ray.

'It went right out my head earlier,' Colin said, 'but supposing we do strike lucky tomorrow ... Have you done the flying bit all right?'

'I've got in thirty-four hours. It's no sweat.'

'Thirty-four hours! Is that all?'

'Plenty for what we'll need,' Ray told him confidently. 'I know it doesn't sound much, but it's surprising how long it takes to accumulate flying time, especially when you're just learning. It's not like driving around in a car. Once you reach the solo stage it becomes easier, but the first twelve – fifteen hours takes about two weeks to get in. Once you've got hold of the basics you can work a bit faster.'

'You can fly solo then?'

'No bother! Went solo in ten hours – two better than anyone else on the course.'

'Reckon you can handle this DC-3 plane all right?'

237

'Definitely!' Ray was emphatic. 'One of the reasons I've only got the thirty-four hours in is that I decided to spend a fair bit of money putting time in on a twin-engine job – a Piper Aztec. It's small, but I reckoned it would give me useful experience with the twin throttles and dual instrumentation. I got quite good at it,' he added, with a self-satisfied smile.

'Is it anything like a DC-3?'

'It's nothing like a DC-3 as regards size,' Ray admitted. 'But the basic flying instruments are almost identical, and that's what I was after . . . getting used to twin-engine controls and instruments.'

'And you can definitely handle this plane tomorrow if things work out for us?'

Ray's voice was suddenly dead serious. 'Let's not kid ourselves that I'm suddenly a hot-shot pilot, but I've worked hard and paid attention. On top of that I've managed to log in about four hours on an actual DC-3. I found out that a small airline flew one-man-operated cargo flights from Southend to Ostend in Belgium. One of the pilots happened to be a part-time flying instructor with the club. I offered him instructor's rates to let me sit with him for experience. He was glad of the money and took me on three round-trips doing his instructor bit. I learned a lot from him, including how to operate the autopilot.'

'Jesus Christ, that's terrific!' Colin said, before smothering his enthusiasm with a frown. 'Everything's working out for us except for that fucking helicopter.'

'Yeah, well . . .' Ray looked thoughtful. 'I still reckon we're in with a good shout. And if they do use the plane and we get control of it, I'll manage. As long as the weather is clear, I have a horizon and I can see the ground, I'll be able to hold or alter course, maintain height or lose height. I could even manage gentle turns. But if visibility is bad, or there's high winds or turbulence – it won't be on.'

'Jesus,' Colin blew his cheeks out and shook his head. 'We're asking for an awful lot of luck on this job all right.'

'Yeah,' Ray agreed, 'I know that. But at least we're ready, and if everything works out we can go ahead.'

'Aye,' Colin agreed. 'We're ready. And here come Bert and Doc,' he pointed at two men who had just walked into view. 'At least . . .' he hesitated, 'I recognise Doc, but . . .' He eyed the unfamiliar figure accompanying him.

'It's Bert all right,' Ray assured him. 'He's shaved his head completely bald. It puts years on him and makes him look thinner in the face; all part of his smother. He's been practising like a quick change artist for weeks.'

Colin got out of the car and waved, attracting their attention.

'Good to see you.' They exchanged subdued greetings, both Bert and Doc looking more serious than their usual cheery selves.

'Look,' Colin flashed his watch as he ushered them into the car, getting Ray to move into the rear seat so as to make room for Doc in the front. 'We haven't got time to waste, so we'll do our talking on the move, okay?' He turned to Doc. 'And I want you to pay attention to the route we're taking. You'll be driving this motor back after we've done the business tomorrow.' The car rolled into motion as he spoke. 'You two happy with the parachute jumping?' he asked when the car was out of the main road.

'Great!' Doc enthused. 'Really great! I've done over twenty jumps already. It's no bother.'

'Don't hear you saying much,' Colin looked in his rear-view mirror, trying not to smile at Bert's sweating dome.

'I'll manage,' he snuffled, rubbing nervously at his nose. 'I've done the basic course and enough jumps to know the business.'

'You don't sound too keen.'

'I'm not "too keen" as you put it,' Bert growled. 'Leaping out of a perfectly good plane miles up in the sky isn't exactly my idea of having a good time.'

240

'You'll be all right, old mate.' Doc annoyed him by reaching back and patting affectionately at the top of his head, grinning and fending off a clumsy retaliation. 'Eight jumps he's done,' he told Colin. 'He'll be fine.'

'Only because of the gold,' Bert snapped at him. 'You wouldn't get me doing it for fun.'

'But you are happy about it?' Colin pursued him. 'You are confident enough?'

'Yeah, yeah. Nothing to it,' Bert finally admitted, glaring angrily at an unrepentant Doc. 'It's only a matter of pulling the ripcord and the parachute does the rest.'

★

'We're heading for Cape Coast,' Colin explained, as he drove the car along at a fair clip. 'I'll show you the landing site and the place where the motor will be parked. Then Doc can drive us back to Accra so's he gets at least one run over the getaway route.'

It took them just over an hour to reach Cape Coast, the buildings of the university sparkling white in the bright sunlight as they approached. Colin turned off the main road, following a sign that directed him into the university car park. He wasted no time, halting just long enough to explain: 'I'll have this motor sitting here for you tomorrow – keys on top of the offside front wheel. You should make it to Accra in well under an hour if you put the boot down.'

★

At the deserted village he showed them his preparations and explained his signalling plan as they inspected the drop zone. Ray, as the expert, ranged further afield, checking the texture of the earth and looking for dangerous rocks or potholes. Finally he pronounced the terrain: 'A pretty fair DZ.'

'Thing is,' Bert asked. 'Will you be able to find the place?'

'I've spent a lot of time on navigation,' Ray told him. 'It'll be easy enough finding the plain and, with the arrangements Colin has made, I don't see any problem getting us here.'

'That's the reason I painted the end of the building and prepared the fire,' Colin pointed out. 'They'll give you something to aim for.'

'They'll be useful,' Ray agreed. 'But remember, I'll be coming in at about 150 miles an hour and I'll have to be spot-on first time. I won't be making any second runs – that's for sure.'

'You're saying you can deliver us?' Bert demanded, his face puckered up in enquiry.

'Course he can,' Doc spoke confidently. 'He spent enough fucking money learning, didn't he?'

'I'm asking him.' Bert stared at Ray with steady, penetrating eyes.

Ray squared his shoulders and looked at the horizon, staring at the low, haze-shrouded hills before replying. 'I can do it,' he said. 'I'll deliver you all right.'

'So it's settled?' Colin broke in.

'I've seen enough,' Ray agreed. 'All I need now is a good map covering the flight route and this area of the coast.'

'Right then,' Colin hurried them on. 'There's nothing else here and I've still got a lot of travelling to do.' He led them back to the car. 'Bert, you'll be coming back to Takoradi with me tonight.'

'Takoradi?' Bert's voice was sharp with surprise. 'What about the hotel?' The car bumped along the neglected road as they talked.

'You and Doc are sharing a room, right?' Colin didn't wait for a reply. 'So no one will be any the wiser if one of you happens to disappear for the night.'

'I was thinking of disappearing myself,' Doc leered. 'Know what I mean?' He nudged Colin suggestively.

'I've thought it all out,' Colin continued, ignoring

243

Doc's flippancy. 'You stay the night in Takoradi, Bert, and join the plane there. That way one of you will already be on board when it arrives at Kumasi. It also saves the three of you travelling together from Accra and maybe attracting attention.'

'You've certainly got it all worked out,' Bert acknowledged.

'Besides I'll be needing someone to give me a hand tomorrow morning with placing your getaway car at the uni.'

'I'll be looking for overtime rates!' Bert warned.

'Then you can start working now,' Colin said as he bounced the car on to the main road and brought it to a halt. 'You drive to Accra from here. Get in at least one run over the route.'

Doc drove hard but took no real chances as he made the one and only rehearsal of their escape. Forty-five minutes later he entered the industrial outskirts of the capital to merge easily with the heavy evening traffic. 'That's it.' He relaxed his concentration. 'If we get this far we're home and dry.' He nodded at the heavy traffic. 'S'like Oxford Street out there.'

★

The bedroom in the Ambassador Hotel seemed crowded as they gathered round the map Colin had provided. Ray adjusted it to his satisfaction on top of the coffee table and drew a line between Kumasi and Accra. 'There,' he said, making a mark with his pencil. 'I'll follow the normal flight path to here,' he touched the map at a point approximately forty miles south-east of Kumasi. 'Turn on to 235 degrees here,' his pencil moved south of the established flight path. 'And in thirty minutes . . .' the pencil stabbed – 'Uturri! That gives you a full twenty-five minutes to get control of the passengers and prepare for the drop.'

'If we handle everything properly we should be fine,' Bert said in his slow, careful speech. 'As far as I can find out, there's actually never been any trouble with passengers during a hijack.'

'That's a fact,' Ray agreed. 'But you still have to handle it properly, put on the right kind of show and make them believe that you really will shoot.'

Bert's finger tapped hard on the paper map, making it crackle like distant pistol shots. 'Yeah, right. We'll give them a fright all right. But it all starts with you. You've got to get control of the cockpit before we can make a move.'

'Don't you worry about that,' Ray grinned. 'I can be quite scary when I want to.' He turned to Colin. 'What's the story about the cockpit crew?'

'There's just the pilot and co-pilot in the cockpit,'

Colin told him. 'And a stewardess always goes in to them with a coffee just after take off.'

'Do they take any anti-hijack precautions on board? Cockpit door locked, no passengers beyond a certain point . . . stuff like that?' Ray asked.

'I've made the trip four times,' Colin replied. 'The last time was just one week ago, and when the plane is in flight the stewardess just walks in and out of the cockpit without knocking, no keys or anything.'

'So it's just a matter of getting into the cockpit sweet and pulling the gun on them,' Ray observed. 'I hope you've bought decent-looking replicas, Colin. Proper frighteners I mean.'

'The guns are fine,' Colin told him. 'I went for quality, the best on the market. Believe me, they look really lethal.'

'What models did you buy?'

'Big ones, Ray. I knew you'd want that.' Colin grinned. 'Real scary .45 Colt automatics. And they're not just replicas; they can fire blanks and eject the casings just like a real gun. Believe me, they look and sound the part all right.'

'Okay then,' Bert joined in. 'So we've got the guns. Now how do we get them on board? Airport security is supposed to be really tight these days.'

'Not out here,' Colin told him, 'especially not on internal flights. There will be no problem getting the

246

guns on board. They've never had any hint of trouble here, so security is really slack. Definitely no worries on that score.'

'Yeah, that sounds about right,' Ray nodded. 'But we'll be catching the plane north tomorrow,' he pointed out. 'How are you going to get the weapons to us?'

'You and Doc will be flying out of Accra,' Colin explained. 'It's just possible that with all the comings and goings of the big fight they'll step up security in the airport. I noticed a lot more uniforms than usual there today, as a matter of fact. So it'll be safer if Bert carries them via Takoradi. There's no question of security checks there and he can pass them over to you at Kumasi.'

At the end of the discussion Colin pulled a long envelope from one of his pockets and handed it to Doc. 'Return flight tickets to Kumasi. I booked them weeks ago to guarantee seats and picked them up at Accra post office to avoid ID problems. You'll see that the names are Braun and Steiner; that's just to throw them off a bit – make them think it was Germans or something. It'll cause a bit of confusion during the initial investigation.' He turned to Bert. 'I've got your ticket in Takoradi.'

'You've done a good job,' Ray said, nodding his appreciation. 'You lay out a good plan.'

247

'Thanks,' Colin acknowledged the compliment and sat back in his chair. 'This is your case, Doc,' he kicked at the suitcase he had carried up from the car. 'And yours is still in the motor, Ray. I'll be dropping you and your case off at your hotel when Bert and me head back to Takoradi.'

'Yeah,' Ray agreed. 'That'll do me.' He got up and stretched himself. 'I'm going to make an early night of it. Big day tomorrow.'

'I'll keep to myself as well,' Doc nodded seriously as he spoke. 'Maybe take a walk just to get the feel of the place.'

Ray folded the map. 'I'll take this with me and study it tonight.'

'Right then! Ready to move?' Colin looked at Bert. 'You won't be needing any luggage in Takoradi, so leave your gear here and just bring your smother with you. I've already booked a hotel and I can sort you out with a clean shirt and shaving gear. Now . . .' he looked at each of them in turn. 'Is there anything else you can think of before we break this up?'

Ray held his hand out to Bert. 'I've been thinking,' he said. 'With the fight on, this plane's bound to be fully booked. I don't want to have to walk down the length of the plane to get into the cabin.'

'I'll make sure I'm first on board at Takoradi,'

Bert promised. 'I'll get a seat right up front for you.'

'Then all we need is a little bit of luck and we're in business,' Ray's glance at Colin meant nothing to the others.

Colin stared back at him for a long moment before speaking. 'Everyone feel okay? Quite happy?'

'We've covered it all,' Doc agreed. 'If anything does go wrong it won't be our fault.'

Once again Colin met Ray's eyes, an imperceptible nod bridging the air between them.

'There'll be no accidents,' Colin stated confidently. 'The last thing they're expecting out here is a hijacking.' He turned to punch Bert lightly on the shoulder. 'Come on. You too, Ray. Bert and me still have to get back to Takoradi tonight.'

Colin hung back a little as the three of them moved towards the door. 'Well, Doc,' he said, 'this is the big 'un we all dream about. I'll be waiting for you to leap out of that plane tomorrow and make me a millionaire.'

Doc's face tightened as he stiffened his chin. 'It's the big 'un all right. Thousands of miles from London, hijacking aeroplanes, leaping out on parachutes and running about the fucking jungle. Yeah! It's the big 'un all right.'

'You happy about it?'

'It's looking good,' Doc admitted. 'I've been on a lot rougher jobs for a lot less money. Yeah.' He nodded. 'I'm happy about it.'

'Be lucky,' Colin gave him the thumbs-up, turning the movement into a quick salute as he let the door close and hurried after Ray and Bert.

★

'Well, we're committed now.' Colin stood at the rear of the car, retrieving Ray's suitcase from the boot.

'It's the right way,' Ray assured him. 'There's always the chance we'll strike lucky in Kumasi.'

'Well, you seem to be calling the shots now, Ray. I only hope it all works out for us tomorrow.'

'No.' Ray put his hand on Colin's arm. 'It's your operation. I'm only making suggestions based on my experience in the army. You discovered this job and your plan is first class. If that gold goes on the Dakota tomorrow, we'll take it. Your plan will take it!'

'*If* it goes on the Dakota.' Colin sounded very pessimistic.

'Believe me, Colin, if I didn't think there was a genuine possibility of that happening, we wouldn't be talking now.'

'Right,' Colin nodded, grateful for the moral support, even if he did have his doubts.

250

They walked round to the side of the car, Ray speaking louder now for the benefit of Bert. 'Christ!' he exclaimed, shaking his head as he looked along a wide avenue of tall palm trees. 'A few weeks ago I was hacking a taxi down the Fulham Road . . . Now look where I am. It's better than the fucking SAS!'

'Well, it'll be up to you tomorrow, soldier,' Bert grinned up at him. 'Feel confident, do you?'

'I am confident.' Ray looked straight at Colin. 'Confident about everything.' He stood on the wide pavement, lightly swinging his suitcase as Colin climbed into the car. Then, almost simultaneously, the three of them uttered the villain's timeworn prayer.

'Be lucky!'

The car accelerated away through a patchwork shadow of palm trees cast by the overhead street lighting, brake lights glowing as it approached a junction. Thoughtfully, Ray looked at the disappearing rear lights. *'Be lucky?'* he repeated the words quietly to himself. 'Well, as you told me once yourself, Colin: *You've got to work at being lucky in this business.'*

Fifteen minutes later, after depositing the suitcase in his room and changing into darker clothes, Ray was back on the street, making enquiries about the

251

nearest all-night marketplace. Later, after visiting the market and making his purchases, he hailed a taxi.

'How many pounds you take me for Kumasi?' he asked the delighted driver.

24

Colin turned into the cinema car park and pulled on the handbrake. 'You're booked into the Atlantic Hotel – name of Watson,' he told Bert as they got out of the car. 'You can carry the case with your kit in it as luggage and I'll get an overnight bag to you later on this evening.'

Bert lifted the case from the boot and weighted it experimentally in his hand. 'No bother,' he said. 'But if I'm to carry this, along with the two duffle bags tomorrow, it'll be a bit of a load. I helped Ray pack them and they've got a lot of extra bits and pieces inside.'

'Everything will be going into the one hold-all tomorrow,' Colin told him. 'But keep it out of sight when you check-in, just in case they decide it's too big for hand baggage.'

'Yeah, I'll watch that. Now, what about the replicas? When am I getting them?'

'You'll have them when I bring you your overnight bag. Put two of them in the holdall and carry the

253

other one on you to pass to Ray in Kumasi. Just make sure you don't go bumping into anyone with it and you should be all right.'

'Fuck me! I'll be like Arnold Schwarzenegger by the time this is over.' Bert flexed his arms in demonstration.

'You'll manage.'

'Yeah,' Bert nodded approvingly. 'You've got it all sussed out, Colin. Just like old times, eh?'

'I'll meet you near the hotel later on,' Colin told him over a beer in the cinema lounge. 'We can go for a meal this evening; there's a club in Sekondi that does a good steak and it's well out of the way of Takoradi.'

'I could do with a kip right now,' Bert admitted. 'I've been on the go since the minute I arrived here.'

'Aye,' Colin agreed. 'It's all been a bit of a rush and a rest will do you good. I'll give you a couple of hours before I pick you up, then we'll head for Sekondi for a meal and a pint. You can even try a bit of the old 'High Life' dancing at the Jamboree Club; you'll like it there. Mind you, it'll have to be an early night, so no heavy drinking or getting involved with women. We've still got a lot of work to do in the morning.'

Bert made a face at him. 'Is that all you ever think about?' he asked. 'Work, work, work?'

'As far as this job is concerned it is,' Colin agreed. 'Remember, you keep yourself in good nick for tomorrow and we can all forget about ever having to work again.'

'You're the boss. If you say no heavy boozing and no women . . .' Bert spread his arms. 'That's it!'

★

'Bit of all right that,' Bert remarked, pushing his plate away and wiping his mouth with a napkin as he looked round the club's interior; he didn't notice a gold-bedecked African man nod his head at two of the girls sitting at the bar. 'And look at the birds; a few tasty lookers there.' He nodded to a string of attractive young black women sitting along the bar. 'Wouldn't mind a shot on the swings with one of them. There you go,' he smiled happily. 'I'm getting the eye from a couple of them already.'

'Forget it, Bert,' Colin said. 'You're just a meal ticket to them, so don't show out or they'll be all over you and harder to get rid of than fleas on a camel's arse. A quiet meal and a drink, that's all we're here for.'

'Yeah, I know,' Bert nodded despondently. 'But what a waste, eh? Oh oh, there's a couple of them coming towards us.'

'Just be polite,' Colin told him, 'but don't let them

255

sit down or offer to buy them a drink; they'll take that as an invitation and pester us all night to take them home.'

'Wish I could,' Bert lasciviously licked his lips. 'What a body!' he said, looking up at the approaching girls.

'We sit beside you?' One of the girls placed her hand on Bert's shoulder. 'We keep company for you. Have good time.'

'Sorry, girls,' Colin spoke up. 'Maybe some other time, but not tonight.'

'I don't speak to you,' the girl turned a petulant face towards him. 'I speak to him,' she smiled down at Bert, moving her hand to caress his cheek. 'You like me?' she said, smiling at him and moving to take a seat. The second girl curled her arm round Colin's neck and bent her head to his face.

'You like me? You buy me drink?'

'Look, girls,' Colin pushed her hand away. 'We have things to talk about, so just leave us alone. Maybe another night.'

'You not like me?' the girl persisted, placing her arm round Colin's neck again and talking into his ear. 'I good girl, we have fun together. Come on, you buy me drink then we go have fun.'

Bert was having a struggle to prevent his girl sitting on his lap as she writhed her body against him. 'Hey, you've been told! We're not interested. Get off me.' He pushed her away. 'Now leave us in peace to have a drink.'

'My girls not good enough for you?' Bert heard a voice and turned to the gold-wearing African standing behind him. 'Why you come here if you don't like girls?'

'Look pal,' Colin, pushed the girl away and rose to his feet. 'We only came in for a drink and a meal. We've had that, and now we're leaving, okay?'

'You pay girls some money, *then* you leave.' The African looked at Colin then stared into Bert's face. 'They at your table, so now you pay.'

'Pay for what?' Bert demanded, rising to his feet. 'They came and stuck themselves on us. We didn't ask them to come over.'

'They at your table, so you pay,' the man demanded, rubbing his forefinger and thumb in that international gesture. 'You pay me for my girls.'

'I'll pay you fuck all,' Bert growled. 'Come on, Colin. Time we got out of here.' Bert moved to walk away from the table when the African swung a punch at him, catching him full on the eye. 'You bastard!' Bert snarled, retaliating with a roundhouse punch that knocked the man to the floor.

'Come on!' Colin grabbed Bert as he bent to hit the man again. 'We can't afford this sort of trouble.

Come on, before the others join in.' He pushed a still angry Bert towards the door and out into the street, quickly getting into the car and driving off as the first man ran out from the bar.

'Bastard!' Bert said angrily. 'Caught me proper, he did.' He turned down the sun visor and looked into the vanity mirror, gingerly touching the swelling around his eye. 'Look at it!'

'It could've been worse,' Colin inspected at Bert's eye. 'At least it didn't break the skin. But I think we'll call it a night now; we've got a lot to do in the morning.' He turned in the direction of Bert's hotel. 'Nine o'clock sharp, right!'

'Nine o'clock sharp,' Bert repeated. 'Don't worry, I'll be up and ready to go.'

*

'Jesus Christ!' Colin exclaimed when he saw Bert walking towards him. Even behind the sunglasses the heavy bruising on Bert's face was obvious. 'Your eye, it's a real shiner.'

'Yeah, ain't it,' Bert agreed. 'Came right up during the night.'

'We're fucked!' Colin said in disgust. 'That's the job gone clean out of the window.'

'How?' Bert demanded. 'A black eye won't stop me working.'

258

'Aye,' Colin agreed, the stress making him revert to his native Scots. 'It maybe won't stop you working, but if you do work you can guarantee it'll get you done.'

'Done?' Bert looked at him. 'What d'you mean, done?'

'Look at you,' Colin held out his hands. 'You can't go on board that plane. A white man with a black eye! Christ, Bert, once your description goes out you wouldn't last ten minutes on the street.' He made an exasperated sound through his teeth. 'That's it, the job's fucked!'

'What about a bit of make-up?' Bert groped for a solution. 'Some of that pan-stick stuff and the dark glasses. Should be all right with that.'

'No, it's not on,' Colin shook his head. 'You would be close up and in their faces. Christ, even Steven Spielberg couldn't hide that eye.'

'What's to be done, then?' Bert finally asked. 'Job off?'

Colin scratched his head, deep in thought. 'I don't know . . . there's maybe still a chance.'

'How?' Bert asked eagerly. 'What can we do?'

Colin thought hard, his lips pursed in concentration, before finally nodding his head. 'Aye,' he said, repeating the word again as he voiced his thoughts. 'Aye, it could be done.'

'What could be done?' Bert pressed him. 'What have you come up with?'

Colin stared into Bert's face, his mind still taking in the momentous decision he had come to. 'We could swap places, you and I. Change jobs,' he said. 'You on the ground, me in the plane.' You've been to the site and know what's to be done. All we need to do is swap jobs.'

Bert held up a hand. 'C'mon, Colin. That's just not on. The parachute jump . . . You've never had any training.'

'I know that,' Colin retorted. 'But you said yourself there was nothing to it.'

'Yeah, I know I said that. But I still did the training. You? You've never even strapped on a parachute. Fuck me, you could kill yourself.'

'I'm not giving up on this job, Bert. This is a one-off! A chance of a lifetime, and I'm not throwing in the towel for the sake of making a parachute jump. There's plenty of people that jumped from planes who never had any training.'

'Well, yeah,' Bert agreed. 'But they were all emergencies, life or death situations.'

'Aye, I know that. And as far as I'm concerned this is life or death for me; secure my future once and for all, or carry on with all the rubbish stuff we've been doing for years.'

'It's up to you, Colin,' Bert's face was deadly serious. 'The jumping bit is easy; it's remembering to pull the ripcord that's important. Once you do that the 'chute will automatically bring you down.'

'Right,' Colin came to a decision. 'We'll take the parachute gear up to your room and you can give me a run-through with the parachute harness – how to put it on and stuff like that. And then you can show me how to pull the ripcord.'

'Jesus Christ, you don't even know where the ripcord is!' Bert shook his head. 'Man, you're taking on an awful lot.'

Colin gripped Bert's forearm and squeezed hard. 'Listen,' his voice was as serious as Bert had ever heard it. 'As far as I'm concerned it's all or nothing now. We've all worked too hard on this job to throw in the towel at this stage. We're going ahead with it, whatever it takes. And even if that means I have to make a parachute jump, then that's the way it is. So let's get up to your room and you can give me a crash course on this parachuting business. I want to practise getting in and out of the harness a couple of times, become a bit familiar with it and learn how to pull the ripcord. After all,' he reminded Bert, 'according to you it's only a matter of pulling the ripcord and the parachute does the rest.' He opened the boot of the car and lifted out a small case. 'C'mon,' he said. 'It's time we got on with it.'

★

Bert looked doubtful as he draped the parachute across Colin's back and guided his arms through the harness, showing him how to tighten the shoulder straps, clip and lock the chest belt and pull the leg straps firmly against his hips and thighs.

'Just make sure everything fits nice and tight,' he told Colin. 'In fact I'll adjust the straps for you now – that way you'll just have to put the harness on like a jacket and clip up the chest and leg straps.' He was working away as he spoke, adjusting and pulling until he was satisfied the harness fitted snugly against Colin's chest and hips. 'Now,' he said, 'the ripcord.' He took Colin's right hand and pushed it back towards the parachute pack. 'Feel for this metal hand-grip.' He moved Colin's hand onto a metal ring. It was easy to find, falling naturally into Colin's palm as he reached backwards, and he practised the movement several times until he was confident that he would have no problem finding it when the time came.

'As soon as you exit the plane push your hand back onto the ripcord,' Bert moved Colin's hand as he spoke. Count to three and pull the ring firmly

262

forward. You will feel as if you are being jerked upwards, but it will only be the canopy opening and slowing you down. Once you start floating you will have plenty of time to locate the target and once you do find it, you keep your eye on it all the way down so you know which direction to run when you hit the ground.'

'Sounds straightforward enough,' Colin told him. 'As you said before; *pull the ripcord and the parachute will do the rest.* But what about the landing?'

'Well,' Bert said, 'you need to keep both feet tight together, knees touching, legs slightly bent ready to roll your body forward.' He adopted the position to demonstrate. 'Get set up like this and you should roll out fine.'

'Feet together, knees together . . .' Colin copied Bert's movements, 'legs bent, roll forward. Okay?'

'That's about it, Colin. Just remember that position and you should be fine.' Bert pushed the release catch on Colin's chest, catching the parachute as it slipped from his shoulders. 'Just keep cool, remember what I've told you and you should be all right.'

'I'll be fine, Bert,' Colin nodded his head, repeating the words as if reassuring himself, 'I'll be fine. Now come on,' he looked at his watch. 'Get that parachute packed up again and down to the motor.

Then you'll be taking my Peugeot and following me to Cape Coast, where I'll set up the getaway car. When that's done we'll be heading back to Takoradi so you can check me in for the Kumasi flight.'

*

The university car park was half-empty when Colin pulled into it and he had no trouble finding a shaded, unobtrusive spot in a quiet corner. He locked the vehicle up and placed the keys on top of the offside front wheel before strolling casually over to where Bert was waiting. A few minutes later the Peugeot was stopping again, opposite the worn road that led to Uturri, the same road that Bert would soon be traversing on his way to the drop zone. 'There's no other road for miles,' Colin explained to Bert. 'And it becomes even more of a track after couple of miles until it finally runs into a dead end at Uturri, so you can't go wrong. I've been up and down that road several times in the last couple of months and never once seen a soul on it.'

'Yeah, that's good,' Bert nodded thoughtfully. 'No people, no witnesses.'

'Aye,' Colin agreed, 'That's the way I like it.' He took a last look at the road to Uturri. 'So you think you'll be all right then? No problems about finding your way?'

264

'No probs, mate,' Bert nodded, twisting the key in the ignition and pulling away. 'Couldn't be sweeter.'

★

The drive to Cape Coast had revitalised them and Colin was more like his usual self as they headed towards Takoradi. They had plenty of time in hand and stopped off at Sekondi for a final discussion and to sort out some final details.

'I'll hold on to the bag while you do the check-in and collect the boarding pass, Bert. I've been through that airport a few times recently and a check-in girl might recognise me,' Colin told him as they sat outside a café overlooking the wide Bay of Sekondi. 'And pass me your smother; I'll have to put it on before we get to Takoradi.'

Bert passed over a package. 'Wig and false moustache, good ones too. And you'll have the hat and shades on of course.' He straightened his own sunglasses on his nose.

'Should be enough,' Colin agreed. 'Besides, I can't see any of the passengers being very willing to step forward as witnesses. The people to worry about are the soldiers and the plane's crew, and they should have no reason to pay us any particular attention until we stand up and declare ourselves.'

'The routine for the plane is well sorted out,' Bert

assured him. 'Doc will keep you right. You shouldn't have any trouble.'

'One thing's for sure,' Colin added. 'If anything does go wrong – we're done! There's no place to go on board a plane.'

'Nothing'll go wrong, Colin. We've been going over and over it for the last few weeks and got it all sorted out. If you make the jump, it'll all be done and dusted.'

Colin smiled at his enthusiasm. 'Aye, we can do it all right,' almost adding aloud, *providing the gold is on the plane.*

An hour before the Kumasi flight was due to depart Takoradi they went back to the car where Colin spent several minutes in the rear seat attaching a realistic moustache and adjusting a wig on his head. When he added a wide-brimmed sunhat and dark glasses, even Bert had to admit the disguise looked good.

'You look well,' Bert complimented him. 'A good smother.'

'Right,' Colin consulted his watch and took a deep breath. 'Time to make a move.'

25

Ray peered anxiously from the window of the plane as the mid-morning flight from Accra touched down at Kumasi. At first he could see only rolling bush through the starboard window, then the plane turned off the runway, its wingtip moving like a pointer as more of the airfield came into view. He saw the helicopter immediately and felt bitter disappointment at the sight of it standing firmly on its hard-pad. He thought of the work he had done the night before: the three-hour taxi ride north; penetrating the airfield's perimeter fence; two hours of patient, painstaking work sawing at the underside of the struts supporting the Lynx's landing gear; the return trip to Accra – all for nothing.

Dejected, he trudged behind Doc towards the arrivals gate, knowing now that the job was irretrievably lost. He turned to stare at the crouching helicopter one last time. He appeared cool but every nerve in his body screamed in frustrated anger, and he tortured himself for not simply setting it ablaze.

But deep down he knew that that would have been a mistake – such obvious sabotage would have stirred up a hornet's nest of activity. With time so short it would have been impossible to risk the return trip to Accra. No . . . without sophisticated timing devices and explosives, weakening the struts so that they would snap under the strain of landing after its routine morning test flight had been the best he could do. *If only he had cut deeper.*

*

The city of Kumasi was about three miles north of the airport and, rather than be seen loitering about the terminal, Doc and Ray took a taxi into town, planning to return when the first of the boxing charters were scheduled to leave and they could mingle with the crowd.

Morosely silent, Ray trooped behind Doc as they threaded their way through yet another local bazaar, brooding on the helicopter and his failure to im-mobilise it. Yet, despite his failure, he felt an almost masochistic desire to be near the airport, even if only to see the gold that might have become their own.

'Jesus Christ!' Doc trudged along, panting like a hard-run canine, mopping his forehead with an already sodden handkerchief. 'It's like a fucking hothouse out here. I've got to get out of this sun.'

Ray grasped his opportunity. 'We'd be better off at the airport,' he said. 'The lounge is air-conditioned and the fans should be gathering by now.' The urge to return was so strong that he found no difficulty in finding excuses to head back.

'Anywhere would be cooler than this,' Doc agreed, turning his head to locate a taxi.

*

The airport was indeed beginning to fill with fight fans as they slipped into the lounge, thankfully sinking into low-slung armchairs that faced onto the aircraft parking area. Ray stared towards the helicopter pad, but his view was obscured by a loading plane. Finally a last hurrying passenger crossed the tarmac and climbed the shallow steps, turning before he entered the dark oval to wave a Union Jack triumphantly at the fans still waiting for their flight. The door closed over and in another minute the propellers spun into life. The plane began to move, slowly at first, then more smoothly as it gathered speed.

Ray inched forward on the edge of his seat as the large tailfin of the departing plane sailed slowly across his line of vision, aware of a deep thudding in his chest as the ominous, shark shape of the helicopter shimmered into sight through the distorting ripples of rising heat. Ray stared at the lethal Lynx, wishing he had a Browning anti-tank gun in his hands; he would have used it too! He decided to say nothing to Doc, knowing he would be angry at not being put properly in the picture.

There was a stir of activity outside and a three-vehicle convoy drove past, heading for the helicopter. At the same time, loudspeakers announced that flight GA 670 from Takoradi was on schedule and would arrive in Kumasi in a few minutes' time.

Doc looked at his watch and raised his eyes to Ray, his face growing several degrees more serious. 'Thirty minutes,' he said. 'Thirty minutes and we're up and running,' his tongue wetted the bristles of his false moustache between phrases.

Might as well be thirty years, Ray grunted to himself, watching the convoy head towards the helicopter hard-pad.

'He ... e ... y,' Doc breathed out in a whisper. 'Those motors out there ... One of them is an armoured car and there's a truck and a jeep too! Isn't that what we're waiting for?'

'Routine convoy,' Ray told him, still reluctant to admit the truth. 'Probably arming the chopper for a patrol.'

'Yeah,' Doc accepted the explanation without question. 'They certainly look a bit busy, don't they?'

Three white-overalled mechanics were fussing over the helicopter and two of them turned towards the convoy as it approached. The third man hung back, something seeming to have attracted his attention. Ray saw him put his hand out to feel round the strut where he had made his cut. Suddenly the mechanic was on his knees, peering closely at the underside of the steel tubing where it curved away from the body of the aircraft. Ray was too far away to hear, but he could see the man's mouth open and close as he shouted for attention. Several men rushed forward, another of the ground crew going under the machine to excitedly confirm his colleague's discovery.

Ray leant forward, eyes fixed on an officer who had leapt from the armoured car to stride purposefully towards the excited group. The officer, Judas Akaba, knelt and inspected the strut, moving to the rear support when a check revealed similar damage there. He rose to his feet, cane pointing urgently at the struts as he stepped clear of the machine. One of the ground crew stood in front of him and they appeared to be arguing, the mechanic shaking his head as if refusing an order. Akaba's cane rose and slashed viciously across the mechanic's face knocking him to his knees as the soldiers cocked their weapons, pointing them in readiness. Then two of the ground crew were being escorted under armed guard towards a service hanger. Moments later they reappeared, pushing a trolley bearing welding equipment towards the damaged helicopter.

Ray looked on bleakly as one of the ground crew knelt under the belly of the Lynx, striking sparks into the nozzle of his welding torch to ignite a long, wavering, yellow flame of acetylene gas before catalysing oxygen was fed into the mixing valve at more than 2000 pounds per square inch pressure. Suddenly, like Doctor Jekyll's brew, the oxygen forced the innocuous acetylene gas into a volatile, blue-point flame capable of slicing through the thickest steel. The mechanic pulled dark goggles over his eyes and under the guns of the military escort bent to weld the fractured strut, his head disappearing in a burst of smoke as the flamehead touched the painted surface. In seconds the metal melted and merged under the concentrated heat of the torch, quickly undoing Ray's crude sabotage as the sides of the cut fused solidly together.

Ray looked down on the activity despondently, scowling as the welder moved to the rear strut to complete the repair that would make the helicopter fully operational again. He took some satisfaction from the fact that the workman seemed to be having problems in positioning himself to complete the repair, remembering the difficulty he had experienced himself by being too close to the fuselage. Finally the mechanic ended up flat on his back to weld in the overhead position.

Hope he burns himself to death, Ray thought, watching morbidly as the welding torch forced molten metal to drip dangerously close to the face of the prone welder. Suddenly the man convulsed, jerking his head to one side and throwing his arms across his face as a huge white-hot blob of metal exploded like lava under the pressurised flame of his torch. The searing flame scorched across the underside of the helicopter, destroying aluminium fuselage like thin ice in a furnace and atomising a fragile fuel pipe with the power of a space age laser beam.

Ray leapt to his feet as a jet of flame erupted under the helicopter. He saw the welder abandon his torch and race for his life as blazing flames spread quickly across the belly of the machine. Even in the lounge the yells could be heard as men shouted for fire-fighting equipment. But it was too late. Akaba screamed an order and the convoy accelerated clear as flames totally engulfed the doomed machine.

The explosion sent a black pall of smoke and whirling debris skywards and spectators dived for the floor of the lounge. Ammunition from the helicopter's ordnance exploded in all directions; tracer bullets leaving smoking trails against the blue sky, cannon shells pounding madly into the ground like demented pneumatic hammers as ricochets screeched through the smoke like banshees mourning the dead. Finally the explosions died away and all that could be heard was the roar of flames pushing a pillar of black smoke skywards in the windless air.

Stunned fight fans leapt to their feet, staring at the scene like unexpected spectators in a front-line trench. Through the torn veil of drifting smoke the distant wail of approaching fire tenders gradually grew loud.

In the tower, anxious air traffic controllers ordered flight GA 670 to orbit in the holding area and await further landing instructions.

26

When GA 670 finally landed, Colin found himself entering a lounge full of boisterously singing fight fans, the patriotic sea of red, white and blue regalia almost making him feel that he had gatecrashed a royal garden party!

His eyes swept the crowd, missing Doc and Ray the first time round, and for a moment he felt a surge of panic. Then he realised they would be wearing their smother and calmed himself, taking more time with his second scan of the room. This time, he located a serious-faced Doc staring at the incoming passengers and a worried looking Ray craning his neck, obviously expecting to see Bert. If he hadn't known about their disguises he would never have recognised them. Both wore wigs, and Ray, like himself, had suddenly sprouted a thick moustache. Doc was the least recognisable; his dark head now covered by a thick thatch of fair hair, along with a bristling, military looking moustache above his upper lip that had transformed him into a typically belligerent looking English colonialist.

Colin was almost within speaking distance when the shocked expression on Ray's face told him he had been recognised.

'What the . . .' Ray looked stunned. 'What are you doing here?' he blurted out, obviously shocked to see Colin in front of him.

'Long story,' Colin mouthed back at him before nodding in the direction of the Gents and carrying on through the throng, leaving a worried-looking Ray to follow him inside.

'What happened out there?' Colin asked quietly. 'All that smoke and fire . . . Was there an accident?'

'You could say that,' Ray smiled. 'They were doing some work on the helicopter when all hell broke loose. One second they were working away then suddenly the thing went up in smoke. Within a minute it blew sky high. It's a wonder no one was killed.'

'The chopper's gone?' Colin gasped. 'Jesus, what a result! Looks like we're on!'

'Yeah, I'd say that's a definite,' Ray agreed. 'Things are definitely back on track. But what the hell are you doing here?' Ray hissed, keeping his voice low. 'What the fuck's happened to Bert?'

'He had an accident,' Colin told him in a low

voice. 'There's no way he could board the plane the state his face is in. I'm taking his place; he's doing my job on the ground.'

'You're going to do a jump! Jesus! Do you think you can handle it?'

Colin looked him in the eye. 'I talked all of you into this so it's my responsibility and I'm not scrubbing things now.' He stared into Ray's anxious face. 'We've all put too much into it. So if things have worked out here I'm going to make the jump. That's a definite, and nothing's going to stop me from trying.'

A cubicle door opened behind them and they slipped into the vacant toilet together.

'But you've never even trained,' Ray said, shaking his head. 'You would be risking your life.'

'Bert and Doc were prepared to do it,' Colin reminded him. 'Sure, they did a quick course, but they had to do a first jump too, and even Bert said it was a piece of cake.'

'Well . . .' Ray looked doubtful. 'If you've got the confidence you should be fine. But what if you freeze up? Don't make the pull?'

'I'll make the pull,' Colin nodded. 'My fucking life will depend on it! So don't you worry, I'll make the pull all right.'

'You're sure of this, Colin?

'I'd sooner it was Bert than me,' Colin admitted. 'But he's out of it and I'm in. Everything's set up and I've made up my mind.' Colin passed over one of the replica guns. 'Give this to Doc. I've still got yours on the plane and I'll pass it to you when we get on board.'

'Good idea,' Ray praised him as he pushed the gun into his belt, under the loose jacket he was wearing. He posed, his arms by his sides. 'Look all right?'

Colin examined the line of Ray's jacket, giving it a tug to pull the front a little closer together. 'Fine. Just don't let it flap open.'

'You've managed to get me a seat up front?'

'Row one. You can press your feet against the cockpit door if you like.'

'That's good.'

'What about the mob out there?' Colin asked. 'I hope to fuck we're not going to be lumbered with a planeload of drunks. Could be very dodgy that.'

'Nah,' Ray assured him. 'We're on a scheduled service. Probably get one or two on board our plane, but most of them are booked on specials.'

'Better get moving.' Impatient hands were pushing at the toilet door. 'These guys outside will think we're a couple of gayboys.'

Back in the lounge, Ray slipped the replica gun to

278

Doc and explained what had happened as he checked the scene outside. The Dakota was well within his field of vision and he just couldn't help the satisfied smile that crossed his face as he watched the ground crew hurriedly unloading seats through its passenger door.

Ray looked at Doc, then over at Colin, who had moved to get a better view from the window, where he could watch the operation as the armoured van backed up to the aircraft's steps. Five minutes later the van pulled away, leaving only the soldiers and the gun-mounted Land Rover on guard. Their collective concentration was broken by the crackling Tannoy announcement: 'Will all passengers on flight GA 670 to Accra please board the aircraft immediately. Flight GA 670 to Accra is now boarding at Gate Number One.'

★

The plane's captain was busy with Akaba, checking the wooden boxes, when Ray squeezed past, carefully turning his head away to avoid any direct looks from them, but his heart pounded with excitement at his first sight of the prize. He tried a quick count of the boxes as he went by, but bending bodies obscured his view and he could not afford to linger.

Colin slipped past as Akaba bent to inspect a seal on one of the boxes and closed up behind Ray, speaking softly, so as not to attract attention. 'Our seats are in the front row on the right. I left the bags on them in case someone tried to step in.'

'That's fine,' Ray muttered, sneaking a look behind. 'Doc's just moved into a seat at the back and both stewardesses are busy in the galley behind him. Everything's looking good. I reckon it's a go.' They settled into their seats, sitting in a tense, almost self-conscious silence as the other passengers filed aboard.

The activity in the centre of the plane ended with the pilot signing a receipt and suddenly Judas Akaba was standing in the plane's exit, looking sternly at the sergeant and private soldier detailed to guard the gold. He gave a last lingering look down the length of the cabin as if to reassure himself, then his swagger stick rose to touch his cap as the plane's captain politely ushered him outside. A dull thud was heard as the door thumped tightly shut, cutting off all external noise.

With the door closed, the scene outside took on the surreal quality of a silent ballet as Akaba appeared and twelve pairs of army issue boots stamped soundlessly into the tarmac, bringing their owners smartly to attention. Sweat stood out on

Colin's forehead as he watched. *Why didn't the engines start? Did someone suspect something?* Perhaps someone in the toilets spotted us and became suspicious? He turned his head, looking for support. But Ray was looking composed, sitting comfortably in his seat. Colin's face was pale as one of the stewardesses made a final seat belt check, moving towards the small galley at the rear of the plane and the jump seat beside her colleague, ready for take off.

A thump sounded through the plane and for a moment Colin thought the door was being opened again. But no, he settled back as the port engine kicked over a second time before settling into an even roar. In a minute the second engine burst into healthy-sounding life and the aircraft vibrated with power. Then the brakes were released and the plane rolled smoothly forward.

'We're off then?' Colin's voice was strained.

'Just about,' Ray's voice reached him. 'We're just taxi-ing out. Did you see the stuff?'

'Yeah. It's there all right,' Colin said. Then ... 'Christ!' The plane dipped to a sudden halt and he pressed his cheek against the window, craning his neck to look backwards. 'What is it?' What the fuck have we stopped for?'

The plane's engines rose to a crescendo of

screaming sound then died to a whisper before returning to an even roar again. Ray looked at Colin. 'It's only checks,' he said. 'Routine power checks.'

'Everything's okay?' Colin whispered back. 'Nothing to hold us up?'

'Everything is A-okay,' Ray assured him as the plane began to roll again. 'We'll be lining-up now, waiting for take-off clearance.'

There was no mistaking the surge of power that catapulted the Dakota down the runway, or the sudden change when the rumbling, lurching motion altered into smooth flowing movement as the aircraft lifted off and found its element.

Colin looked at his watch – 4.20. If Ray had calculated correctly they would reach the turn-off point in eighteen minutes. But they were running more than an hour late. He wondered what Bert would think when they didn't show up on schedule. *Surely he would wait a while.*

Colin casually turned his head and let his eyes flick over the soldiers, wincing inwardly at the sight of stubby barrelled Uzi sub-machine guns lying easily across their knees – *Jesus Christ! Where were the Lee-Enfields . . . the unloaded 'frighteners' he had been so positive about?* The helicopter! That was it! They had intended using the helicopter right up until the fire and there had been no time to reorganise the soldier's hardware. Instead of useless, empty rifles the escort now had the massive firepower of modern nine-millimetre machine guns. The replica in Colin's pocket suddenly felt puny, the taking of the plane had become infinitely more dangerous. He studied the rest of the passengers. They were all men, the majority of them well into middle age. Steady-looking people, people sensible enough to avoid heroics. Except for the soldiers, the job *should* be a doddle. He pressed his arm against the gun in his side pocket, as if seeking reassurance, and knew that neutralising the soldiers hard and fast would be the key.

Doc was sitting in an aisle seat right at the back of the cabin when Colin passed him and entered the toilet. He leant back against the door of the claustro-phobic cubicle and closed his eyes. First the heli-copter, now two heavily armed soldiers and himself subbing for Bert. He gave serious consideration to calling the job off – it always had been a last-minute option. But striking out went against the grain. The helicopter had been a stroke of bad luck, but then again, somehow or other the game had turned for them; maybe the job was starting to go their way. *What if the soldiers did have guns?* he asked himself – *They didn't suspect anything, and up until recently the escort job had always been a soft, regular weekly duty –*

something of a skive in fact. But even though they were trained men, an actual hijack would be the last thing on their minds. And trained men wouldn't argue with what they thought were loaded guns, especially when innocent civilians were involved. A firm hand, along with the element of surprise was all that was needed here. Colin was confident he could handle things, but did he have the right to jeopardise the lives of Ray and Doc and everybody else on board the plane too, for that matter? He took out the replica gun from his pocket and pulled the trigger. The hammer fell with an emphatic click, like a full stop to his doubts, and he made up his mind. They might have to make slight alterations to the plan, but they *were going ahead*. A smiling stewardess made way for him as he returned to his seat.

'How'd it look?' Ray whispered as Colin settled down beside him.

'Couldn't expect much better,' he said convincingly. 'As far as the passengers go anyway. They all look too sensible to start anything and the stewardesses are busy in the galley. The squaddies ignored me when I walked past them but they could still be a bit tasty; seems they've swapped the Lee-Enfields for machine guns. But then again, they won't be expecting anything to go wrong. So as long as we act hard and fast we should catch them napping.'

'Right . . . Especially when they see the size of our shooters.' Ray nudged him and grinned wickedly. 'It'll be a straight case of hands up and don't shoot me, Kameraden.'

'Yeah, as long as it's properly handled,' Colin agreed.

'What d'you mean?'

'They might feel obliged to put on a show, offer some resistance. Next thing some of the passengers could join in and bingo! We've got a problem.'

'There's always the chance of a problem,' Ray admitted. 'But our guns really look the business, Colin, and I can't see the squaddies arguing with them; especially on an aircraft.' He seemed to think for a moment or two before speaking again. 'You know, I think it would be better if I actually took on the soldiers myself,' Ray told him. 'I have a better idea than you or Doc on how they'll react, and it's not a big change in the plan. You only have to take over from me when I bring the crew out of the cockpit. I'll have the plane on automatic pilot by then and that will leave me free to tackle the soldiers.'

'Don't you have to stay in the cockpit?' Colin looked at him doubtfully. 'Surely you have to keep control of the plane?'

'I told you, the plane will be on automatic pilot and once that's set up it'll fly itself. You only have to

285

take control of the crew when I bring them out of the cockpit, then I'll neutralise the soldiers. It'll happen so fast they won't know what hit them.'

'As long as you're sure,' Colin said, looking serious. 'Once it's started I'll do whatever's needed to pull it off.'

'Okay then, we handle it my way,' Ray told him. 'You take over control of the crew and leave the soldiers to me.'

'Right,' Colin nodded. 'I'll do that. But what about Doc, will he be all right?

'Doc will be fine. His job stays the same and he knows what to do when things kick off.'

'And you think you'll be okay in there?' Colin's eyes flashed to the cockpit door.

'Don't worry about me,' Ray said. 'Things are in my favour. The pilot's first consideration is always the safety of his passengers. He definitely won't give any trouble if I show I mean business.'

'There's two of them.'

'All the same. They won't take any chances if they think I've got a loaded gun at their heads.' Ray looked at his watch: twelve minutes since take-off. He reached into a pocket and withdrew a black hooded mask and for about five seconds sat perfectly still, steeling himself. Then he spoke quietly. 'I want you to stand in the aisle and mess about in the luggage rack,

286

give me a bit of cover in case the squaddies are looking this way.' He waited until Colin's body blocked the aisle, then took a deep breath.

'Here goes, mate. It's boom or bust time now!' He stood up and calmly moved towards the cockpit door. The handle turned easily and he stepped inside, allowing the door to close behind him as he slipped the hood over his head.

Holding his breath, Colin fiddled in the luggage rack and watched the cabin door. After a minute had passed he knew it was all right and sank back into his seat.

Captain Okebo Udeh abandoned his usual welcoming smile when he realised that the intruder was one of the passengers and not, as he had expected, the stewardess with his customary cup of coffee.

'I'm sorry, sir. Passengers are not allowed on the flight deck.' He raised his eyes to the visitor's face, his voice very English. Very correct. 'I'm afraid I must ask you to . . .'

The young co-pilot looked round in mild curiosity as the captain's voice petered out in a gasp.

'Keep your hands in sight and don't touch anything,' Ray grated, swinging his gun in an arc between the two men.

Captain Udeh's mouth opened and closed as he tried to grasp the situation. The co-pilot sat stunned, twisted awkwardly in his seat like a cripple in a wheelchair looking backwards. The whites of his eyes grew huge in his black face and he gaped uncomprehendingly at Ray.

'What ... what ...' stuttered Udeh, trying to string some words together. 'What are you doing, sir?' Force of habit maintained his politeness.

'I'm taking over this plane, that's what I'm doing. Now turn round and face away from me. You too!' He almost had to tap the co-pilot on the head. 'Face forward and keep your hands away from any buttons and switches – right?'

'What do you intend to do?' This time Udeh dropped his habitual 'sir' as he turned to face Ray again.

'I've already done it!' Ray pushed the gun into Udeh's face. 'You've just been hijacked. Now face the fucking front!' He noisily cocked the automatic. 'Another question ... one single move I don't like ... and you are one dead pilot!' Ray warned. 'I won't tell you again.'

Captain Udeh tried to form a reply, his mouth opening and closing as he struggled to come to terms with this sudden nightmare. His co-pilot looked on, naked fear in his staring eyes and gaping mouth.

Udeh swallowed. He knew that he must regain full

288

control of himself; acutely aware that the safety of his passengers depended on him.

'I will do as you ask.' His voice was pitched a little higher than usual, but he sounded reasonably calm. 'What do you want me to do?'

Ray checked the compass heading on the instrument panel, noting that the course was only two degrees out from the one he had plotted on the Michelin road map.

'Fly one-three-four,' he instructed.

Captain Udeh took the control column in both hands and settled down to flying his plane. 'One-three-four,' he repeated, stretching a hand forward in a natural movement towards a bank of switches, one of which would transmit a hijack in progress signal. He felt the cold touch of the gun's muzzle on the flesh at the back of his neck.

'Keep your hands on the control column,' Ray threatened. 'I told you, no switches, no buttons.'

'I must operate the ailerons.' Udeh's voice sounded almost convincing. But the gun nudged harder, making his head jerk forward.

'And you *don't* operate the ailerons with *that* switch,' Ray told him. 'So any more of your *"operating the aileron"* shit and I'll blow your fucking head off. Now get your hand on that yoke and alter course.' The gun jabbed emphatically into Udeh's neck.

'Yes. I understand.' Udeh nodded, faster this time, and moved the column in a gentle turn. 'One-three-four,' he called out as the compass needle swung over two degrees.

Ray had his map out and held it in front of the pilot. He pointed to the cross he had pencilled in about one quarter of the way along the line between Kumasi and Accra. 'That's your course change,' he ordered. 'When you reach this point you'll turn onto a heading of two-five-three.' He looked at the cabin clock, then at the airspeed indicator. 'I estimate about seven . . . eight minutes. Just carry out my orders and everything will be okay. Your aircraft and its passengers will be safe as long as you do as you are told. Do you understand me?'

'Yes. I understand.'

'And you?' Ray spoke to the young co-pilot. 'Do you understand?'

The man's tightly curled head nodded rapidly in agreement. 'Yes, suh. I understand. I make no trouble.' Nerves had reduced his speech to 'bush' English.

'Right then. We should all get along fine. Now, Captain . . .' Ray touched the man's neck with the gun barrel and positioned himself where he could see all that was going on.

Colin reached for the canvas holdall, using his

body as a shield to place it on the window seat. He withdrew the two smaller duffle bags and loosened the rope ties. From the first one he withdrew a packet of plastic zip-tapes and a polythene bag containing half a dozen black hoods, carefully laying them out on Ray's vacant seat and covering them with a magazine. From the other duffle, he withdrew three tightly wrapped bundles, checking them for his personal mark before unfolding his own package to reveal a one-piece jump suit, a cyclist's helmet and swimming goggles bulging out from one of its many zip-up pockets.

Unobtrusively, he folded down the dark-coloured material and began to step into the legs of his jump suit, gradually working the material under his backside and over his shoulders until he could slip his arms into the sleeves and pull the long zip halfway up his chest. From a side pocket he extracted a pair of ladies' fine leather gloves and held them ready in his hands. Neither of the two passengers across the aisle so much as glanced at him. Finally he took his weapon from his belt and slipped it into another of the large zip pockets. Then he pulled back an elasticated cuff and looked at his watch. They had been airborne for fifteen minutes. He tore open the packet of zip-tapes and stuffed them into a breast pocket, ready to pass them to Ray. Behind him he could hear a subdued murmuring as passengers chatted, unaware of the drama already unfolding. A stewardess came by bearing a coffee tray for the flight deck, her smile tailing off as she took in Colin's clothing. Faint creases were beginning to etch lines around her eyes as she disappeared into the cockpit.

Inside the cockpit the stewardess jerked to a halt, gasping in shock, unaware of the coffee cups flying over the head of the co-pilot. Ray thrust out a hand, stopping her from falling forward as she appeared to almost faint. The co-pilot moaned in pain, his hand raised to the back of his neck where the hot coffee had scalded him and stained his immaculate white shirt a muddy brown.

'Don't move!' Ray's voice was harsh. 'Don't anyone fucking move! Try anything and *she* gets it!' He put the onus on the pilot to behave. 'One minute to course change.' Captain Udeh's voice sounded out, an oasis of calmness in the highly charged atmosphere.

'Keep it like that, Captain,' Ray warned. 'Keep it cool and no one gets hurt.'

'I will do exactly as you say,' Udeh replied earnestly. 'There is no need for violence. But if you are hijacking this aircraft . . . what is your final destination? This aircraft has only a short range and the course you have given me will take us out over the ocean.'

'Just do as you're told,' Ray replied. 'I know where we're going, that's all you need to know.'

'I'm beginning the turn . . . now.' Captain Udeh tilted the control column to his right.

'Keep it gentle – rate three.'

Udeh's earlier suspicions were confirmed by Ray's order. The man was obviously a pilot himself.

'And when you're on 253 I want 130 knots at 3000 feet. Do you understand me?'

'Course 253. 130 knots at 3000 feet,' Udeh chanted back at him.

'And then engage the autopilot.' The revolver tapped the back of the man's head, demanding obedience.

Colin felt the gentle turn because he was waiting for it and looked back along the cabin. No one seemed to have noticed anything amiss. He struggled to pull a thin piece of black nylon cloth from his jacket pocket and spread a hooded mask across his knees, carefully rolling its bottom edge into a thick hem so he wouldn't fumble when he slipped it over his head. He pulled on the gloves, rubbing the backs of his hands to draw the fine leather skin-tight and watched the cockpit door. Then he saw the handle turn.

As soon as he caught sight of the pilot's drawn face, Colin slipped the black hood over his head and gave the hem a tug to settle it round his neck. Ready,

293

he drew his gun and rose to his feet, a terrifying figure in his sinister black outfit as he stepped forward to push his weapon into the pilot's chest. Ray grabbed the zip-tapes as he darted by, storming up the aisle toward the soldiers, neither of whom realised anything was amiss until he suddenly loomed over them, thrusting a huge automatic pistol into their faces.

'Don't move! Don't move a fucking inch!' Ray grated the words out hoarsely. There was a smooth metallic sliding sound as both soldiers cocked their guns, pushing high-velocity 9mm shells into the breeches of their weapons. Behind them, Doc rose from his seat and stepped quietly into the aisle.

The sergeant glared grimly at Ray and trained his weapon on his heart. Beside him, Private Akempo licked his lips in indecision as the enormous barrel of the revolver settled its aim on his head. First trigger pressure had been taken up and he *knew* that even if he fired first, reflex action would cause the madman's weapon to blast him into eternity. The sergeant also held his fire, but for a different reason. He knew what a burst of high-velocity machine gun bullets could do to the flimsy structure of a passenger plane. And there were civilians well within his field of fire. His thumb slid forward, pushing his fire-selector to single shot mode. At least now there would be no lethal spray of bullets mowing down innocent people. He would make his single shots count.

'Don't even think about it, Sarge,' Ray aimed his words at the sergeant but kept his gun trained on the private.

'Put down your weapon or you will force me to kill you.' The sergeant jerked his gun, as if to draw attention to it. But he had already waited too long.

'No!' Ray kept his eyes on the private, his pistol clamped in the two-handed marksman's grip. 'You shoot – he dies.' He knew this responsibility would weigh heavily with the sergeant.

'He is a soldier.' The sergeant ignored the huge beads of sweat oozing from Private Akempo's forehead. 'He is prepared to die.'

'And are you prepared to let innocent civilians die too?' Ray's eyes flashed and he tossed a nod backwards, more eloquent than words.

The sergeant's eyes flicked beyond Ray and locked onto the huddled crew members being threatened by a second masked gunman hiding unashamedly behind the clutch of bodies.

'Please!' The captain's voice entreated. 'You must do nothing to endanger the safety of the aircraft.'

Stunned passengers tore their eyes away from the masked figure menacing the soldiers and were shocked to see the dishevelled crew gathered in front of the cockpit door. A sobbing stewardess had an automatic pistol held against her head by a second masked figure.

'Please . . .' The captain spoke into the forward telephone link, allowing his voice to be heard by everyone on the plane. 'I must ask you to pay attention to me.' Heads at the rear of the plane lifted, some of them unaware until now that anything untoward was going on. 'The aircraft has been taken over . . . hijacked! I must ask you to follow any instructions issued by the hijackers immediately.'

'You see,' Ray told the sergeant, 'we have nothing to lose now. You shoot me, I shoot him and my partner shoots the pilot. That way everybody gets to die. Everybody!' he emphasised. 'So either lay down your weapon, or go ahead and shoot.' This time he stared directly into the sergeant's face, his iron-grey eyes implacable in the dark holes of his mask.

There was an unbelieving hush as the passengers turned to look at one another in amazement. A man in the rear of the cabin rose to his feet and stepped into the aisle.

'I say! This is prepos . . .'

His words were suddenly cut off as Doc's heavy hand landed on his shoulder from behind and thrust him back into his seat.

'Shut up!' A masked face glared down at him. 'Just sit on your fucking arse, mister, or you'll be getting some of this.' Doc's gun jabbed out. 'Do as you're told, all of you.' He swung his gun at the other shocked passengers, who gaped in bewilderment at the appearance of yet another masked and armed figure.

'Yes,' Ray addressed the sergeant again. 'There are more of us.' His gun jerked. 'Put down your gun or the killing starts now.'

The sergeant licked his lips. At his side, Private Akempo was rigid in the fire position, but not rigid in readiness – a paralysis of fear held him tight in its grasp. He knew that the threat from the masked man was all too real.

'Sergeant!' the pilot shouted. 'I am in command of this aircraft and I order you to put down your weapons. I am the captain and I accept full responsibility for this decision. Put your weapons down . . . Now!'

For a moment it seemed that the sergeant would defy him, then his body sagged along with the muzzle of his gun.

'Use your left hand,' Ray instructed. 'Take your weapon by the barrel and place it on the floor in front of you.' He waited until both soldiers had complied with his order. 'Now kick them towards me. Steady now . . .' he warned, as both men reluctantly obeyed. Quickly he scooped up one of the machine guns before shoving his own weapon into his belt and ordering them to stand up and turn around. In moments their wrists were securely zip-taped and he was draping black hoods over their heads before allowing them to sit down again, their effectiveness totally neutralised.

'I must ask all of you to remain seated,' the captain pleaded. 'Acts of violence will only endanger the safety of the aircraft and the lives of all of us on board.'

His words had an immediate sobering effect on the passengers. A lone voice asked: 'But where are they taking us?'

Captain Udeh turned to the hooded figure behind him before replying. 'I am afraid I do not yet know that, gentlemen. No doubt our destination will be revealed in due course. In the meantime I must insist that you offer no resistance to these armed men. Any such action can lead only to catastrophe.'

The warning delivered, Colin shepherded his three captives along the aisle. 'And no funny stuff,' he warned. 'I'm right behind you.' He forced the crew the length of the cabin, holding them at gunpoint as Doc hurried forward to assist Ray in zipping the soldiers' ankles together. After the soldiers had been dealt with, the protesting pilot and co-pilot were quickly given the same zip-tape treatment and pushed into a small galley at the rear of the plane, the second stewardess being dragged from her hiding place to make room for them. Both terrified girls were only too happy to be bundled into the toilet, the door clicking over to 'Engaged' as they locked themselves inside.

Ray tapped urgently at his wristwatch, speaking staccato fashion. 'You've got fifteen minutes. I'm going forward to the cockpit now to get used to the plane. I'll call out the approach times at intervals as we get closer. Okay?' He was already moving towards the cockpit door.

'Right,' Colin's hooded head nodded after him. 'Everything's gone well so far. But don't forget the reminder to this lot,' he jerked his head at the craning passengers. 'We don't want any of them getting ideas.'

Ray's hand was lifted in understanding as he hurried forward, stopping only to collect his suitcase and jumpsuit from Colin's seat before disappearing inside the cockpit.

Working fast, Colin and Doc carried their own luggage and the second machine gun to the rear of the plane as the Tannoy crackled into life.

'Attention! Attention everyone!' The passengers

jerked their eyes away from the activity in the cabin and looked towards the cockpit, like children waiting to see a Punch and Judy show. There was plenty of punch for them, even if it was only vocal. 'We have taken over the aircraft. I repeat. We have taken over the aircraft.' Ray's voice introduced an agreed speech. 'You will all remain seated and make no attempt to interfere with anyone or anything going on in the cabin beside you. We are well armed and will have no hesitation is using our weapons if we are provoked. For your own sakes do nothing to make any further violence necessary. Remember, we have nothing to lose. If you all remain calm and stay seated no harm will come to you, and the captain will be back in control in thirty minutes.' The Tannoy clicked off to a suddenly vociferous audience as the passengers discussed their plight.

At the rear of the plane Doc scrambled into his jumpsuit and donned the leather crash helmet. While he was doing this, Colin opened up both suitcases to expose the bulky parachute equipment. From a pocket on the underside of each lid he extracted a heavy canvas sack, shaking both of them out to show a line of brass rings fitted neatly round their wide necks. Each sack had a nylon drawstring snaking through the brass eyelets, their ends securely spliced on to heavy metal D-rings.

'Ten minutes! Ten minutes to target!' The speakers rapped out the first of Ray's time checks.

★

Bert looked anxiously at the sky above Uturri, trying to visualise the drop. He still had strong misgivings about Colin making the jump but the decision had been made and all he could do now was get ready for the aircraft to appear. Face puckered with concern, he began setting things into position, dragging the bales of hessian from their hiding place and spreading them evenly along the length of the trenches Colin had so painstakingly dug. Then he quickly began saturating the material in a heavy mixture of oil and petrol from the store of five-gallon containers Colin had secreted in the village. When he was done he looked at his watch: if the plane had left on time and Ray's estimates were accurate, he should only have about fifteen minutes to wait. He looked anxiously up at the sky again, his thoughts revolving around one thing: *Jesus,* he repeated to himself, *I wonder what's going on up there?*

★

Colin and Doc began manhandling the bullion boxes to the rear of the plane with Ray's one-minute reminders urging them on.

As each sack received its quota of ten boxes their

drawstrings were pulled tight and the laden sacks, too heavy and unwieldy to lift, were dragged over to the door of the plane where a final push would despatch them earthwards. Now the duffle bags were emptied to reveal the olive green oblongs of United States Army emergency parachutes. The many dry runs Doc had practised in Bert's living room now paid dividends as he efficiently connected the D-rings to the harness, Colin following his instructions as they both drew sweat and panted under the pressure and speed of the work.

Ray sat awkwardly in his parachute harness, sweating uncomfortably at the controls of the old Dakota. He had failed to pick up any identifiable landmark and peered anxiously ahead in an effort to locate his target. *How are they getting on back there?* He must have asked himself the same question a dozen times over. The temptation to leave the cockpit and check was almost overwhelming, but he resisted and looked at the plane's clock again before reaching for the intercom button. 'Five minutes!' he rapped out. 'Five minutes to target!'

Ray scanned the ground ahead, eyes narrowed, thoughts running wild as he saw only unremitting greenery below. *Five minutes left and still no recognisable landmark. Jesus! I should be almost on top of the place.* He picked up the intercom again.

'Four minutes! Four minutes to target!'

Time was running out when suddenly he leant forward, screwing up his eyes as the monotonous green of the jungle canopy petered out into a stark scrubland. The alluvial plain!

'Three minutes! Three minutes to target!' *Christ!* He had almost missed his check time there.

★

Almost forty-five minutes behind the scheduled time, Bert's flame of hope was fading fast. Totally depressed and feeling lost and alone, he decided he had had enough. The job was off. There was no way the plane could be this late. It seemed obvious that they had failed; he only hoped that the plan had simply been aborted and his mates were now travelling as bona fide passengers. Frustrated, he wanted to scream at the empty, mocking sky. Hopes now hollow, he bent to strike his lighter into the trough of hessian, a funeral pyre to mourn the death of the plan.

★

'Two minutes!' Ray's voice spurred Doc and Colin on to more frantic efforts. 'Two minutes to target!'

Doc snatched up Colin's parachute and helped him into it, snapping the clips tight before turning to get help with his own harness. Then each checked the other's equipment, making sure everything was secure.

'One minute! One minute to target!'

They turned urgently to the locking lever of the aircraft's door.

*

The lighter clicked several times, somehow its wheel failing to dispatch sparks into the hissing gas. 'More fucking trouble,' Bert cursed aloud as he pulled the flint holder free and inspected it. A few turns of the screw forced the worn flint against the ribbed wheel and he tried it again. This time the lighter spewed a stream of sparks, the liquid gas igniting with a soft explosion that was audible in the silence of the plain. He worked the gas control, sending a foot-long jet of flame whooshing into the air, cutting it on and off once or twice like a child playing with a toy. With a last, longing look to the north, Bert knelt and caught a handful of dry hessian. It ignited easily, making a faint crackling as it flared. He held the burning torch in his hand and let the flames grow higher, just as another noise intruded to override the soft plopping sounds the flames were making. He cocked his head. It wasn't a mosquito, much too low a buzz for that. The sound grew louder, and suddenly every sense in his body became alert. *The plane! It had to be the plane!* An exultant whoop left his lips and he threw the burning cloth into the fire, moving immediately to aim the lighter in another place. The droning was quite loud now as he ran to the other side. In seconds a yellow glare ran the length of both trenches and thick smoke billowed into the air. He could see the plane now, lower than he had been expecting and far off to his right.

'Over here!' he screamed. 'Over here! Over here you stupid bastard!'

But the plane flew on, oblivious to his screaming, as Bert sank slowly to his knees, the euphoria of the moment before turning to ashes in his mouth.

*

The oval door of the plane flew wide, Doc barely managing to avoid being dragged out by the slip-stream as the sound of the screaming engines suddenly disconcerted him. Then Colin was tossing the empty duffle bags and suitcases past him; if the police wanted them they would have to look for them. The machine gun followed the luggage into space.

Bracing himself, Doc dragged one of the loaded sacks to the edge of the door then helped Colin to place the other one in position, ready to be pushed out. Both of them leant forward, fists firmly gripping the setting key of the spring-loaded automatic openers. Ray had chosen a five-second delay and Doc had only to release the key to activate the timer. Tight with tension, they crouched over the gold, heads craned upwards, eyes focused on the unlit sign above the passenger seats.

*

Ray's eyes swept over the ground ahead, scanning right and left across the bleak countryside. He knew the dropping zone was approximately six miles in front of the low mountain range and he concentrated his gaze on that area, searching desperately for the target.

Christ! If I don't spot the fire soon I'll overfly the fucking DZ! His head swivelled anxiously, searching for the elusive signal.

A red light flared into angry life on his instrument panel. *Jesus!* Then his eyes caught sight of black overprinting on the warning glow – 'Rear Passenger Door.' He sighed in relief, realising that Colin and Doc were prepared. Now all he had to do was spot the signal fire.

He flew on for another half minute, hands tight but impotent on the control column. Then, almost at the bottom-right-hand corner of his windscreen, he spotted a waver of grey smoke and the flicker of yellow flames.

Too near! Even as Ray's heart pumped adrenaline the flames drifted past parallel with the plane. His timing had been good, but he was nearly a mile off target. Bitter bile rose in his throat as he realised he could never make the turn in time. He thumped his fist on the control column in rage and frustration. Suddenly, the plane was diving. *Jesus Christ!* He had disengaged the autopilot. He snatched the column towards his stomach, dragging the plane's nose up until it pointed at the horizon again. He was flying it. He *had* to fly it!

★

'What the . . . !' Colin burst out as he grabbed at the back of a seat. 'What the fuck's going on?' His words were almost drowned out by the screaming noise from the engines. Doc lay groaning on top of a sack of gold, his parachute pack saving his back from injury against the sharp-edged boxes. He struggled painfully to his feet, Colin's willing hand helping him to stand as the plane recovered from its dive and began to regain height. They stared at the unlit 'Fasten Seat Belts' sign, willing it into illumination. The passengers were alarmed too, raising their voices, some of them getting to their feet to stare up and down the cabin, a few of them on the razor edge of panic.

'Shut up!' Colin screamed. 'Shut up and sit down!' He looked at the passengers. Most of them were on their feet, some even stepping out into the aisle. 'Sit fucking down!' Colin roared, pointing his gun towards the roof of the plane and pulling the trigger. 'Sit down or I'll fucking well drop you!' The explosion from the blank cartridge brought a stunned silence as every face turned towards Colin, mouths wide in shock and fear.

'Next bullet goes into you!' He pointed his gun at one of the passengers who had stepped into the aisle. 'Now get back to your fucking seats! Get back into your seats or we'll all go fucking down!'

As the plane steadied and settled down to normal flight the disturbed passengers sank back into their seats, faces scared, voices quietened as the stark scent of fear permeated the cabin.

Colin stared at Doc with worried eyes and threw him a questioning look. Doc could only shrug. The thundering engines made conversation almost impossible, but they both knew that something had gone drastically wrong.

Tapping his chest, Colin pointed down the aisle at the cockpit door then back at his chest again. Doc nodded back in understanding and drew his automatic, making sure that the passengers saw it. With a tight nod Colin turned and made for the cockpit, silencing the rising murmur with a wave of his still smoking gun.

★

On the ground, Bert stared at the Dakota as it droned steadily past, far over to his right. Sick at heart, his throat hoarse from shouting, he watched helplessly as the plane flew on towards the coast.

★

Ray looked to his right as he regained control of the plane. Already the fire had slipped under the wing and out of sight behind him. His eyes scanned the instruments, his experience with the Dakota at Southend making them familiar to him. In fact the basic flying instruments – airspeed indicator, artificial horizon, altimeter and compass – were very similar to the instruments on the light aircraft he had trained on. Concentrating hard, he tried to recall all he had learned from the compact flying course. The control column was pushing back against his hands, as if some weight was forcing the plane's nose upwards. *The gold!* Almost 600 pounds of it must be sitting at the rear door now. He spun the trim control forward until the joystick felt light to his touch and flew on, straight and level. They were less than two minutes from the range of hills that shielded the coast.

'Fucked!' Ray cursed aloud. 'Three million quid lost! And so close too.' He picked up the microphone to pass jumping instructions to Bert and Doc when the door burst open behind him. The microphone dropped from his hand as he grabbed the machine gun from the co-pilot's seat.

'It's me!' He heard Colin's voice as he spun round, finger already caressing the trigger of the deadly weapon. 'What the fuck's going on? What's happening?'

'Jesus!' Ray tossed the gun on the seat again. 'You scared the shit out of me. What's going on out there? I thought I heard a shot!'

'You did! I had to let one go to settle things down. They were going crazy out there. *But what the fuck's going on in here?*'

'I've blown it! That's what's going on,' Ray admitted. 'I missed the DZ by about a mile. You better get back and jump before we fly over the hills. You've got about one minute.'

'But . . . but can't you turn it?' Colin demanded. 'Fuck me! You spent nearly three grand at that fucking flying club. Surely they taught you how to *turn*, for Christ's sake?'

'Light aircraft, Colin. Light aircraft. Not these fucking things!' Ray shook his head. 'Not these!'

'You said you could put us there!' Colin yelled.

'You've got about thirty seconds before we're over the hills,' Ray roared back at him. 'I'll have to reset the autopilot and jump with you.'

'Fuck the autopilot! Turn the fucking thing round. You're flying it all right just now, aren't you? Surely it can't be all that hard to turn? Come on . . . At least give it a try. Fuck me, I'm risking my own life now on this.'

Ray sweated, his brain performing somersaults as he sought a decision. 'Who Dares Wins'. His old motto flared into his brain and the decision was made for him.

'Okay! I'll give it a go!'

'Good on you.' Colin slapped his hand on Ray's shoulder. 'D'you need any help?'

'Do I need any help?' Ray's eyes rolled upwards. *'I need a fucking miracle, mate!'* His grip tightened on the control column, his eyes riveted on the 'turn and bank' indicator. 'Better let Doc know what's going on.' He nodded at the microphone.

Colin stretched the coiled wire across the cabin as he keyed the transmit button. 'We're going round again! We're having another go!' he shouted into the mike.

*

Bert watched the DC-3 as it flew southwards. It was

almost over the hills and still no one had jumped. Worriedly, he watched the plane grow smaller, narrowing his eyes when it seemed to turn to the right. At first he thought it was his imagination, a distortion caused by the distance. But no! Now he could clearly see it side on. The plane was definitely turning! *The crazy bastard's having another go!* A wide grin split his face and he looked at his fire. The flames were rapidly dying. Quickly, ignoring the pain in his hands, he began tearing up clumps of scrubbush, heaping them on to the fading flames, unaware of the words he was yelling out.

'Burn! Burn!' He was working frantically, tearing his hands to shreds on the dry thorny bushes as he gathered in more fuel. 'Burn! Burn!' His cries rose into the air.

★

'Anything I can do?' Colin asked, slipping into the co-pilot's seat.

'Don't touch anything,' Ray pleaded. 'Just sit still and keep quiet, that's all. Once we start flying inland again you can look out for the fire. That's the point I'm aiming for. It should appear somewhere down to your right on your side of the plane. Keep your eyes peeled for it.' Nervously he scanned his instruments and leant further into the turn.

Nose on the horizon. Back pressure on the column.
Ray followed the drill he had practised so often on
the twin-engined Aztec at Southend. *Speed . . . 130
knots. Ball . . . in the middle.* He eyed the turn and
bank indicator and the artificial horizon, trying
desperately to keep the miniature wings at a steady
ten degrees. But still, as if they had a mind of their
own, the wings tilted more and more steeply.

Beeep . . . ! Beeep . . . ! Beeep . . . !

A chill of fear shivered down Ray's sweating back
at the piercing scream of the stall warning. The first
staggering shudder hit the plane and he surprised
himself as his hand shot out to slam the dual throttles
wide and put the plane into a shallow dive in standard emergency procedure. The screaming faded as
speed increased, the acceleration making the aircraft
lighter and easier to control. As soon as the controls
felt more responsive he dragged the plane's nose back
to the horizon and went back into the turn.

'Jesus!' Colin exclaimed. 'I thought we were well
away there.'

'It's okay. I've got control now. Just you keep
looking for the fire. I've got to have that to aim for.'

The plane had turned through 180 degrees and
was now flying back the way it had come.

'Can't you see it yet?' Ray demanded, reluctant to
take his eyes off the instruments.

'I'm looking. I'm looking.'

'Now you know how hard it was for me,' Ray told him. 'And I was flying this thing.'

'Okay . . . okay,' Colin snapped back at him. 'I can see what you mean.' He was silent for a moment or two. 'Jesus!' he said again. 'It all looks the same.'

'Split the ground up into small areas,' Ray advised. 'Don't try to cover everywhere at the same time. Section it up.'

Colin stiffened in his seat as an area of ground showed paler than the rest. The paleness spread and he realised it was smoke, then he picked out the two lines of fire and the arrowhead shape of the ruined building.

'Gottit!' he yelled. *'Gottit!'*

'You're sure?' Ray turned his head, trying to locate the site.

'There!' Colin pointed at right angles. 'We're passing it now!'

Ray breathed a prayer of thanks. He'd never have spotted it on his own, that much was certain. Now he focused his gaze on the feather of white smoke. 'I'll fly on for a bit,' he said. 'Give myself a better chance at lining up for the drop.' He nodded at the microphone. 'You better give Doc the word. He'll be wondering what's going on.'

A minute later he was coaxing the Dakota into a

314

gentle, more confident turn, exhorting Colin to keep his eyes fixed on the signal. At last he was lined up on it and throttling the engines back to their original 130 knots.

'You better get back to Doc now.' He told Colin. 'You've got about one minute to set up the drop. Same signal as before.'

Colin was already moving, a relieved slap on Ray's shoulder his only acknowledgement.

★

'What the fuck's going on?' Doc turned on Colin when he arrived back at the gaping passenger door. 'Up and down like a fucking yo-yo! Twice I've nearly been out the fucking door! And these bastards!' He waved his gun at the passengers, letting them hear his voice. 'They've been creating murder. I thought I was going to have to use this on them.'

'It's all right,' Colin's voice was tense. 'We're on the run-in again. *It's definitely on this time.*' He pointed to the seat belt sign. 'Same signal as before.'

Doc shook his head in amazement. 'And they call this *easy money*!'

Ray kept the plane's nose lined up on the smudge of smoke. When he estimated he was ten seconds away he flicked the 'Fasten Seat Belts' sign twice. The smoke disappeared under the plane's nosecone

315

and he counted up to three before flicking the switch repeatedly.

On the second signal Colin and Doc levered the heavy sacks over the sill of the door, releasing their grip on the automatic openers as the parachutes fell away. Hesitating only a fraction, Doc launched himself into space, snapping his head round in a textbook exit to see Colin hesitating in the aircraft's door. *'Fucking jump!'* he screamed, flinching inwardly when Colin, arms flailing, tumbled awkwardly out of the plane. Then Doc was in the stable position and reaching for his ripcord.

*

Bert followed the DC3's course with mounting tension, his hands balling into tight fists as the plane appeared to accelerate towards him, then jumping with excitement when two black objects fell away from the plane. The two bundles seemed to drop forever, plunging almost halfway down before silently swelling out into plump clouds of camouflaged nylon. Below them, suspended on invisible rigging, his future swung to and fro in the clean bright air. Then another two shapes dropped from the plane and a feeling of exultation charged through Bert like a bolt of electricity. His chest swelled, and he raised his arms in victory as an animal scream of triumph ripped free from his throat.

'Ye . . . e . . . e . . . e . . . ah!'

He broke his mad run in dismay, stumbling to a horrified halt as he watched a black mass accelerating earthwards, flailing arms and legs telling him it was a human body.

'The ripcord,' he screamed, his cry rising high in the air. 'For Christ's sake, Colin! Pull the fucking ripcord!' he yelled. Almost as if his voice had been heard, a small square of cloth shot out from the hurtling mass dragging an explosion of silk behind and Bert gasped in relief. But the parachute had only half developed when it crashed into the ground, less than 100 yards from where he stood. Horrified, Bert rushed forward, tears already streaming down his face as the white canopy settled over the still figure, like an undertaker's shroud. 'Jesus, Colin. I fucking told you.' He stumbled to his knees beside the inert shape and lifted the silk away from the body, only to start back in surprise at the sight of Doc's dead face.

'Doc!' Bert stared in total shock.

*

Ray engaged the autopilot, wrenched the two hand-microphones from their sockets and smashed their casings hard against a bulkhead. He mangled the

317

wire-slim mouthpiece of the headphones and used the butt of his gun to destroy the plane's two radio sets. There was little he could do about the hijack warning switch, but with no radio communications the pilot would be unable to give any details until he landed. With just two and a half minutes before the plane flew out over the South Atlantic, he worked furiously at coupling a coil of wire to a cabinet handle, paying it out as he opened the door and re-entered the passenger section. Some of the passengers had risen to their feet after Colin and Doc had jumped, looking undecidedly at the cabin door. They stood back when Ray burst out brandishing the Uzi machine gun.

'Sit down!' he yelled. 'Sit down or you'll all fucking get it!' He threw an electric detonator and a quarter pound of mock gelignite on to an empty seat. 'Show that to the pilot,' he snarled. 'Tell him the other half is wired to a timer on that door and if anyone tries to open it the cockpit will be destroyed and all of you with it. The plane is on autopilot and in thirty minutes the timer will switch itself off and he can open the door. *Half an hour and it will be safe.*'

Two or three of the men gasped, faces paling as they took in the warning.

'Thirty minutes! No sooner!' Ray hurled the words at them as he raced up the aisle, knocked a

318

sluggish passenger out of the way, threw the suitcase and the machine gun out of the door, jerked off his mask and leapt into space.

The rushing wind rumpled his cheeks and he settled quickly into the free-fall position, arms and legs spread wide to stabilise himself, automatically ticking off the seconds as he fell. The plane was already out over the Atlantic, but he allowed himself a full ten seconds of free-fall before pulling his ripcord. In that time he estimated himself to be 400 or 500 yards offshore and reckoned he'd need about 600 feet of controlled descent to make it to dry land. On the count of ten the ripcord of his Strato-Cloud sports parachute sent 260 square feet of sculptured nylon billowing out above him, trapping a massive cushion of air as the harness snapped tight against his body.

Shaped like a wing, the Strato-Cloud could be flown by opening or closing vents in its canopy, the escaping air ramming the chute in the required direction and allowing forward speed of up to fifteen miles per hour. Under the right conditions, and with skilled handling, a parachutist could maintain control over his direction, speed and rate of descent.

Ray flew the parachute in a long shallow glide, using the shaped vents to push him forward and allowing a drop-rate of about ten feet per second.

This gave him approximately sixty seconds of controlled descent; long enough for him to check the ground below and pick out a landing site. The huge canopy curved gracefully to the right as he selected a small clearing just short of the road. His glide angle had been shallow, but as the ground neared he pulled downwards on the steering toggles, opening the vents and going into a steep, almost vertical descent. The ground suddenly leapt up at him, but he averted a collision by raising his arms to close the vents and flatten out his flight, flaring into a faultlessly controlled stall inches above the ground, which allowed him to land on his feet in a textbook touchdown. A punch on the harness release and, like a snake shedding its skin, the canopy fell away, tumbling backwards on bubbles of trapped air to tangle in the undergrowth surrounding the clearing.

He did not waste time hiding the parachute; there was no point. Besides, it was highly unlikely that the valuable canopy and rigging would be handed in to the authorities even if they were found. The jumpsuit, helmet and goggles were torn off and thrown aside as he hurried towards the road.

He had walked half a mile before he had to plunge into thick undergrowth to avoid the first chattering locals as they trotted past, pointing and gesticulating skywards, obviously discussing the recent aerial phenomena. Ten minutes later he walked into the university car park at Cape Coast, recovered the keys from their hiding place and climbed thankfully into the parked Escort to wait for the others to appear.

★

Bert knelt over Doc's broken body, oblivious to the gold, unaware of Colin pounding towards him white-faced with shock. Together they tenderly removed the helmet and mask from Doc's unmarked face and untangled the harness of webbing that seemed to bind him in a death grip.

'Jesus Christ! I thought it was you, Colin.' Bert wept openly, flinging his arms wide in appeal. 'How . . . what happened?'

'His 'chute,' Colin said. 'It didn't open right. Look.' He pointed to a safety clip that was twisted out of shape. 'That's what's done the damage. He . . . he fell in the plane', Colin recalled. 'Went down fucking hard too. He must have fallen on that clip and damaged it.' Bert stared at the clip, eyes shedding tears. 'Why couldn't he have been more careful?'

Colin sighed and raised his eyes to Bert. 'It doesn't matter now,' he said. 'He's been careless once too often, the stupid bastard!' His tears came then, dropping unashamedly on to the strangely serene face of his dead friend.

'Come on.' It was Colin who rose first. 'We've still got to get away from here, Doc or no Doc.'

'Yeah,' Bert rose to his feet. 'But we're not leaving him here, not in this Godforsaken place. He's coming with us.' He put words into action, bending to catch Doc's body under the armpits and draping him across his shoulders in a fireman's lift. 'C'mon, we'll get Doc into the car then we can drive round and pick up the gold and the parachutes. It'll be a lot quicker than trying to hump everything back to the car on foot.'

'Aye,' Colin agreed. 'Good thinking. We've got to get clear of here rapid.'

Struggling with the unfamiliar awkwardness of handling a dead body, they managed to wedge Doc upright in the rear of the car, then, breathing heavily, with sweat pouring from both of them, Colin skittered and skidded across the loose shale towards the parachutes and the first sack of gold.

Working as a team, they unclipped the sack and began pulling out the gold-filled boxes, the rope handles making the job a little easier. Grunting with effort, Colin swung each box to a panting Bert, who placed them on the floor of the car and on the rear seat alongside Doc's body.

Time was passing fast as they hurried on to the next load then raced round to collect in the other

322

parachutes. But they kept up the pace, racing against the clock as they crammed everything into the car, unwilling to leave any evidence behind. Their teamwork paid dividends and, quicker than expected, they were done, the gold and equipment stowed safely away inside the car. Finally, both men stripped off their jumpsuits and stuffed them into the boot along with their other equipment, with the final parachute thrown over the distinctive green ammunition boxes, hiding them from a casual glance. Satisfied that they had gathered in any evidence or clues, they got into the car, nerves jangling, bodies reeking with the stale smell of sweat, and set off along the hill road to Cape Coast.

They sat silently for the first lurching miles, like two screws in the death cell, ignoring the grisly subject uppermost in their minds. Silently they stared ahead, both wishing themselves 1000 miles away from the horror of their situation.

'What are we going to do about Doc?' Colin finally broke the unnerving silence as the Peugeot plunged into the dark shadows of the forest and began to labour uphill.

'Well, we're not leaving him here,' Bert declared. 'He's going home for a decent burial.' He stared stubbornly at Colin, his face pugnacious. 'We owe him that at least.'

323

'Aye.' Colin's face twisted in pain, feeling he was to blame for what happened. 'Aye, he'll have to go home. But we can't just turn up with his body and ask for a ticket. There'll be questions – a lot of them. Especially after this.' He pointed at the gold.

'Yeah,' Bert's face screwed up in thought. 'We could always dump the gold where they would find it. That would take the heat out of the investigation. Make them less determined.'

'You know Doc wouldn't want that.' Colin shook his head. 'You know what he was like ... always giving them the finger. He'd hate to have done all this for nothing, even if he is ...' He gave a sigh. 'You know what I mean.'

Bert nodded slowly in agreement. 'Yeah. He'd be as sick as a parrot if we handed the gold back ... especially now.'

'So we'll have to fake his death, make it look like an accident. That way they'll allow the body home.'

'Jesus!' Bert objected. 'Fucking about with his body!'

'It's the only way,' Colin insisted. 'Either that or they'll tie him in with the hijack. If that happens it'll put the law on to you, then ...'

'Yeah. Yeah.' Bert rubbed his forehead with both hands. 'Jesus! What a mess.'

'You'll have to get him back to Accra. Anything that happens will have to happen there.'

'What d'you think?'

'What sort of accident, you mean?'

'Yeah.' Bert shifted uncomfortably in his seat, finding the subject ghoulish.

A large flying insect splattered itself into a bloody pulpy mess on the windscreen.

'Hit and run.' Colin whispered the words.

Bert wiped sweat from his face with clammy hands. 'I suppose so.'

'It's no good *supposing*. You've got to be sure.'

'There's no fucking alternative, is there?' Bert barked, his nerves jangling. 'It's out of our hands now.'

'Right.' Colin pressed his foot down as they crested the hill. 'We'll be at the car park in about five minutes.'

They were just two minutes from the junction with the main highway when they caught sight of a police barricade being pushed into position on the road below; the sight of flashing blue lights stunning them with the power of a high-voltage shock.

'No!' A disbelieving scream burst from Colin's mouth as he stood on the brakes and threw the gears into reverse to regain the cover of an embankment.

'Jesus Christ!' Bert burst out accusingly. 'An hour at least, you said!'

'But it *had* to be an hour,' Colin retaliated. 'Unless Ray fucked up in the plane.'

'If he fucked up on the plane, he's fucked us on the ground. Look!' Bert pointed down at the road. 'Fucking cops are everywhere!'

'But they haven't got us yet,' Colin replied, still trying to get his thoughts together. 'You can still get away.' He pointed into high grass. 'Through there! Cross the road a couple of hundred yards down and the uni car park's on your right.'

'And what about Doc? What are we going to do about him?'

Colin's face twisted in torment. 'I don't know,' he confessed. 'I never expected anything like this to happen. Never thought they could react so fast.' His head spun as he tried to think positively. 'We'll have to hide Doc's body and take our chances. If I get clear I could come back later and bury him.'

'What?' Bert was shocked. 'Leave our mate out here in the bush!' He got to his feet and glared at Colin.

'God knows, Bert, I don't like it. But what the fuck else can we do?'

'I'd sooner do time!' Bert wrenched open the rear door. 'He's coming with me.'

'Do you think you can make it?' Colin got out of the car and helped to lift Doc's limp body from the rear seat.

'I'm going to give it a good fucking try,' Bert told him. 'And if I make it, I'll make it carrying Doc.' He let the body lean loosely against the side of the car before bending to pick it up in a fireman's lift again. Seconds later he was swallowed up by the dense undergrowth.

Colin cautiously raised his head above the embankment and eyed the scene below; two police jeeps, and a minibus with flashing blue lights were drawn up by the roadside as a squad of uniformed police manhandled a barrier into position. The first cars were already pulling up. He saw the minibus disgorge a dozen policemen and watched as they formed two ranks at the side of the road looking onto the barrier.

The first driver was being questioned, one officer checking papers while two others inspected the car's interior and opened the boot, looking briefly inside before waving the car on. An inspector let out a bellow and marched towards them waving his arms angrily. Colin couldn't hear, but the inspector was obviously ordering his men to open the boot again and remove the spare wheel. In the meantime other cars passed through the roadblock unmolested.

He narrowed his eyes, noticing for the first time the blue cap-bands of the police manning the barricade. *Cadets!* They were all cadets. And the police training college was nearby. Colin watched with mounting hope as his suspicions were confirmed. They were cadets from Cape Coast Police College out on a practical training exercise! While the 'check' was being made, a sergeant waved following traffic through, waiting until the 'students' had satisfactorily finished with one vehicle before allowing them to stop and search another.

Colin turned out on to the main road about seventy yards short of the barricade, keeping a careful eye on activities. The sergeant was waving cars through and he took his chance. He couldn't afford to wait any longer, knowing all hell would break loose in the next half an hour or so.

The traffic slowed as one of the cleared cars pulled out and the sergeant marched importantly on to the crown of the road.

Move! Move! Colin closed up on the car in front, urging it forward, anxiously eyeing the search team as they scanned the approaching vehicles for another victim. His stomach lurched when he saw the sergeant's eyes focus on him. He recognised the interest in his look and knew he had been chosen. Desperately, he touched the brakes, making room to swerve round the car in front. Whatever happened, he had no intention of surrendering meekly to a search. Determinedly, he gripped the steering wheel in sweating hands and chose his path, preparing to crash through the barrier. Then he saw an arm stretch lazily from the window of the car in front and casually toss an empty Coca-Cola can onto the surface of the road.

Colin heard the anger in the sergeant's voice and braked violently as the car in front screeched to a halt allowing a posse of zealous cadets to pounce on the offender, grateful to have discovered a real criminal.

Breathless, eyes almost closed in relief, Colin saw himself waved through, positive that the sergeant could hear the pounding of his heart as he passed by. Four hundred yards on he came to a halt and, opening the car's door, vomited on to the road, his body heaving, the car's interior stinking with the stale scent of sweat and fear.

It was two full minutes before he could bring himself to continue to Takoradi.

27

Ray straightened in his seat as Bert appeared at the car park's entrance looking dishevelled and more than a little distraught. Sensing something amiss, he started up the car and drove towards him, leaning over to open the passenger door as he drew level.

'Jesus!' Bert exclaimed. 'I didn't expect to see you here.'

'What are you talking about?' Ray demanded. 'You knew the arrangements.'

'Something must have gone wrong. They must have been able to report in . . . send out an alarm.'

'No way!' Ray was positive. 'No one would have gone into that cockpit with that "bomb" on the door. No one would have chanced it, at least not until the half-hour was up. And even if they did, I fucked up all their communications.'

'Well, something must have gone wrong,' Bert gasped. 'Doc's dead and there are cops all over the fucking place. The whole thing's turned into a right fuck-up.'

'Doc's dead!' Ray interrupted, paling beneath his tan. 'Jesus Christ! What went wrong?'

'Chute never opened. He's dead all right,' Bert panted, breathless from carrying Doc's body nearly a quarter of a mile through thick bush. 'And there's a police roadblock just up the road.' He pointed to the left as they turned on to the main road, heading in the opposite direction.

'A roadblock!' Ray turned horrified eyes on him.

'Yeah. So much for our one-hour start! And Colin's stuck up there with a car-load of fucking gold! It's a right fucking mess, so it is. Over there!' He pointed at a clump of bushes. 'I've got Doc stashed in there.'

'You brought him with you!'

'Of course I brought him with me. You don't think I'd leave my mate lying dead in the fucking bush, do you?'

'Well . . . no,' Ray admitted. 'But without him we're clean. If we run into another roadblock with a dead body in the car we've got no chance,' he pointed out as he drew into the side of the road beside the bushes.

'Tough!' Bert stated bluntly. 'Anyway, if we leave him here his body will be found and they'd get on to us anyway. Come on. Give me a hand. We've got to get him back to Accra so we can set up an "accident".'

For a moment it looked as if Ray was going to

refuse, then he switched off the engine and hurried round to help Bert. Two minutes later they were heading east as fast as the Ford could move.

*

Ray vetoed the hit and run idea. 'No use,' he said. 'We'd attract attention rather than divert it. Start people asking awkward questions.'

'How's that?' Bert looked at him, puzzled. 'The way these fucking locals drive I should imagine road accidents are common out here.'

'Exactly! And because they're common they'll be used to the type and severity of injuries sustained. Doc fell more than half a mile out of the sky. You wouldn't get broken up like that if a car hit you.'

'Got any better ideas?'

'It's got to be a fall!'

'Again?'

'Have to be. It's the only way the injuries will be consistent.'

'Christ,' Bert stared, as if seeing Ray for the first time. 'You're a right callous bastard.'

'C'mon Bert,' Ray pleaded. 'We're talking survival here. If they become suspicious about his death they won't be long adding two and two together; they're not stupid you know. We're talking about our lives here. You do realise that, don't you?'

Bert sat quiet, seeing the sense in the argument but hating himself for being part of it – for making himself part of it. He nodded soberly, features rigid. 'Yeah,' he mouthed the word almost silently. 'Yeah, you're right.' He straightened in his seat. 'What are we arguing about anyway? We've not even made it to Accra yet.'

'I've been thinking about that,' Ray said. 'And I've a feeling we might be all right. We're clear of Cape Coast and there are only a couple of villages between here and Accra. That roadblock you saw must have been the only one they could find the manpower for in a hurry. It'll be different once they get them-selves organised.' His foot pressed harder on the accelerator.

'I hope you're right,' Bert spoke sincerely. 'I hope to fuck you're right.'

*

They were entering the industrial outskirts of the city when the first convoy of police and army vehicles shrieked by, frenziedly caterwauling up the centre-line of the highway, anxiously flickering blue lights and flashing headlamps, forcing traffic to swerve wildly to avoid their furious passage.

It was almost 6.30pm, the last of the daylight gone, when Ray found his way into the car park of the Ambassador Hotel. Bert went quickly to the room he should have been sharing with Doc and collected some supporter's regalia.

Feeling like ghouls, they draped Doc in a red, white and blue scarf, set a Union Jack-patterned cap on his head and pinned an enormous, patriotic rosette on his chest. They waited until a mob of roistering Cooper fans approached the entrance and, supporting Doc between them, they entered the foyer, mixing with the crowd, just another trio of drunken supporters. No one paid any attention as they staggered into the lift and pressed the button for the sixth floor.

Inside the room, they cut the jump suit from Doc's body and liberally sprinkled whisky on his face and chest, leaving the open bottle on the table next to a half-filled glass.

'Jesus,' Bert wiped his sweating forehead. 'Why didn't we just leave him below the window? This . . . this is fucking awful.'

'Witnesses, Bert. We need real live witnesses for this. It's got to look like a genuine accident.'

'Oh, shit . . . I know,' he grimaced. 'It just seems so . . . so cold-blooded.'

'Got to be done.' Ray's voice was steady. 'And talking of witnesses, you better get yourself downstairs and into the bar.'

'Downstairs to the bar?'

'Yeah. And put yourself about a bit. Make sure you're noticed. That way the law won't bother you with too many questions.'

'Jesus, you are a cool bastard,' Bert admitted, shaking his head.

'I've had the best training in the world,' Ray told him. 'Now, move! On your way. I'll do the necessary with Doc.'

'Well, thanks for that anyway,' Bert said, moving to the door. 'How long will I give you?'

'You'll know how long when the screaming starts. Now hurry up before I lose my fucking nerve and end up drunk myself. I'll give you five minutes to establish your presence in the bar – then it's a go. I'll sneak back to my own hotel when I've . . . finished.'

Five minutes later Ray was ready. 'Sorry, mate.' He squeezed Doc's shoulder as if he was still alive and carefully toppled his body into the night. Seconds later, just as Bert was loudly ordering a drink in the lounge, the screaming started.

28

Colin drove the Peugeot into the garage behind his uncle's bungalow, switched off the engine and cradled his head in his arms against the steering wheel with a long, drawn-out sigh. He had always thought the firm could do it and now they had, but at what cost? He sighed again, thinking of Doc and his cheery, slapdash attitude to life. At this very moment he would have swapped all the gold in the world if it could have brought his friend back. Yes, and considered it a good exchange too. For the first time in his life he sincerely regretted his involvement in villainy. Since the moment of Doc's death he had been too preoccupied with his own safety to think of anything other than getting clear with the booty. But now, in the safety and coolness of the darkened garage, Doc occupied his thoughts infinitely more than the gold did. At last he stirred himself. Recriminations would do no good. They had the gold and he could start to think of the future. All he had to do was get it home and he could begin a future free from the dangers of crime. A future with Lesley. *Poor old Doc,* he sighed again. *One of the best.*

He made sure that the distinctive green boxes were out of sight under the folds of parachute material before locking the car and going into the bungalow.

The Cooper-Alloteh fight almost faded into insignificance against the challenge of the hijacking. Radio and television programmes were constantly interrupted as fresh information was released; each more distorted than the one before as newscasters vied for an exclusive. All that was really certain was that flight GA 670 from Kumasi had been hijacked and robbed of its cargo of gold bullion and the white mercenaries, terrorists, or criminals – as they were indiscriminately labelled – had parachuted to safety with their loot. A gigantic manhunt was in progress along the central coastal region and there were high hopes of an early arrest.

*

'Professionals, Colin. Professionals. That's what they were. Paid mercenaries recruited by one of the anti-government factions. A political group tried to steal the gold from the mine last year, you know. But it all went rather badly for them.'

'I heard they were shot.'

337

'True,' George nodded sadly. 'But not so much for trying to steal the gold, as the purpose they intended to put it to.'

'What was that?'

'Anti-government propaganda. Publicising political activities. Exposing corruption and organising rallies, all that sort of thing. And with the state the country's in right now the situation is ripe for another coup. All that's been missing is something to set it off, and this gold robbery could very well be the spark that ignites it.'

Colin nodded in agreement with everything George said, fervently hoping that this was the line being taken by the authorities. It would divert enquiries from the purely criminal aspect of the robbery.

Later, as he was sipping a welcome beer on the verandah after dinner, George asked him about his plans for the evening.

'You'll be coming along to the club tonight?' he queried. 'They've managed to arrange one of these TV projectors with a satellite link-up; it'll be as good as a ringside seat.'

'I heard about it,' Colin told him. 'But it's being beamed straight into the Princess on the big screen, and that'll be ten times better than the club's set up.'

'The Princess! My God, the place will be packed

with screaming locals! We've even had to give the back-shift the evening off and close down the mill. It'll be bedlam down there tonight.'

'No more so than the stadium itself,' Colin countered. 'Besides, the crowd's all part of the big fight atmosphere. It'll be more like the real thing.'

'You don't have to make excuses, m'lad.' George rose from his chair. 'You please yourself where you go to watch the fight. But it does seem to me that you've been spending a bit too much time with the Africans lately.' It was as close as he had ever come to telling him off and Colin had nothing to say as the door closed on him. Ten minutes later George emerged from his room, ready to leave for the club.

'Just watch yourself.' His voice was friendlier now. 'These Africans can become very excitable you know.'

'I'll be all right.' Colin thankfully accepted the olive branch. 'Once the fight's over I'll come along to the club for the party.'

'That'll be fine,' George's voice expressed pleasure. 'I'll be looking for you. But don't leave it too late or that mob down there will have finished off all the beer!' He threw the warning over his shoulder as he got into his car, leaving a friendly 'parp parp' hanging in the air as he drove away.

★

The factory was deserted when Colin parked his car at the entrance to the loading-bay and made his way to the packing section. Once there, he selected twenty empty cartons from the store, placing one of them in position under the nozzle of the cocoa butter tap and pulled the lever, keenly watching the scales. At six kilos the carton contained a four-inch layer of butter and within ten minutes the rest of the cartons contained a similar amount. When he was finished he wheeled the twenty part-filled cartons into the refrigerator and hurried back to his car; he still had plenty to do while the butter hardened.

It took three trips to pile the gear in front of the oil-fired furnace and a further five minutes to stuff everything through an inspection hatch into the roaring inferno. Parachutes, harnesses, jumpsuits, gloves, helmets and goggles were all fed into the searing flames and he watched as the flimsy, swirling materials of the canopy and lines flash-burned into a fine ash. The heavier canvas harnesses took a little longer, but in a couple of minutes only the metal buckles and fasteners were left glowing hotly on the floor of the furnace. Finally he reached inside with a long, metal, rake-like tool and fished out the melting metal parts, hosing them down with cold water before carrying them back to his car to put them into a bag that already contained the guns used in the robbery. Now he turned his attention to the bullion boxes, their thick rope handles making carrying easy. With one in either hand he made ten trips between his car and the packing section.

Every time he forced one of the wooden boxes open Colin just couldn't help grinning in satisfaction, the sight of the gold even making him forget for the moment his sadness at Doc's death. *Pick up a bar and you can keep it.* He could hear Fred O'Hara's voice in his head and he laughed aloud, counting: 'One, two, three, four . . .' until twenty bars of gleaming Ashanti gold winked back at him from the table he had stacked them on.

Ready now, he brought the part-filled cartons through from the refrigerator section and placed one of them in position under the cocoa butter valve. Working quickly, he lowered a gold bar onto the layer of hardened butter and opened the valve, using the skills he had gained at his practice sessions to cut off the flow at precisely twenty-five kilos. A frown crossed his face; he had not considered the weight-to-mass ratio of the gold and the carton was barely half full. As soon as any weight went on top of the carton it would collapse – a dead giveaway.

Swearing to himself, he studied the problem. Maybe he was working too fast. He took deep breaths in an effort to slow his pounding heart and began to think things out. Finally he went into the bagging area and brought back a number of the large hessian sacks. Rolling up his sleeves, he plunged both arms into the carton and grabbed the hidden bar. Obuasi again! The heavy bar, slippery with butter, refused to budge. He tried forcing his fingers under the gold, but the layer of frozen butter was too hard. His arms coated to the elbow, he stopped to reconsider.

Slow . . . Slow . . . he told himself. *Think it out.* He picked up one of the hessian sacks and pushed it down into the soft cocoa butter, kneading the loosely woven cloth in the thick, viscous cream so that it was soon soaked through, causing the level of the cocoa butter in the carton to rise substantially. Two more of the sacks brought the butter level up to the carton's rim and added only a few ounces to the total weight. When the cocoa butter hardened the saturated sacks would give enough strength to prevent the boxes from buckling too easily, and he would help matters by seeing that the finished packages were placed on the top layer in the cargo hold. Colin was satisfied with the job and attended to the remaining cartons in the same way. By 10.30pm the prepared cartons were back in the refrigerator. Sweating hard, he collected the broken bullion boxes and carried them to the furnace, watching as they disappeared in a blazing inferno. A final inspection of the weighing room for any incriminating evidence and he headed for his car, hurrying so that he could catch the last few rounds of the fight and make people aware of his presence.

On his way to the Princess he made a short detour and lobbed the bag of guns and metal pieces into the deep, dark water of the harbour.

29

Bert didn't need to pretend grief. Doc's death had been a genuine blow and the subsequent handling of his body had affected him deeply. The huge police inspector was both sympathetic and censorious.

'Your friend was obviously under the influence of strong drink,' he said, his voice an impressive basso profundo. 'I have your admission that you both spent the entire afternoon touring city bars and returned to your hotel to continue drinking in the evening.' He shook his head, heavy jowls sagging on his sad face. 'It is not surprising that such accidents occur.'

'We didn't drink that much,' Bert said, feeling it would be natural to object a little. 'Just a few beers and the odd glass of whisky. That's all we had.'

The inspector's black Brillo pad of an eyebrow curved sceptically upwards. 'Perhaps the heat affected him?' the inspector suggested, not unkindly. 'However, what is done cannot be undone and now I must ask you to formally identify the body.'

Bert blanched, looking worse than ever. 'Must I?'

'I am sorry. But yes, it must be done.'

'But you've got his passport . . . You know his identity.'

'Formalities in Ghana are no different from those in your own country, sir. In fact it was your colonial ancestors who instituted such proceedings here, and our government saw no reason to alter them. As there are no members of the deceased's family available, the duty falls upon you.' His jowls quivered again and he rose to his feet, surprisingly light for a man of his bulk. 'I would like the matter dealt with as soon as possible.'

Bert's reluctant face twisted uncomfortably. 'Will his body be ready to go home once I've done the identification thing?'

'I am sorry, sir. Your colonial predecessors were very pedantic about these formalities. First there will be an autopsy, then a hearing in the Coroner's Court. I am afraid that it will be at least three days before the needs of bureaucracy are satisfied and the body of your friend is released either for burial or to be flown home.' He flung a look at his wristwatch.

'I have just enough time to take you to the morgue before I report for duty at the sports stadium.' Fight time wasn't very far away and, like most of the

345

sports-minded citizens of Accra, the inspector intended to be there when the Ghanaian champion defeated the upstart challenger from England.

30

By the time Colin arrived at the sports club a rowdy party was in full swing, celebrating an easy eight-round knock-out by Cooper. His uncle waved to him, but he had already spotted Lesley and pushed his way towards her.

'Hi!' He gave a broad smile, the tension of the last few weeks erased by the success of his plan, his mind so involved in playing out his part that he had temporarily blanked the memory of Doc.

Lesley stared at him for a long, wordless moment and he wondered at the troubled expression on her face.

'I want to speak to you, Colin,' she said, avoiding his arms as he stepped closer.

'Yes?' He stopped, feeling awkward, the rebuff registering and puzzling him.

'Not here.' She moved towards the door which led to the living quarters, leaving him to follow on behind, her back stiff with disapproval.

The living room was quiet after the revelry of the

347

lounge and when she turned to face him, standing just out of his reach, her attitude warned him to keep his distance.

She gave him a deep, searching look, making him feel uncomfortable as he tried to figure out what was bothering her.

'Well?' She spoke one word and compressed her lips into a tight red line.

A wave of confusion swept over him. 'Well what?'

'Isn't there something you want to tell me, Colin?' Her face was a mask of accusation.

'Tell you what?' He looked at her, his brain racing, trying to figure out what had provoked her attitude. 'What are you talking about?'

'Colin!' Her whole body stamped at him.

Christ! He thought. *Surely she can't suspect me of . . . No!* He dismissed the burgeoning thought. *How could she? But, then again, what else was there?* He stared into her eyes, seeing both pain and concern in them.

'I don't know what you're talking about,' he finally answered.

'Why are you telling me lies, Colin?' She clasped her hands in front of her chest, creating a barrier between them.

He searched his mind for some clue to her behaviour, the feeling growing in him that the only possible explanation was the robbery. He continued to stare at her and felt trapped. What if it was just a jealous tantrum? He had neglected her more than just a little over the last few weeks. *That must be it,* he told himself. *It couldn't be the robbery.*

'Look, Lesley.' He moved closer and reached for one of her hands. 'I'm sorry I haven't been much company for you lately.'

She snatched her hand back. 'Why can't you tell me what you have done?'

He felt the snare tighten, yet still clung to the hope that it was something else that was troubling her. He searched for a way to resolve his predicament without making an outright admission.

'I haven't any idea what you're talking about,' he finally said, forestalling her obviously rising ire by adding, 'but if you tell me what you think it is, and you're right – I'll admit it.'

'Colin!' She looked at him and furiously shook her head. 'You are so transparent.'

He stared back confidently. She *couldn't* know anything.

'You had something to do with that gold bullion robbery!' Her face was set.

Strangely, her accusation didn't surprise him. In fact it was almost a relief to have it out in the open. But even after his promise he fought a last-ditch battle of denial.

'Who, me?'

'Yes, you.' She pursued him relentlessly. 'For weeks now I've hardly set eyes on you and on the odd occasion when you have appeared you've either been exhausted or totally preoccupied. I put it down to the heat at first. At one time I even began to wonder if you had found someone else. Then this evening I was talking to your uncle and it was obvious that he thought we had spent the day together. I had no idea what you were up to, so I didn't tell him that I hadn't set eyes on you all week, never mind today! Then I heard the news of the robbery. I was busy the first time I heard it and didn't pay much attention. But when the details started coming in, hijacking a plane and escaping by parachute, it all fell into place. That day at Cape Coast, the way you stared at that plane, as if it was some sort of miracle. Then rushing me round the museum and dumping me back here as if I had a nasty disease. Then there was your unexpected boat trip to God knows where. Your whole attitude changed from that moment. It was as if you had something constantly on your mind. And you had too! You've been planning to steal that gold ever since you saw that plane at Cape Coast!'

'Aye.' His voice sounded far away, as if someone else was doing his talking for him. 'Aye,' he repeated, trying to regain some of his self-control. 'You're right.' He had to sit down.

'Why, why, why?' She held her hands out to him, jerking them in time to her words. Then she clasped both hands to the side of her head as if shutting out the facts.

'Our future. I did it for our future.'

'You think I want a future with someone who can casually hijack an aeroplane?'

'I had nothing to offer you,' he appealed. 'This sets us up. Gets me away from villainy forever. We'll never need to worry about money again.'

'But it's not your gold!'

'And it's not the government's either,' he argued. 'They've been stealing it for years. Driving the country into poverty.'

'Oh! So now you're an authority on Ghanaian politics?'

'I met this guy . . . a lawyer. He told me what was going on.'

'And who was this lawyer?'

'A Ghanaian, Yarty Okufu. He helped me with my visa, then I bumped into him on the plane. He told me he was the son of the Asantehene, King of the Ashanti or something. Anyway, he's some sort of a big shot and he seemed to know a lot about things.'

'And he told you about the gold?'

351

'Not exactly. He just told me about the general state of things: corruption in the government, systems breaking down, workers being ripped off and stuff like that. He was really bitter about it. Said he was coming home to try and help his people.'

'And it's all true,' she agreed. 'But that doesn't entitle *you* to steal their gold.' She gripped his hands. 'You must give it back, Colin. If not to the government then, at least, to the people who will benefit most from it.'

'I can't,' he said. 'There are other people involved. I couldn't hand it back now, even if I wanted to.'

'And you don't want to?'

He looked her straight in the eye. 'If I was the only one involved, and it meant so much to you . . . yes, I would give it back. But the decision's not mine to make. I'm sorry.'

'Oh, Colin!' A tear rolled slowly down each cheek and he rose to hold her, feeling her body tremble against him. 'What are we going to do?'

The rest of the evening was an anti-climax for him and at one in the morning he made his excuses and headed back to the cocoa mill, stopping only to deposit a letter in the company's mailbox as he passed the post office. This time he went straight to the refrigerator and transferred his cartons to the packing department. It took him over three hours to

352

make a passable job of sewing the cartons into their hessian sacks. His final task, before stacking the finished packages in a secluded corner, was to stitch labels onto each of them. They read:

Mr J. Thompson (Purchases)
Hansel Of London (Confectioners)
632 Goldhawk Road
Shepherds Bush
London UK

Tomorrow morning, or more correctly, in a few hours' time, George would be surprised to find a cash order for 500 kilos of cocoa butter in the morning mail. The International Money Order to cover the purchase price and shipping costs might cause some comment, but it would certainly ensure that the Hansel of London order received prompt attention.

31

At the airport, happy Cooper fans were becoming restless as yet another delay was announced. Few of them realised the reason for the hold-up; they were too busy celebrating their champion's success to appreciate the local news, however sensational. But Bert was very conscious of the heavy police and military presence. There seemed to be uniforms everywhere. One fan struggling with a heavy suitcase was approached by two armed soldiers to have his suitcase unceremoniously torn from his grasp and thrown open to display a selection of wood carvings. With no apologies the soldiers moved on, their eyes already tracking another heavily laden fan.

Bert looked around, thankful for his immediate companions. Attending the morgue the night before had been a harrowing experience. An officious administrative clerk insisted on questioning him regarding the disposal of the body, taking notes and asking questions regarding payment for the undertaker's services and air-freight charges to fly 'The

Deceased' home, as if he was dispatching a piece of machinery or furniture. However, the man had been ruthlessly efficient and had quickly ascertained that Doc's travel insurance would indeed meet all charges. This put a smile on his face and an end to his questions. On his return to the hotel several of the supporters who were aware of what happened had invited Bert to join them. Strangers had become supportive friends, and he had gone to the fight to shout his support for Cooper along with them, consciously choosing to become 'one of the boys'. He just wished that Doc had been there with him to celebrate their own particular victory.

*

Behind the scenes angry airline officials were locked in combat with the authorities as pressure was brought to bear.

'I warn you,' the local British Airways agent raised his voice above that of the airport manager, 'the Ghanaian government will be held fully responsible for all charges or debts incurred by any delay.'

'I have two international flights arriving within the hour. I must have space,' the airport manager demanded, glaring angrily at the sinister-looking army officer who seemed determined to disrupt the smooth running of his airport.

Major Judas Akaba controlled himself with an effort, his basilisk eyes flickering between the carping men. Straight-backed, he stared them down, his own silence demanding silence in return. When he spoke his voice was calm, but inside he quivered like a bowstring, taut with the strain of suppressed anger. The hijacking and theft of the gold, *his gold*, gnawed deeply at him. He was well aware of his failure and already his superiors at General Headquarters had hinted at strong career repercussions should he fail to retrieve the stolen gold and bring the culprits to justice. The more he thought about the robbery coinciding with the influx of visitors for the big fight, the more convinced he became that the two incidents were connected. With so much at stake and with nothing else to work on, it was a possibility he could not overlook.

'Gentlemen,' he spoke through angry lips. 'A serious crime has been committed against the government. It is known that the terrorists are white men and almost certainly English, despite their foreign-sounding names. Is it not reasonable to suspect that they could be amongst this crowd?'

'I would imagine that to be extremely unlikely,' the tour organiser spoke drily. 'These people only arrived here on Tuesday morning, barely forty-eight hours ago. Hardly long enough for anyone to organise and carry out a robbery of this magnitude.'

'It is possible that the criminals entered the country some time ago,' Akaba countered. 'No one pays any attention to routine arrivals. But after the deed, when the alarm has been raised, they would need some camouflage to leave safely. What would be better?' He used his cane to point at the crowded concourse. 'I cannot overlook the possibility. The plane will not leave until I am satisfied that neither the gold nor the criminals are on board.'

'But the delay!' The airport manager pleaded. 'Other traffic is due.'

'What you are suggesting, Major,' the tour organiser interrupted, 'about passengers joining the plane for the return flight . . . *Camouflage*, I think you said?'

'Yes?' The weal above Akaba's eye pulsed convulsively, the skin throbbing visibly in an angry, shiny swelling.

'It's impossible! Every seat was occupied on the outward journey.'

'And why would this make it impossible?' Reptilian eyes narrowed maliciously.

'This is a special *round-trip* charter flight,' the tour manager spoke pedantically, 'and it is fully booked. Therefore if anyone intended to use only the return flight, it would have meant empty seats on the outward trip. However, as I have already mentioned, the flight was fully booked on the outward leg and there were no empty seats. It follows then that the return flight is also fully booked, leaving no seats available for new passengers. Ergo, your culprits cannot hope to board this plane.'

Judas Akaba was a logical man by nature and by training, and what the tour organiser said made sense. It seemed ridiculous to argue against such obvious logic, and he had just received a call suggesting that a body in the city morgue might be connected to the robbery. It was something he would have to check. But he sensed a connection between this plane and the robbery and a deep gut feeling told him not to let it fly. He would go to the hospital, but in the meantime he would issue an order that would delay the departure of this plane a while longer.

For a moment he stared balefully at the organiser. 'They could be using accomplices,' he said. 'The gold may even be hidden on the aircraft itself.'

'No!' The airport manager interrupted the verbal battle on the side of the tour organiser. 'The plane arrived direct from Rome less than three hours ago. It has been refuelled and pushed to its allocated parking stand and no one,' he emphasised, '*No one* has been allowed on board. Wherever your gold is, Major, it is most certainly not on board that aircraft.'

'I will order a body and baggage search of every passenger,' Akaba told them, confident that a painstaking search of over 250 passengers would give him time to visit the morgue and return again before the plane was cleared to take off.

'Then I suggest you set your men to work,' the airport manager quietly advised him. 'The facilities here cannot cope much longer with these numbers. Already half the toilets are out of order through vandalism. There has been sickness, even some fighting, and the first aid post is overcrowded.'

*

Alert for any change, Bert became aware of increased activity as workmen helped customs officers and airport security staff erect extra tables alongside the permanent counters. Then a loud cheer went up when the loudspeaker chimed musically into life with the announcement: 'Special Flight BA 142 to London is now boarding. Will all passengers of this flight please make their way to customs and passport control.'

The airport manager bustled about behind the tables like an agitated ant. He could not ignore Akaba's order but the extra tables and staff would certainly speed up the search process. In thirty minutes a long haul jet would be depositing another 250 passengers in his lap, and twenty minutes after that a 707 would be coming in with more passengers. He looked at his watch, winced, and ordered his men to hurry.

There were loud cries of protest as bags were roughly opened, their contents tipped on to the counter and ransacked by at least two officers in an orgy of efficiency. There were more protests as black hands squeezed and probed at bodies, feeling for any suspicious lumps or bulges. Finally a metal detector was run over the complaining travellers, every response disappointing the seekers as innocent bunches of keys or heavy belt buckles activated the alert. Then, quickly, the protesting fans were herded to the exit doors to run a gauntlet of police, soldiers and airport officials on their way to the waiting plane.

Bert dumped his canvas holdall on the worn customs table, pulling the long zip open to expose the bag's meagre contents. Nothing found; he was waved on to the body search. He wasn't in the least worried; he hadn't even been aboard the hijacked plane. With a satisfied smile on his face he stepped through the exit and walked towards the plane.

To Bert, it was almost like coming home. *That's it!*

he told himself as he settled into his seat. *Done it! Now let's get off the ground and out of here!* He looked down from his window seat, mentally urging the last of the stragglers to hurry.

★

The scent of death did not disturb Judas Akaba when he entered the mortuary in Accra City Hospital. Unperturbed, he waited alone in the frigid atmosphere, casually eyeing the shrouded cadaver which lay on a marble slab. He was beginning to enjoy the cold when the door hissed open to admit the sparse, blood-spotted, almost ghoulish figure of Doctor Benjamin Boesak, the hospital pathologist and undisputed ruler of this labyrinth of death.

'Ah, yes, Major Akaba,' Doctor Boesak held out a hand as clammy and eerily loose-skinned as the thin rubber gloves of his profession.

'You sent word that you had a body that might be of interest to me.' Akaba dry-washed his hands as he spoke. The dead didn't worry him, but those clammy hands and what they might have handled did.

'Ah, yes.' Boesak smiled, exposing teeth like worn tombstones, and moving to the draped figure on the marble slab. Slowly, like a curtain rising on a horror film, he drew the shroud from the body. Akaba swallowed and tightened his lips as the cloth

361

slithered to the floor to expose a scalpel-ravaged corpse. The deep exploratory chest incision began just below the bulge of the Adam's apple. From there it widened, huge chrome clamps pulling at sawn pink ribs, as if they were trying to tear the carcass apart. The slashing incision carried on over the soft belly flesh, forking left and right below the navel like lines to unmarked destinations on a map. Neatly placed to one side lay several enamel dishes. Akaba thought he recognised the heart, and there was some darker meat that might have been the liver or kidneys. A pale loop of glistening intestine drew his eyes to a bowl containing the sludge-like contents of the stomach and he almost retched, swallowing deeply to hold down his gorge. What was left of the body was a bloodless, blue-tinged mass of dead, white flesh, against which some heavy bruising across the hips and shoulders framed a sickening, surrealistic picture of the mutilated chest. Under the glaring overhead lights, it looked like some hideous detail by Hieronymus Bosch.

'And why should this body be of particular interest to me?' Akaba tore his fascinated gaze from the ruined remains.

Doctor Boesak referred to a clipboard he held in his hand.

'Joseph Docherty. Male Caucasian. Twenty-eight

years old. Native of the United Kingdom. DOA at this hospital at 19.15 hours yesterday evening. Cause of death: multiple fractures sustained in a fall from hotel balcony.'

'And why should the death of this man require my attention?' Akaba looked at him curiously.

'When the body arrived here the time of death was accepted without question. There were several witnesses who saw it on the ground seconds after the fall.'

'But you do not accept this?'

Boesak shook his head. 'I do not,' he replied, turning to the body on the slab. 'I began my post-mortem examination at precisely . . .' he referred to his board again, '10.25 this morning. It was immediately obvious from the stasis line,' he pointed at a faint, purplish 'plimsoll' line on the carcass at waist level, 'that Mr Docherty had died, I would estimate, anything between two and five hours before his body fell from the balcony of his room. And the damage is also inconsistent with a fall of around fifty feet, even if it was on to the surface of a concrete car park. In fact, I am able to identify several fractures that must have occurred a few hours after death, which would indicate that the body suffered a second fall some time after the original fatal injuries were sustained.'

'So you are suggesting that he was the victim of murder, disguised as an accidental death by falling?' Akaba anticipated him. 'But what has this to do with me?' he asked impatiently. 'It is surely a matter for the police department?'

'Normally, yes.' Boesak agreed. 'But I heard about the bullion robbery last night, and read in the morning paper that you were in overall charge of the investigation. I felt that you should be the first to hear my suspicions.'

'Suspicions?' Akaba looked at him, eyes suddenly slitted.

'Observe this heavy bruising between the legs and across the hips.' The blunt side of his scalpel traced the marks. 'And here.' The scalpel moved to the shoulders. 'These marks indicate a severe blow or jolt to the skin and musculature. After I qualified as a doctor I served two years with the military forces, Major Akaba, and I recognise this bruising as similar to the damage caused by a badly fitted parachute harness snapping too hard against the body. That, along with a smashed pelvis, broken ankles and compacted fractures of the spinal column, lead me to believe that this man was the victim of a failed parachute drop.'

'You are certain of this?' Major Akaba felt an excitement well within him.

'Yes, I am certain,' Boesak stated confidently. 'There is no doubt in my mind that there has been an amateurish attempt to cover up the true cause of this man's death.'

'You have his personal effects?'

'The police left them at the hospital reception desk.'

Minutes later Major Akaba was on the phone, talking to the police inspector who had interviewed Bert the night before. With growing excitement, he heard the inspector confirm his suspicions that the dead man was a boxing fan who had arrived in the company of another man on the special charter flight from London.

'You know the identity of this other man?' Akaba demanded.

'I cannot recall it offhand,' the deep voice told him. 'But he filled in the identification forms with his full name and address at the hospital last night.'

Two minutes later Akaba was at the reception desk scanning the DOA file headed 'Joseph Docherty'. Quickly, he turned to the identification entry. 'Albert Frederick Maddren, 26 Eustace Road, Fulham, London.' The name leapt out at him and he felt the comfortable glow of success suffuse his body as he reached for a telephone. 'Special flight BA 142 to London is grounded,' he barked into the mouthpiece once he was connected to the airport manager's extension. 'Have passenger Albert Frederick Maddren arrested immediately and hold him in secure custody until I return.'

'But that is impossible,' the plaintive voice of the airport manager sounded in his ear.

'Impossible!' roared Akaba. 'I am ordering you, with the power invested in me as a representative of our government, *to arrest that man!*'

'I am sorry, Major Akaba,' came the apologetic voice again. 'Special flight BA 142 took off more than half an hour ago.'

Akaba sagged against the wall, the sense of loss threatening to overwhelm him as victory seemed to be snatched from his grasp. One man dead, another gone, the gold God only knew where. A feeling of failure rose in him like a black tide of despair. Then a ray of hope appeared as he cogitated over his problem. The ray grew brighter and finally burst into full-blooded light. *Three men! There had been three men on board the DC-3!* And there must have been *yet* another man on the ground – the one who prepared the fire-pit and painted the end of the building. He must have been the one who set up the job. He must live in Ghana. Akaba straightened up and replaced the whining phone on its hook. There had to be a connection between the corpse in the mortuary,

Albert Frederick Maddren, the third man on the plane and whoever had been on the ground. It was axiomatic. And he had a positive lead now; much more than he had had a scant hour before. He was confident that Albert Frederick Maddren's name would be known to the police in the United Kingdom; Joseph Docherty's too – honest men did not suddenly involve themselves in serious crime – and through them the names of the others would come to light. Marshalling his thoughts, he dialled police headquarters and asked to be connected with the local Interpol liaison officer.

32

Colin couldn't help feeling he shared a secret as he entered the passenger cabin of the DC-3 at Takoradi airport.

'Going home?'

He dragged his eyes and his thoughts away from the centre section and turned to the man who had spoken. It was two days after the robbery before he had managed to book this flight to Accra. At this time of the year flights were heavily booked as most Europeans, particularly the British, took their annual leave to avoid the torrential, West African rainy season.

'Wish I was,' he replied with an ironic smile. 'But I'm only going to Accra to pick up my car.'

'Not another one!' The stranger grinned and held out his hand. 'Bill . . . Bill Keen.'

'Colin Grant.' They shook hands in the loose, easy manner of strangers who knew they would get along together.

'What did you mean then, *Not another one?*'

Colin wrestled with his seat belt and looked at him again.

'Left your car in Accra,' Bill grinned knowingly. 'Too much to drink after the fight the other night and had to cadge a lift home. That right?'

The explanation suited Colin and he nodded agreement. 'Well,' he said, 'after that result the booze went over easy.'

'Cooper! Cooper!' Bill held up two fists and gave a victory chant. 'Terrific result!'

'Same thing happen to you?'

'What?' Bill looked puzzled.

'Did you leave your car in Accra?'

'Oh, that! No,' Bill shook his head. 'I'm going home on a bit of leave. But I was at the fight and got lumbered with some guy afterwards. Blind drunk he was too. All I could get out of him was that he lived in Takoradi – at least that's what it sounded like to me. Anyway, I drove him to Tak' and dumped him outside the Post Office. S'pect he got home from there all right.'

'Probably couldn't have cared less anyway after that result,' Colin said with a smile. 'But I bet his wife won the other fight!'

'What other fight?' Bill looked quizzically at him.

'The fight he had with her when he arrived home without his car!'

They laughed together at the image.

'Have any trouble on the road home from the fight?' Colin asked when they had settled down again.

'Trouble!' Bill gave a wry shake of his head. 'Thank Christ I don't drink, that's all I can say. There were uniforms everywhere. I must have been pulled over every ten or twenty bloody miles and searched at roadblocks by police and army units looking for the guys that stole the gold.'

'Bit of a do, that,' Colin agreed with him. 'Give you a good spin, did they?'

'Had us out on the road while they searched the car,' Bill complained. 'Personally, I think they were getting at us because Cooper beat their boy in the ring. At least that's what the drunk kept telling them at Cape Coast, stupid bastard! Nearly got us locked up, he did. Still, it was worth it,' he said with a happy smile.

'Aye,' Colin agreed. 'Cooper really did their boy over, didn't he?'

'Cooper! Cooper!' Bill chanted happily. 'Next one's the world title!'

'How long you going on leave for?' Colin asked as the plane lifted off.

'Month.' Bill replied. 'A whole month in the sunny UK while everyone out here gets washed away in the rain. Yahoo!'

370

'Aye,' Colin smiled at him. 'I wish I was going with you.'

★

The keys were on top of the front offside tyre and in a moment Colin was inside the car. It wouldn't start. The starter spun sturdily enough, but the engine refused to be whirled into life. He twisted the key again and again, sending the coughing sound echoing over the parking area. Even if he had noticed, he would have thought nothing of the hotel doorman hurrying inside to make a telephone call.

'Fuck it!' he swore aloud. Cars were for driving as far as he was concerned, and their engines were mysteries for motor mechanics to ponder over. He let the engine rest for five minutes before trying again. In less than a minute the starter motor ground to a chugging halt as the last of the battery power drained off.

'Fuck it!' He swore again in exasperation and pulled on the bonnet release, although he knew that simply looking at it would do him no good. He was right. The engine looked perfectly normal to him, even fairly clean – which was about all he could tell about it.

'Perhaps if you fitted this . . .'

He spun round and found himself looking into the deadpan face of Major Judas Akaba. Panic flooded

371

his chest, but he held it down, forcing back the pressure of air that threatened to escape as a gasp.

Akaba extended an arm, an oddly shaped piece of plastic resting in the open palm of his hand. His face was neutral, but impassive eyes could not hide the excitement that coursed through his cold-blooded body. He recognised Colin immediately; from the mine and from two or more sightings on the plane at Kumasi. Adrenaline surged through him like a drug addict's 'rush'. Colin Grant! The hotel doorman had reported that a man had been helped from his car not long before Joseph Docherty had fallen to his 'death'. The doorman had been unable to identify anyone, but the timing had worried Akaba and he had immobilised the car, instructing the man to report anyone attempting to drive it away. Later, a report came in that a similar car had been seen in the university car park at Cape Coast. He had nurtured a hope that the car would provide him with a clue to the robbery, but this was almost too good to be true. *Colin Grant!* He fitted the mental identikit profile of the man he was trying so desperately to trace.

'What's that?' Colin's voice was hoarse. All of a sudden, speaking had become an effort.

'The rotor arm, Mr Grant.' Akaba was being impeccably polite. 'I had it removed to prevent the car being driven away.'

372

'Why did you have to do that?' Colin was regaining his composure. 'It was safe enough parked here.'

Akaba's predatory eyes flickered. He was confident that he had found his prey, but yet, with no hard evidence, and with Grant a British subject, he would have to tread warily. To arrest Grant now on the basis of guesswork and flimsy circumstantial evidence – evidence not even a Ghanaian court would accept – would only serve to alert his accomplices and destroy any chance of recovering the gold. He knew who he was after now and decided to pay out enough rope to let his suspect hang himself.

'Your car appeared to have been abandoned, Mr Grant, and became the object of suspicion. Unfortunately our car registration department is not as efficient as we would like it to be and they are still trying to trace the owner of this particular vehicle. Had it been traced to you this would not have been necessary.' He held the rotor arm out again. 'However, this car does answer the description of a vehicle seen in the car park of Cape Coast University two days ago – the day of the robbery – and I would like you to accompany me to headquarters so that we may eliminate you from our enquiries. A formality, of course.' His face altered a little to accommodate a slight movement of his lips that passed for a smile from him.

'Enquiries?' Colin looked suitably surprised. 'How could I possibly be of any help with your enquiry?'

Akaba smiled again. He had been correct. Grant would not be easy meat. Unconsciously, he let his tongue flick round his lips, like a snake preparing to swallow a tasty snack.

★

'I do apologise for the inconvenience.' Akaba's voice sounded sincere as he ushered Colin into his office at military headquarters. 'But your car was listed as a suspicious vehicle and I must eliminate it from my enquiries.' He moved a chair into position for Colin. 'I'm sure you understand.'

Nerves keyed to fever pitch, Colin wondered what made him so sure he would *'understand'* as he watched Akaba step round the desk to take his seat.

'I'm sure a short statement will satisfy my superiors.' Akaba's unblinking eyes seemed to be looking right inside his mind.

'Anything to help.' Colin shifted uncomfortably in his chair.

'Yes. I'm sure.'

Colin heard the man's intonation and wondered just exactly what was going through Akaba's mind. There was *nothing* he could possibly know.

The ritual of name and address was gone through. Easy questions. Easy answers. Ease the tension.

'If you will just tell me how your car came to be left for two days in the hotel car park?' His eyes bored into Colin.

Colin could hear his brain giving him advice: *Appear to be as helpful as you can. If there's something they don't know, but you know they will find out anyway, and it won't do you any harm – offer it up. It looks good to appear to be helpful.*

'It isn't my car,' he said. 'I only hired it to come through from Takoradi for the fight.'

'You don't have a car of your own?' Akaba's eyebrow became more offset in exaggerated surprise.

'Clapped out old Peugeot,' Colin told him. 'Couldn't chance it on a trip to Accra.'

'So you hired the Ford and left it sitting in Accra for two days?' There was very definitely scepticism in his voice.

'Not intentionally,' Colin told him. 'But after the fight, well . . . you know the result. We drank more than one bar dry that night. I could hardly stand, let alone drive a car.'

'So how *did* you get home?' The question was casually conversational rather than interrogative.

'Some guy at the fight. Bill . . . Bill . . .' He didn't have to pretend to struggle for the man's name; for

375

the moment it really did elude him. He screwed up his face in concentration. 'Bill Keen! That's it. He ran me back to Takoradi and dropped me off at the Post Office.'

'At about what time did you leave Accra?' This time Akaba stared hard at him.

'Jesus! I don't know for sure. But it must have been well on in the morning. I wasn't paying an awful lot of attention,' he grinned knowingly at Akaba.

Akaba said nothing, but rose and pulled open a filing cabinet. For a few minutes he studied several sheets of paper containing long lists of car numbers that had passed through the roadblocks that night. His eyelid twitched when he found it. '02.23hrs – BMW. TK 1025. Metallic Blue. William Keen c/o Fred Hill sawmills, Takoradi. One passenger – intoxicated.'

He looked up, eyes warily slitted. 'Mr Keen will bear witness to this?'

'We didn't talk much,' Colin grinned. 'But he'll remember me all right. Apparently I offended some of your soldier boys at a roadblock in Cape Coast over the fight result and nearly got the two of us arrested.' Silently he blessed his meeting on the plane and the fact that Bill Keen was at this very moment flying north at about 500 or 600 miles an hour.

Akaba raised his head and looked over at him. 'So you left your car at the hotel because you were too drunk to drive.' It was a statement that saved Colin explaining himself.

'That's it,' Colin moved his hands. 'I would have come back for the car the following day, but all the flights were booked. That's the reason it sat here so long.'

'I wish every mystery was so easily explained.' Akaba pushed the paper aside as his office door opened and an aide handed him a piece of paper.

'A telex from London, sir, regarding the Joseph Docherty accident.'

It was a reply to Akaba's request to Scotland Yard for any information on one Joseph Docherty, date of birth 15–01–47. Place of birth London. Listed among his 'known associates', the name Colin Grant stood out like a beacon. And alongside Grant's name blazed Albert Frederick Maddren. It was all Akaba could do to restrain a scream of triumph.

'Thank you.' He read through the message again, savouring the information, then placed it face down on his desk and asked the man to bring two coffees. 'How do you like your coffee, Mr Grant?' His eyebrows quirked again.

'Don't go to any bother for me,' Colin said, wishing he was elsewhere, the sooner the better too.

'It's the least I can do after inconveniencing you.'

'Well . . . white, no sugar, please.'

Akaba tapped a newspaper that was lying on his desk. 'An unfortunate business this; the boxing fan who fell to his death from the hotel balcony.' He shook his head. 'A long way to come to die in a car park.'

'I never read the report,' Colin told him, feeling a stab of pain at being reminded of Doc in this way.

'I don't suppose you would have known him?' Akaba enquired conversationally, making a space on his desk for the coffee tray and handing Colin a cup. 'Ground beans,' he said, nodding approval. 'Did you?'

The question disconcerted Colin for a moment. 'Did I what?' he asked, looking puzzled.

'I just wondered if, by any chance, you happened to know the man who died . . . a Joseph Docherty of London?'

'No.' Colin shook his head. 'London's a big place, Major. I never knew the man.' He bent his face into his coffee cup, hiding the pain in his eyes.

★

Akaba sat at his office desk after Colin had gone. Grant had made two mistakes: the roadblock at Cape Coast had been fully manned by uniformed police, not by *'soldier boys'*. But better than this, and infinitely more damning, was his denial of Joseph Docherty. He turned the telex message on his desk and read through it again.

'Why did you allow him to leave?' his puzzled aide asked, when told of the development. 'We could have made him tell us where he has hidden the gold.'

'No.' Akaba rubbed a finger on the smooth skin of his scar. 'If I arrest Grant now his associates will be alerted and the gold might disappear forever. Besides, three hijackers on the plane and one man on the ground makes four. So we let Grant run, but on a very short leash. As of now I want him under full twenty-four-hour surveillance. He will lead me to the gold – and the fourth man will be a welcome bonus.'

33

There was something about Major Akaba that worried Colin. Those dark, unblinking eyes had never once reflected the apparently casual tenor of their meeting. And he had been just that little bit too ready to accept his explanation. Then there had been his questions about Doc; too close for comfort. An eerie premonition disturbed Colin, and his hands tightened on the steering wheel. *The telex*. Why would the authorities in London be in contact with Akaba over a visitor's accidental death? Such accidents were very definitely a matter for the civilian police force, and a nuisance to them at that, wasting valuable time and generating unwelcome paperwork. It didn't make sense. Unless . . . his grip tightened further, unless Akaba had somehow or other connected Doc's balcony 'death' with the hijackers. And if he had made that connection, it would only be a matter of time before he discovered Doc's association with himself, an association he had already denied. He recalled the old con's advice about fear and went over everything in his mind. There was nothing in Ghana to connect him in any way with the hijacking – the white-hot furnace and the cold waters of the harbour had seen to that. The gold was safely away; he had personally seen it loaded and stowed for Tilbury on the *Lagos Palm* the day after the robbery. There was nothing he could think of that would point to him. Yet, just two days after the robbery, he had found himself facing Akaba over a desk, being asked if he had known Joseph Docherty. Coincidence? Or did the man suspect, or even worse, did he *know* something? He looked long and hard into his rear-view mirror and realised the same red Peugeot had been behind him for the last half-hour. *Coincidence or what?* he asked himself. After all, there was only the one road along the coastline. Yet when he slowed down the other car fell back, only to reappear a few miles along the road when Colin put his foot down again.

Hoping it was only a touch of paranoia, Colin kept his eye on his mirror as he turned off the main road and drove into the shelter of the cocoa mill. Behind him he saw the red Peugeot pull into the side of the road just beyond the gates. *Forget paranoia!* he told himself, feeling sweat suddenly bead out on his forehead and trickle down his face. *Definitely* time to be thinking about getting out of Ghana before

Akaba dug up any more information and decided to pull him in for a more physical form of interrogation.

★

'So you're thinking of going home?' George looked over the rim of his tumbler as they relaxed on the cool verandah.

'It's time I went home. You can get too used to this sort of life, you know. I've got to get back to real living again. Find a decent job and try to settle down.' He looked over at George. 'Lesley will be going home herself soon and I'd like to have something to offer her by the time she arrives.'

'That's wonderful,' George enthused. 'I had the impression that you two had fallen out.'

'We have had a bit of an argument,' Colin understated. 'But I think she'll come round.'

He was less certain than he sounded about Lesley. He had called at the club every day since she had denounced him, and although they had spoken, she had remained distant, allowing none of their former closeness. He sighed, and found himself wishing once again, and for more than one reason, that he could turn the clock back.

'Penny for them?' He jerked at the sound of George's voice.

'Just thinking of how much I've enjoyed it out here. The lifestyle . . . the people . . . the weather . . . It's been really nice.'

'You could always come back. Perhaps when it's more settled politically and there are jobs for Europeans again. Who knows?' George winked. 'You might even bring Lesley with you.'

Lesley! Colin agonised. It was going to be hard leaving her.

*

'You're going home?' They sat facing each other across a table in the club's empty lounge.

'I have to,' he said, longing to stretch his hand towards her, yet scared of inviting a rebuff.

'Have to?' She gave him a knowing look, but kept her thoughts to herself. 'When will you be leaving?' her voice was cool, the question a convention rather than a caring enquiry as they fenced like a divorced couple meeting unexpectedly.

'There's a Wednesday-night direct flight to London. I'm booking a ticket tomorrow.' He took a deep breath and reached across for her. Lesley's hand slipped to the edge of the table, but she let him reach out and gradually he teased her fingers forward until her hand was in his.

'I'm sorry,' he began.

383

'Don't!' She held her free hand up, as if to block his words. 'Don't make apologies, Colin. You made your decision. Did what you wanted. I don't want to talk about it.'

'But I love you, Lesley.' He squeezed her hand. 'We've never really spoken properly since . . .' He saw her flinch at the immense, unmentionable secret that lay between them. 'Look, Lesley,' he committed himself. 'I'm finished with all that business now. It's over for me.'

She looked at him incredulously. 'It's only over because you've got the gold, not because you've suddenly seen the light!'

'No, no, Lesley.' He lowered his head, thinking about Doc. He hadn't told her what had happened and the news media had failed to connect Doc's 'accident' with the hijack. There had only been a brief newspaper report about a drunken Cooper fan falling to his death from a hotel balcony. 'I . . . I can't explain it, but something happened that day. It completely changed my ideas. I can't tell you about it. But even if the gold wasn't involved, I'm finished with villainy for good. I want you to know that. And I want to see you when you come home.'

'As long as you keep that gold, Colin, I don't think we'll ever have a relationship with each other again.

384

I'm sorry, but I think that that gold should be put to use for the improvement of the Ghanaian people. They have little enough as it is. So if you really do want to see me again, you must see that the gold is returned.'

'Be realistic, Lesley,' Colin begged. 'Who could I give the gold to anyway, even if I did want to hand it back?'

'There's always Yarty Okufu,' she said. 'He has always fought for his people and against corruption in this country. He would know how to use the gold for the best.'

*

Colin parked outside the Kingsway supermarket in Takoradi and entered its cool interior. From behind a food rack he watched as a car drew in and parked on the opposite side of the road, its driver making no sign of leaving as he opened a newspaper and began to read. He didn't appear to notice when Colin slipped out through a side entrance and crossed the road to a small travel agent's shop.

It took Colin less than five minutes to purchase a flight ticket home and two minutes later he was getting back into his car outside the Kingsway store. Smiling to himself, he watched his sentinel follow him down into the dock area; there was a ship loading cocoa butter and the stowing had to be checked before it sailed that night.

*

An aide entered Akaba's office in a rush. 'Grant has just purchased a ticket on this evening's flight to London. Do you want him picked up?'

Akaba stared at the anxious man, eyes pinpoints of light in his dark face. Then his lips moved with a reptilian smile of satisfaction; this was a cat and mouse game he liked to play. 'Good,' he said, nodding thoughtfully. 'But no, I do not want Grant picked up, at least not immediately. After all, we know what flight he is on and we will have no problem intercepting him when he is about to board. So let us allow him to think he is free and clear, and then, when he is least expecting it, I will make the arrest myself. And I can assure you, Lieutenant,' his lips thinned in a sinister smirk, 'once I have him in my interrogation room he will be only too willing to tell us all he knows. Good,' he said again, already anticipating a lively interrogation session. 'All we have to do now is wait for Grant to walk into my trap.'

34

Colin boarded the mid-afternoon flight to Accra with ambivalent feelings. On one hand he was glad to be going home, on the other he was not happy about leaving Lesley. There had been a tearful parting in the departure lounge, but Lesley had made it clear that as long as he refused to return the gold there was little hope of them ever having a life together. All his arguments about securing their future had been to no avail; as far as Lesley was concerned he had no right to the gold and it should be returned for the good of the people of Ghana. In the absence of this, she considered their romance over. Sadly, Colin looked down as the plane climbed out over the coastline and headed eastwards on its short journey to Accra.

Back in Takoradi one of the agents assigned to follow Colin punched a number into a telephone. 'Subject one has boarded flight GA 228 to Accra. Agent Yanu is travelling on board the same plane.'

Akaba put down his telephone, satisfied that his

target was behaving exactly as expected. The mouse was heading straight for the cheese and in a few hours' time he, Judas Akaba, would personally spring the trap.

The airport was busy when Colin arrived in Accra but with only hand baggage he was quickly through arrivals and out onto the main concourse. Casually he stood by and watched the other passengers come through the arrivals gate. For the last few days he had been aware of the close surveillance on him and knew he could identify at least two of his satellite shadowers. He casually eyed each passenger as they passed through the arrivals doorway. One man caught his attention, or at least his brightly coloured shirt did. It was the driver of the car who had waited for him outside the Kingsway store that very morning in Takoradi. Colin looked round anxiously and caught sight of another man who was also watching the disembarking arrivals. He saw the Shirt, as he had christened his shadow, stare towards the man and give a slight nod of recognition. Colin felt the noose tighten; how many more of them were there? Acting casual, he made his way over to the café and 'relaxed' into a chair with a coffee, surreptitiously eyeing the other customers. A few moments later the Shirt ambled in and took a seat across the floor from him. Through the open front of the cafeteria he saw the other man take a seat facing the front of the café and pretend to read a newspaper; Colin was beginning to feel boxed in. He looked at his watch; barely four o'clock, more than six hours before the London flight was due. Time enough for him to do what he had planned.

'Where is he now?' Akaba asked for an update on Colin's movements.

'Still waiting at the airport, sir,' his lieutenant reported. 'Sergeant Yanu reports that he appears quite calm and does not suspect that he is being followed.'

'Good,' Akaba nodded approval. 'The more secure he feels the greater the shock when I confront him. I can't wait to witness his collapse.'

Back at the airport, a bored-looking Colin glanced at his watch; still more than four hours to wait. He yawned and stretched a little before deciding to make a move and headed for the taxi rank outside the terminal building. 'City centre,' he instructed the driver. 'Take me to a bar, a good bar. One with nice girls in it. You know what I mean?'

The taxi driver aimed gleaming white teeth at him. 'Yes, sah! I know what you mean. You like black woman, that what you mean. I take you to good bar. Always plenty ladies there.' He pulled away just as the Shirt and his colleague clambered into a car and fell in two vehicles behind.

The taxi driver pulled up outside a bar in a busy part of the city and turned to his customer. 'Here, sah,' he said, smiling all over his face. 'Plenty girls inside this place. Good girls; good beds. Always busy. You like very much, I think.'

'Aye,' Colin grinned back at him. 'Nice way to pass the time when you're bored waiting for a plane.' He looked at the man's meter and handed over his fare along with a substantial tip. 'I hope she doesn't make me miss my flight,' he said, giving the driver a knowing leer. Two minutes later he was at the bar and ordering himself a drink.

Outside the bar the taxi driver was still counting his windfall, when his door was yanked open and the Shirt spoke to him brusquely. 'Your passenger,' he barked. 'Why did you bring him here and what did you talk about?'

'I don't talk about my customers,' the driver protested. 'That none of your business.'

The Shirt pulled a badge from his pocket and held it in front of the taxi driver's face, making him swallow nervously at seeing the insignia of the secret police.

'Don't waste my time,' the Shirt snarled. 'You tell me now or I take you down to headquarters and chop off your hands. Now, why did you bring your passenger here and what did he talk about?'

The taxi driver stammered an answer. 'He he ask
m . . . m . . . me to take him to a b . . . b . . . bar with
girls.'

'He say anything else? Quick now, you tell me. Did
he say anything else?'

The taxi driver was still stuttering. 'He . . . he only
say that he b . . . b . . . bored waiting for plane. He,
he say he want nice way to pass the t . . . t . . . time.
That is all, sir. My heart to holy Jesus.' He blessed
himself as his door slammed and he was left sitting
alone.

Colin didn't look up when the Shirt entered the
bar and ordered a beer, but he saw that he had taken
up a position with a clear view of the mirror.
Ignoring the Shirt, Colin ordered another beer and
nodded over to a girl who had caught his eye and
smiled when she looked up at him. A minute later
she was at his table, happy to find an obvious
customer and sipping a cold Coca-Cola.

'You like me?' she asked, arching her eyebrows at
him. 'I good girl. Give you good time,' she leant
towards him, exposing a generous cleavage. 'You
see?'

Colin grinned at her and placed a hand on her
shoulder. 'I like you,' he drew her closer. 'I like you
very much,' his hand slipped down almost to her
breast, but the girl drew back.

'I am working girl. I give you good time, but you have to pay.' She rubbed her fingers together. 'You have to pay me for good time.'

'You give me good time, I pay,' Colin assured her. 'I pay you good. Come, we go to your room and have a party. Yes?'

'Yes, I like to party,' the girl rose to her feet and held out her hand. 'My room is upstairs. You come with me now.' She pulled him up from his chair to the accompaniment of whistles from her friends still at the bar.

'A bottle of champagne!' Colin ordered as he led him to the stairs. 'Send it upstairs along with some ice and a couple of glasses.'

The girl squealed with delight and turned to give him a full embrace.

'Better make that two bottles,' Colin called down to a delighted barman. 'It looks like this is going to be a long night.' The last words were shouted as he disappeared up the stairs.

The Shirt was already speaking to his superiors. 'He is in the Eros bar on Maxwell Street. He picked up a bar-girl and has taken her upstairs along with two bottles of champagne. It seems he will be there for some time.'

'Do not leave the place,' Akaba instructed him. 'But do not disturb Grant. Let him enjoy his last few hours of freedom. The shock of arrest will be all the more severe after his enjoyable evening.'

Inside the girl's room she turned to embrace Colin and was surprised when he ignored her open arms and walked quickly past her, going over to the window and looking outside. He had gone from a friendly drunk to a suddenly very serious person.

'There is something wrong?' she asked nervously, a little disturbed by his strange behaviour.

'What's your name?' Colin asked, going over to check that the door had a lock fitted.

'My name is Comfort,' the girl spoke quietly, still a little nervous as Colin tested the strength of the lock. 'We have a party?'

'Well, not exactly,' Colin told her. 'But don't you worry, Comfort, you'll get paid all right. Just wait until they bring up the champagne and I'll tell you what you have to do.' There was a soft knock on the door and Comfort was surprised yet again when Colin grabbed her and threw her on top of the bed. 'Come in!' he shouted, holding onto Comfort and squeezing her tight against himself as a waiter entered the room with an ice-bucket, the bottles of champagne and glasses.

'Put the champagne on ice and leave everything on the table,' Colin instructed. 'I'll be needing a cold drink after this.' He buried his head against

393

Comfort's ample breasts as the waiter followed his instructions before quietly closing the door behind him, a wide smile on his face.

As soon as the door was closed, Colin rose from the bed and turned the lock, making certain it was secure. Comfort rose to a sitting position, looking on apprehensively and wondering what this strange white man was going to do next.

'Right, Comfort,' Colin turned to her, pulling a wad of notes from his pocket. 'This is how you will earn your money.'

★

Downstairs the Shirt was questioning the waiter who had delivered the champagne to the girl's room.

'What were they doing? What did you see?'

The waiter rolled his eyes. 'Man! What I see? That man was hot. I think they have some party going on up there.'

In another minute the Shirt was on the phone again. 'He is holed up in a room with one of the girls here. Looks like he's settling down for a good time.'

'Stay at your post,' Akaba hissed down the line. 'Report in the minute he leaves the bar.'

★

Akaba sat impatiently in the airport manager's

office. It was almost ten o'clock and time was getting short. He looked at the clock again and reached for the telephone.

In the bar the Shirt answered the phone, stiffening automatically when he heard Akaba's voice. 'But he is still upstairs,' he replied to Akaba's question. 'He has been there for nearly four hours now. Yes, sir. Yes, sir. I will go up and check.'

The Shirt listened at the door, hearing the clink of glasses above the sound of music. 'They are still in the room,' he spoke into the open line. 'I can clearly hear them.'

'But his flight leaves in less than forty minutes,' Akaba barked into the phone. 'The passengers have already begun to check in.' He leant forward onto his desk. Something wasn't quite right here, he could feel it in his bones. 'Stand by your post!' he barked. 'I will be there within ten minutes.'

★

Two vehicles stopped outside the Eros bar, discharging Akaba and half a dozen of his men, some of whom he directed to strategic positions around the building. Satisfied he had covered any escape route, Akaba took two of his men and strode imperiously into the bar and, with the Shirt leading the way, climbed the stairs to the bedroom.

Akaba signed for quiet when they reached the landing and with guns drawn the squad crept silently up to the bedroom door. They could hear music and there was the clink of glass; obviously the party was still going strong. Placing a man at each side of the door, Akaba stood back and raised his foot. There was the sound of a giggle and he stepped forward, slamming his foot hard into the woodwork, shattering the lock and sending the door slamming back on its hinges. Akaba leapt into the room, his two men bundling in behind him, their weapons at the ready, to be confronted by the sight of a happily tipsy Comfort sitting on the edge of the bed, obviously alone and completely dressed.

'Where is he?' Akaba demanded, roughly pulling Comfort to her feet as his men quickly searched the room for hiding places. 'The man you were with . . . where did he go?'

Comfort shrugged and moved her shoulders. 'I do not know. I fell asleep and when I woke up he was gone, but there is still champagne so I party by myself.'

Akaba turned and raced out of the room. 'Back to the airport!' he shouted. 'There is still time to stop him.' The cars raced away from the bar, sirens screaming as they cut a swathe through the late evening traffic. It took them seven minutes to make the journey and Akaba quickly checked the names of the already boarded passengers; Grant's name was not among them, but a trickle of late passengers was still coming forward. Relieved, Akaba made his way to the plane and took up a position in the shadows at the foot of the passenger gangway; he would still have his moment of triumph, and looked up hopefully as a bunch of stragglers headed towards the steps.

★

Colin made his approach openly, not wanting to appear suspicious by skulking around. The gangway ahead of him looked clear and he mounted it, greeting the officer of the deck with a handshake. 'Just made it,' he said. 'Ran into a bit of trouble getting here, but better late than never, eh?'

'Had just about given you up for lost,' the officer said. 'Still, you're on board now and we'll be sailing within the hour. Welcome aboard, Mr Grant.'

Twenty-four hours later Colin was once again in an open canoe heading for the riverbank in Lagos. His open ticket was transferable and he could still make a late-night flight to London.

★

Akaba sat at his desk in Accra, his brow furrowed in

thought. Grant had proved cleverer than he had given him credit for. The discovery of an abandoned hire car in the docks at Takoradi had exposed his method of exit. But this had led to a new angle on tracing the stolen gold and he knew he could still recover the situation. Picking up his phone, he instructed the operator to get him a line to Scotland Yard. All he needed now was a little international police cooperation and the gold would be his again, as well as the satisfaction of arresting the remaining members of the gang.

35

Two beaming faces greeted Colin when he entered the main concourse of Gatwick Airport. He looked at Bert and Ray for a moment then a warm feeling of achievement suffused him as they clasped hands. The three of them together – safe – and the *Lagos Palm* was due to dock at Tilbury in just ten days! All they had to do was wait, and it would be all over bar the shouting.

*

The next week or so was a severe test of patience as the days dragged slowly by. But on the tenth day the three of them travelled to Tilbury to watch the *Lagos Palm* nudge gently into her berth. Excitement charged through them as the first hawsers looped round the dockside bollards and the ship was winched slowly alongside.

'How long before the delivery?' Bert asked, unconsciously licking his lips as he stared at the ship.

'The agent says two or three days,' Colin answered.

'I didn't want to press him in case he got curious, but someone will have to wait in the shop all day now, to be on the safe side – starting from tomorrow.'

'I'll be there!' Bert burst out. 'You don't think I'd chance missing out on the delivery of three million in gold?'

Colin gave a good-natured laugh. 'Aye, Bert, you've got a good point there,' he said. 'None of us will want to miss that. We'll all be fucking there.'

'Yeah.' Ray's voice was unusually subdued, as if he had something else on his mind. 'Yeah,' he repeated. 'We'll all be there.'

★

They never really expected delivery the first day, and although there was a better chance the following day, they weren't surprised when it failed to materialise then either. But on the third day their hopes were very definitely high as they settled down with playing cards and flasks of tea and coffee.

Colin was impatiently parting the venetian blinds when a lorry rumbled to a halt outside. It was a flat-platform vehicle and its tarpaulin was folded back, allowing him to see ten hessian-wrapped packages neatly stacked on its back. His sudden tensing and quick intake of breath alerted the others and they rushed forward from their chairs, voices quick with

400

excitement as they peered through the venetian blinds.

'Ye . . . e . . . e . . . ah,' breathed Bert. 'That's it!' He thumped Colin heartily on the back, his face wreathed in a delighted smile.

They could see the lorry driver checking the address against his delivery note. Then he climbed down from his cab and walked towards the shop's entrance.

'Got some stuff 'ere for you, guv.' The driver thumbed over his shoulder. 'Ten packages of cocoa butter – that be about right?'

'I've been waiting for them,' Colin told him straight-faced, trying hard to contain his impatience.

Across the road in an unmarked van a detective thumbed the transmit button of his high-frequency radio. 'It's on!' His voice quivered with excitement. 'Golden Net is a go!'

'Right then . . .' The driver busied himself with untying a rope before clambering up onto the lorry's back. He was surprised when he turned round to see a trio of uncommonly happy-looking faces eagerly waiting to help him unload, each taking a package onto a shoulder and striding urgently into the shop, repeating the process until the delivery was complete. The only job left for him was to obtain a signature for safe and satisfactory delivery.

'Er . . . 'scuse me!' He stood in the shop's doorway

looking at the three men as they stood round the packages. ''Scuse me!' He had to raise his voice to distract them, holding up his clipboard and a stub of well-chewed pencil.

'Oh! Yes . . . sure.' Colin dragged himself away from the booty.

'That's it, guv.' The driver watched Colin scribble along the bottom line. 'You'll be . . . ?' He squinted at the deliberate scrawl. 'Mr Thompson?'

'Yes, that's me.' Colin answered to the name he had given when ordering the cocoa butter.

'Letter 'ere, guv.' The driver held out a thick manila envelope.

Colin impatiently stuffed the letter into a pocket, fumbling for some cash as he shepherded the driver out on to the pavement before joining the victory celebration already beginning inside.

'Come on! Give it a shake!' Ray urged the thick-fingered Bert as he wrestled with the wire on a bottle of champagne and dodged aside when the cork exploded and he was caught in a spray of foam.

The atmosphere was glorious, loud cheerful shouts rising as they ducked and dived to avoid the worst of the spray, trying to catch some of the flying foam in cracked mugs to toast the safe arrival of the gold.

The sound of approaching sirens stopped them in their tracks. They stiffened like three dog foxes in

402

cover, willing the hunt to pass. Suddenly, tyres were screeching, doors slamming and heavy boots thudding across the pavement outside. They looked at each other, eyes wide in shock as once . . . twice . . . three times something heavy battered against the door, sending spears of splintered timber flying as the lock burst and a posse of figures in blue berets, black overalls and flak-jackets stormed into the shop.

'Police! Freeze!' The officers crouched in the firing position, each of them gripping Heckler & Koch nine-millimetre machine guns in their hands. 'Don't move!' More armed men charged through the broken doorway.

'Up against the wall and spread!' a voice screamed. 'I told you! Spread!' Rough hands pushed the stunned trio against the rear wall, kicking at ankles, forcing legs apart and hooking their feet backwards so that they were forced to lean on to the wall on outstretched arms as experienced hands felt expertly over them in a weapons search. Other footsteps entered the shop and Colin felt a hand on his shoulder spinning him round to face his captors.

Colin stared for a moment at the black face confronting him, his mind so numbed that recognition took time. Then he saw an eyebrow twitch, as if deliberately attracting attention, and realisation came to him in a tidal wave of shock.

403

'You!' He gasped into the leering face of Major Judas Akaba. 'But . . . how?' He stuttered into silence.

'I'm sure you know the "why" of it, Mr Grant.' Akaba's voice hissed low and sibilant. 'As to the how? Well, I'm afraid you must blame the death of your friend for pointing the way. And the mistakes you made too. The lies you told when I interviewed you that day. I knew then that you were the one I wanted, but I had to let you go temporarily so that you would lead me to the gold and to the fourth member of your gang. I would have settled this matter in Ghana, but you eluded me with your subterfuge at the bar and doubling back to Takoradi. But it seems my original decision to let you run has finally borne fruit.' He looked at the other two, still spreadeagled against the wall. Then he looked directly at the packages.

'That's my stock.' Colin stepped forward, pale with shock. 'We were just celebrating its arrival. A big day for me.'

'Big day?'

Colin had been so stunned by Akaba's appearance that he had failed to notice Inspector Lambert, but he recognised the voice and raised his eyes to look into the sneering face.

'You know, Grant,' Lambert said. 'I've got the funniest feeling that you're not exactly being truthful with us.'

'What have I got to lie about?' Colin was still reeling, trying to come to grips with the situation. 'This is my shop and this is my stock – cocoa butter, all bought and paid for. There's nothing wrong with that.'

'As long as it is only cocoa butter you've got there,' Lambert emphasised. 'Because we certainly don't want to find anything in these packages that might embarrass Her Majesty's Government, do we?'

'Of course it's only cocoa butter! What else could it be?' Bluff was the only weapon Colin had.

'In that case you have nothing to fear,' Akaba's voice insinuated softly. 'But then, we both know that you do have something to fear, don't we?'

'What have I got to fear?'

Akaba smiled grimly. 'Imprisonment . . . trial . . . Perhaps even death.' His lips thinned even further.

'What the fuck are you talking about?'

'I'm talking about you and your accomplices being taken back to Ghana to stand trial for the hijacking of an airliner and stealing three million pounds' worth of Ashanti gold. Both crimes of which I know you to be guilty.' His voice rose and venomous spittle flew from his mouth in barely suppressed rage. 'Either of those charges merit the death penalty in my country.'

'Ahem!' A polite cough sounded from one of the

figures at the rear. 'I rather think, gentlemen, that before further allegations are made some sort of evidence should be forthcoming.' A slightly stooped, elderly man pushed forward, holding a briefcase in front of him like a badge of office.

'Johnstone-Carruthers; Assistant Under Secretary, Foreign Affairs,' he introduced himself – without shaking hands – to Colin. 'I must witness the actual seizure of the gold so that there will be no delay in issuing extradition documents against the principals involved.'

'Extradition!' Colin stared dumbly.

'A formality, I assure you.' Akaba smiled grimly at him. 'Hijacking an aircraft is an act of international terrorism which no responsible government can, or will, condone. Your government has assured me of its total cooperation in this matter. It will not be many hours before you and your accomplices find yourselves on your way back to Ghana.' His tongue flicked round his lips hungrily, like a viper antici-pating its next meal. 'Then, Grant . . .' His thin-lipped smile never reached his hooded eyes.

'*If* you produce the evidence of the gold, Major Akaba,' the stoop-shouldered Assistant Secretary gently reminded him. 'I must see the gold before I can validate any extradition authorisation.'

Akaba turned back to Colin. 'Once Scotland Yard

sent me the name of your company and the address of this store, your scheme to ship the gold became transparent. It was simply a matter of checking the company records and shipping manifests to discover the hastily arranged Hansel shipment on the *Lagos Palm*. From there it was only a question of waiting until the gold drew all of you into the net.' He held his hands apart like a conjurer completing some sleight of hand. 'And here we are!'

'*If you don't mind,* Major Akaba.' The Assistant Secretary made an impatient sound and pointed at the packages. 'The sooner this unpleasantness is over with, the sooner we can all get back to our offices. So, if you please?' He looked pointedly at the hessian-wrapped packages.

Akaba drew a knife from his pocket and held it in front of Colin's face, pressing a switch that allowed six inches of honed steel to arc out and lock into position. He looked mockingly into Colin's eyes and turned towards the packages.

'That's my stock!' Colin took a step forward, desperately trying to avert the imminent catastrophe. 'If you damage my stock, I'll sue.'

'They can't do this, can they?' Bert's voice sounded hoarse.

Ray, hands high against the wall, turned his head, looking under his arm as Akaba slashed at one of the

407

bales, the hessian parting easily under the attack to expose two of the cardboard cartons.

The stiff cardboard took a little longer, but seconds later it had been peeled away to reveal the carton's contents. Akaba stared at Colin as he sliced confidently into the block of yellow cocoa butter, his avid expression fading as he reduced it to scraps under quick slashes of his knife to reveal . . . nothing. A strangled expression escaped him and he attacked the second carton.

Colin's mouth fell open. He looked at Bert, then at Ray, but could see only the backs of their heads. 'I told you,' his voice was strained as he shrugged off Lambert's slackening grip. 'It's only cocoa butter.'

Akaba was already slashing at the second carton, the scar above his eye pulsating madly as he stabbed wildly into the heart of the innocuous block of butter. Again . . . Nothing! A whimpering sound escaped him and his breath came in short sharp gasps as he slashed the hessian from the next package.

The only sound was the panting of Akaba's breath as the circle of absorbed policemen watched him slash yet another block of butter into pieces to no avail. Akaba became a man possessed and another package was ripped apart, chunks of the hardened cocoa butter exploding wildly as he levered his blade inside, as if disembowelling an enemy.

Colin's mouth was agape. 'I told you . . .' he tried again, not understanding, but keeping up his pretence of outraged innocence. 'You're wasting your time.'

Detective Inspector Lambert glanced up at the man from the Foreign Office. Johnstone-Carruthers' bushy eyebrows were raised like question marks, but he moved his head negatively, returning his fascinated gaze to the spectacle of Akaba hacking hysterically into yet another package. By now half the hessian packs had been ripped apart – their contents violently destroyed as Akaba's voice rose in protest each time his thrusts revealed only pure, unadulterated cocoa butter.

At last Akaba was done, kicking unbelievingly at the slowly liquidising mess he stood amongst. His complexion had gone strangely grey and his eyes were dangerous pits of darkness as he spun round.

'Where is it?' he screamed, thrusting the blade of his knife against Colin's throat. 'Where have you hidden it?'

'I don't know what you're talking about,' Colin spat back. 'You're a raving fucking lunatic!'

Akaba seized Bert's arm, spinning him round and pushing him hard back against the wall. 'You! You must know where it is.' His voice had an almost pleading tone to it.

'Know where what is?' Bert asked, puckering his face up like a puzzled bulldog. 'I haven't the faintest idea what you're on about.'

Like a man desperate for salvation, Akaba grabbed Ray by the shoulders and spun him round. He opened his mouth to speak, and instead froze, his eyes bulging in their sockets as a choking sound came from his throat. It was as if he had suddenly seen a ghost. Slowly he backed away, his hand rising to touch the wide, inflamed scar above his eye which seemed to have suddenly increased in size, the tight skin becoming almost transparent as it pulsed and throbbed like a living thing.

'*You!*' His voice was a whisper of disbelief. '*You are the fourth man!*'

A thin smile curled Ray's lips and he came mockingly to attention. 'Fourth man, Major Akaba? I don't know what you're talking about . . . Sir.' His voice was deliberately goading.

The scarred skin above Akaba's eye bulged, pulsating with a life of its own as blood pumped into it, his face working through astonishment to rage as spittle frothed on his lips. He swayed backwards, like a snake preparing to strike, the blade of his knife gleaming between them. Then, like a man possessed, he lunged forward, thrusting upwards, aiming for Ray's heart.

Ray barely moved. One hand chopped paralysingly on Akaba's wrist, sending the knife spinning to the floor. His other hand, equally fast, closed into a fist and hammered hard on to the pulsating scar tissue above the insane, staring eyes. Blood splattered widely as the drum-tight skin burst and Akaba's eye disappeared behind a curtain of scarlet gore. Then Lambert was on him, clamping his arms around Akaba's chest and swinging him clear. Ray stood his ground, smiling in grim satisfaction at the battered face. The other officers stepped close, positioning themselves between Ray and the frantically struggling Akaba. Colin and Bert looked on in amazement, totally baffled by the turn of events.

'Arrest them!' Akaba screamed, his face a mask of dripping blood. 'Serve your papers!' Released from Lambert's grip, he stood in front of Johnstone-Carruthers breathing heavily. 'Serve them!' he demanded, as if he was shouting orders at a recalcitrant underling. 'These men must return to Ghana with me to stand trial.'

Johnstone-Carruthers looked distastefully at him. 'I'm sorry, Major Akaba. Stand trial for what?' He spoke in a tone that brooked no argument. 'Her Majesty's Government made it abundantly clear that the weight of your circumstantial evidence, on its

411

own, was quite inadequate to justify the extradition of the alleged criminals. The proviso for validating the extradition certificates is quite clear – *the gold must be found in the possession of the men you accuse.* That, and that alone, would have ensured their speedy return to Ghana. However . . .' he looked eloquently at the mass of melting cocoa butter. 'What we have here is, as Mr Grant has repeatedly claimed, merely cocoa butter. I'm sure that I do not have to tell you that the importation of this substance hardly constitutes an offence. Extradition, therefore, can no longer be considered a possibility. As a matter of fact,' he continued drily, 'speaking as a lawyer, I strongly recommend that Mr Grant consults with his solicitors with a view to pursuing a claim for damages against you regarding compensation for his loss and the possible damage to his business through this unfortunate affair. However, that is a matter for his consideration alone. Good day to you, Major Akaba. A pleasure to have made your acquaintance I'm sure.' He smiled smugly at Akaba, shook hands with Lambert and finally threw Colin a quizzical glance before striding majestically out of the store.

'Well,' Lambert turned to the devastated Akaba. 'It looks as if your theory has come unstuck, Major. No gold – no case!'

'They stole the gold! *I know they stole it.* I want these three criminals arrested and held in custody until the rest of the cocoa butter on board the Lagos Palm has been traced and checked. It is possible that the packages were somehow mixed up.'

'Unfortunately what you know and what you can prove are two entirely different things, Major. It happens to me all the time. You'll just have to chalk it up to experience. Besides,' he looked doubtful. 'I never did think this lot had the nous for that level of villainy. A con job here, a blag there, maybe a bit of breaking and entering; that's about their strength. But hijacking a plane and ripping off a load of gold bullion . . . ? Nah!' He shook his head. 'That's way out of their league.'

'But the evidence!' Looking incongruous with blood still pouring down his face, Akaba ticked the known facts off on his fingers. 'Setting up this shop. Tickets for flight 670 purchased by post from an accommodation address in Takoradi. Car hired by Grant seen in the university car park. The faked death of Docherty, and Grant's denial when asked if he had known him. Hired car again; this time in the hotel car park. And if that is not enough, the cocoa butter hurriedly despatched to this address the day after the robbery. Surely that is more than enough evidence to warrant an arrest?'

'Sorry, Major. You're not in Ghana now. And in this country we don't accept coincidence as evidence,' Lambert told him. 'Over a thousand fans travelled from London to see that fight; that's one coincidence explained. You only got the colour and make of the car at the university, so that's no use as evidence – not in this country anyway. And there's no law making it an offence to ship cocoa butter to the UK from Ghana, however speedily it is arranged. Without the gold, all you've got is a series of easily explained coincidences.'

'You seem to be going to great lengths to prove that they didn't hijack that plane.' Akaba looked angrily at him. 'How, then, can you explain away Docherty's injuries?'

'I don't need to. Your own pathologist's report blames the fall from the balcony as the cause of death.'

'It was necessary to falsify the pathologist's report to avoid alerting the criminals.'

Lambert looked at him and shook his head. 'I never really believed this lot pulled that job. But you told a convincing story and the Commissioner went for it. Now you're admitting that you falsified the pathologist's report. Sorry, Major, but your methods stink to high heaven. Your story too, for that matter. I suggest you get out of here before I run you in for possession of an offensive weapon and attempted murder.' He picked the flick-knife up from the floor and nodded at two of his men, looking on impassively as they escorted the protesting Akaba to his car.

36

'You're actually going to sell cocoa butter?' Lambert looked at Colin, his face distorted in query.

'That's what I've been trying to tell you all along,' Colin snapped. 'I've identified a gap in the small, specialist chocolate-makers market. I'm starting small.'

'Very small now,' Lambert grinned, pushing a melting mound of cocoa butter aside with the toe of his well polished shoe. 'Right then,' he signalled the rest of his squad to leave the shop. 'I'll be seeing you. And remember . . .' he menaced them with a stare. 'You're still on my patch. Anything goes off around here and I'll be checking you lot out, sharpish.' He halted at the door and turned to give them a long, thoughtful look. 'Nah!' He shook his head, coming to a final decision. 'Hijack a plane! Nah . . . You lot just don't have the nous for it.' He turned on his heel and strode through the broken doorway with a panache that could have earned him an instant Equity card.

★

416

There was a silence as the three of them stared at one another across the debris of the butter.

'Nothing!' Bert finally broke the silence. 'Not one bloody pennyweight! What the fuck happened to it?'

'He should be able to tell us that.' Colin turned to stare at Ray. 'I bet he knows a lot more about this business than he's letting on.'

Bert's face grew thoughtful and he turned to look at Ray. 'And that black bastard seemed to know you pretty well. How d'you account for that, Ray?'

Ray stared back at them, face drawn, as if he had reached the end of some terrible trial. 'Yeah,' he said quietly, almost to himself. 'I guess you are due an explanation.'

'Well?' Both of them stood waiting.

'That night Eddie sent me round to your flat, Bert, when you propped me about a bit of villainy? I told you then that I wasn't interested in breaking any laws, didn't I?'

'Aye,' Colin agreed for both of them. 'But you soon changed your tune when a planeload of gold was mentioned.'

'Not just *any* planeload of gold, Colin.' Ray turned directly to him. 'A planeload of gold *in* Ghana. That was what Doc said. And that was what made me change my mind. You see,' he said, 'it was in Ghana

417

that I ran into the trouble that got me tossed out of the SAS.'

'And Akaba had something to do with it?' Colin anticipated him.

'That bastard had everything to do with it.' Ray's voice hardened at the memory. 'He had four helpless guys shot and killed; murdered right in front of me because they tried to steal *his* gold. When I interfered and tried to stop him, he laughed at me. So I let him have it. That's my mark on his eye.' He smiled with malicious satisfaction at the memory. 'I was charged with assaulting a senior officer, court martialled, demoted, jailed and drummed out of the regiment. All I could think of was getting my own back on him, and the job you offered me gave me the chance to do just that. I wanted to ruin the bastard, same as he ruined me. I didn't want to steal the gold – I told you that first night that I wasn't a thief and I decided that once the job came off I'd see that the gold got back to the Ashanti people.'

Colin jabbed a middle finger in the air. 'And that to the three mugs who helped you.'

Ray had the grace to look shamefaced. 'Yeah,' he admitted. 'That was what I thought at first. All I could see was the opportunity to get back at Akaba. But later,' he looked at Bert, 'after Colin went back to Ghana and I got to know you and Doc better, saw the way you treated me. Well, it opened my eyes. We became mates and I began to think about keeping the gold. After all, Akaba would still be in the shit no matter who ended up with it. So I kept my options open. It was Doc's death that swung the balance. I knew his body would cause complications; especially when the medics got to him. The safest thing then, for all of us, was to get rid of the gold – the evidence.'

'So you told someone about Hansel of London and left it for them to rip us off.' Colin guessed the rest of his story.

'Colin, *it was the right thing to do.* They were on to us. If that gold had arrived here today as planned, we'd all be in handcuffs right now and on our way back to Ghana. Christ!' He held the tips of his index finger and thumb a millimetre apart and spoke tensely. 'We came as close as *that!* Everyone, including you two, was certain the gold was in those packages. You saw Akaba's face! He *knew* it was there. In fact he was so confident that I began to wonder if they had got it off the boat in time in Ghana.'

'Aye.' Colin was forced to agree. 'My bottle was pouring good style when he stuck his blade into that first block of butter.' His face twisted in an ironic smile. 'I suppose that, in a left-handed sort of way, you actually saved us.'

419

'It worked out, Colin. If Doc hadn't died I would have let things go the way you planned and taken my share of the gold. As it is, I made the right decision for all of us.'

'One of the things you haven't told us,' Colin said as they finished off the bottle of champagne. 'Just who *did* you give the gold to? Who did you know out there who could handle that sort of business?'

'I served six months in Ghana before my court martial,' Ray told them. 'Part of my job was to meet people, observe and report on the political situation and assess morale. It was obvious that the people weren't getting a square deal from the politicians. And there were a lot of things happening to the ordinary people that I didn't like. So I kept my ear to the ground and heard about a group led by some Ashanti chief who seemed genuinely concerned for his people's welfare. I guessed he would be approachable as long as his people were going to benefit. I was right about him and he arranged to have the gold intercepted en-route for Tilbury.'

'So he got the gold and we got left sucking our thumbs,' Bert gloomily observed.

'Back to square one again,' Colin sighed. 'And I've definitely decided to go straight now, especially after what happened to Doc.'

'Yeah. Me too.' Bert snuffled quietly, as if ashamed

of his decision. 'This life's getting to be a bit too hectic for me.'

'Just think,' Colin spoke reminiscently. 'A couple of weeks ago we were millionaires. Now we're practically skint again.'

'Maybe not.' Ray looked pointedly at Colin's hip pocket. 'Didn't the delivery man give you a letter?'

Colin reached behind him and felt for the envelope, his action silencing the others, as if they sensed the importance of the moment. He read through the letter to himself, shaking his head in disbelief before holding it out to them.

'Here,' he said. 'You better read this. It'll save a lot of explanations.'

Bert took the letter from him and, with Ray breathing over his shoulder, read:

> *PALACE OF KUMASI*
> *KUMASI*
> *GHANA*
>
> *Dear Colin,*
>
> *You have succeeded where others failed and my people salute you. For the first time in many years Ashanti gold has come back to its own.*
>
> *I, too, salute you. Your achievement in liberating the gold has done more to unite my people than many years of talk. My people have seen the moguls*

421

of Accra humbled. You have destroyed the myth of their invincibility and because of this my task is made easier.

I must admit that I was taken unawares when Sergeant Quarry approached me in my office at the palace and revealed that he was one of the men responsible for the bullion robbery. But I was totally stunned when he went on to tell me that the gold was being returned for the good of the Ashanti people. Once he was satisfied that it would remain a secret between us, he told me how you conceived the idea and prepared the plan to steal the gold. As we have witnessed, your plan was successful, except for the unfortunate accident to your friend. Please accept my sincere condolences for his untimely death.

Your reasons for returning the gold will always remain a mystery to me. However, one does not look a gift horse in the mouth and I thank you with all my heart.

I am also pleased to be able to tell you that arrangements to fly Mr Docherty's remains to the UK have been satisfactorily completed.

Perhaps I should also tell you that I attended the annual school prize-giving in Takoradi the other day and met a lady friend of yours – a Miss Lesley Farrell. She spoke about the bullion robbery and seemed disturbed that it had occurred. However, *when I told her – in the strictest confidence – that the gold had been returned, she seemed vastly relieved and appeared to be unusually pleased at the information.*

I believe 10% is the usual commission in these matters? Therefore I enclose an International Bankers' Draft for three hundred thousand pounds (£300,000). I am sure you will see to it that the money is properly divided among your men and that the dependants of Mr Docherty will benefit from his efforts too.

I assure you that the gold we have here will be put to good use where it is most needed.

My father, the Asantehene, has decreed that a new link be forged for the chain of Osei Tutu.

You may be assured that your deed will never be forgotten by my people.

Yours sincerely
Yarty Okufu

Colin took the letter back and read it through again, this time taking in its deeper implications for him; Lesley would be coming home soon, and she knew that the gold had been returned. A glow of pleasure suffused his body as he realised that they would soon be together again.

There was something else in the envelope, something hard. Curious, he tipped a small twist of paper into his hand.

'What's that?' Bert asked, looking on as Colin unscrewed the paper and let a small chunk of gold plop into his curled palm.

'That?' Colin stared for a moment, then, slowly, a smile of realisation spread across his face. 'That's my promotion!'

'Promotion?'

Both Bert and Ray turned puzzled eyes on him. 'What d'you mean?' Bert asked. 'What sort of promotion?'

The smile on Colin's face grew broader as he looked at his two friends.

'The bastard's made me an Ashanti chief!' he said, slowly closing his fist over the bright new link of Ashanti gold.